The Bitch of Broadway

I0519644

Harvey L. Bilker

Press One Publishing, Barnegat, NJ

The Bitch of Broadway

by

Harvey L. Bilker

 **Published by:**
Press One Publishing
PO Box 563, Barnegat, NJ 08005-0563
(609) 660-0682, scott@debtsmart.com

Copyright ©1992 by Harvey L. Bilker
First publication date *October 1, 2014*
10 9 8 7 6 5 4 3 2 1
Printed in the United States of America

ISBN 0-9648401-0-3

Table of Contents

About the Author

Harvey L. Bilker (1981)

Harvey L. Bilker (1932-2012), wrote "The Bitch of Broadway," in 1992. He was born in Philadelphia, PA and lived in New York, NY and Los Angeles, CA, before settling in Howell, NJ in 1969 and then retiring in Barnegat, NJ in 1999.

He was a Broadway Stage Manager, member of Actors' Equity, and script reader for Broadway Producers, including Herman Shumlin, the original Producer-Director of the stage play "Inherit the Wind," among other hits, including Robert Redford's first major New York stage performance in "Tall Story."

Harvey was one of the eight editors (Medical and Associated Sciences) for The Random House Dictionary of The English Language and authored over 200 short stories and articles published in anthologies by book houses that include Simon and Schuster, Putnam, Random House and Pocket Books, and in national and local magazines.

He wrote three books published by Contemporary Books: "Photojournalism: A Freelancer's Guide"; co-author (with wife, Audrey) of "Writing Mysteries That Sell"; and "Writing Science Fiction That Sells."

Harvey had over 200 short stories and articles published in magazines and in anthologies (hardcover and paperback), including the following: "Genetic Faux Pas," the first fiction published by Paul Krassner in his Underground Publication, "The Realist," later reprinted in the Random House science fiction anthology, STRANGE BEDFELLOWS, ed., Thomas

N. Scortia. "Apartment Hunting," (collaboration with wife, Audrey) in FUTURE CITY (Simon & Schuster; reprint: Pocket Books), ed., Roger Elwood, published later in slightly different form in the 1975 annual Mystery Writers of America anthology, EVERY CRIME IN THE BOOK (Putnam). ed., Robert L. Fish. "All You Can Eat," (collaboration), in CHILDREN OF INFINITY (Franklin Watts), ed., Roger Elwood. "The Extras are Extra," (collaboration), The Elks Magazine. "Then You Can Do What You Want" (collaboration), in THE LEARNING MAZE (Julian Messner), ed., Roger Elwood. "The Future of Science Fiction" (collaboration) in LONG NIGHT OF WAITING AND OTHER STORIES (Aurora Publishers), ed., Roger Elwood. "Sincerely Yours" (collaboration), Coast Magazine. "The Extras are Extra" (collaboration), The Elks Magazine.

As a Freelance Reporter-Photojournalist for The *New York Times*, Harvey was a contributor to The Times Camera Column. Many front page photographs were published by: The *New York Times*, *New York Times Magazine*, *Star Ledger*, *Asbury Park Press*, and *Tri-Town News*.

Additionally, he was a lecturer on writing, Cable TV Production and Photojournalism at various educational institutions, including The New Jersey Institute of Technology (every year, at their annual New Jersey Writers Conference), Temple University, high schools, and other institutions and groups and an adjunct Instructor of Photojournalism, Photo Editing and Basic Photography at Ocean County College, Toms River, NJ.

Harvey was also a registered Pharmacist for over 40 years, and a consultant to the pharmaceutical industry and medical writer of documents regarding new ethical drugs for submission to the FDA. He also wrote documents for international regulatory agencies for approval of new drugs worldwide. Clients included Johnson & Johnson, Bristol-Myers Squibb, SmithKline Beecham, Merck & Co., Pharmacia & Upjohn, Schering Plough, Abbott Laboratories, and Pfizer.

What they say about Harvey L. Bilker

"...a highly practical guide to becoming a freelance photojournalist."
—*Publishers Weekly*

"Some (dozens of books on Photojournalism) are so much gobbledygook. Recently I came across a book by Harvey L. Bilker...and selling for a modest $7.95 in paperback. I'm impressed. It's like sitting on the front porch with Harvey as he spins his tale of how to succeed. His photo illustrations...bread-and-butter stuff...refreshing ......read this one."—**Associated Press**

"Who is this Harvey Bilker, and where did he get all his energy? He's the consummate freelancer...His advice is on target...I'm glad to see this book come along...Learn from this man's hard work."—**News Photographer** (the magazine of the National Press Photographers Association--for all newspaper and tv photojournalists).

"The best story is by Harvey and Audrey Bilker; it's a biting prediction of what too many people and too few apartments will eventually mean."
—**Library Journal**, on the anthology, "Future City," which includes their short story, "Apartment Hunting." Other authors in the anthology include Dean R. Koonz ("Hideaway"), Frank Herbert ("Dune") , Ray Russell ("The Fly"), Thomas N. Scortia (the movie "The Towering Inferno"), Robert Silverberg, and Harlan Ellison.

"The show topper (and show stopper it turned out) was 'The Memory Machine,' by Harvey Bilker. There are plenty of laughs in this tale of two slightly-cracked college research professors who invent a Rube Goldberg-type gadget and try it out on a not-so-bright student. Author, Bilker, shows a fine talent for funny dialogue and running laugh gimmicks. His talent is complemented by the hilarious performances of the cast..."
—**The Philadelphia Daily News**

"...some valuable nuggets about mysteries and science fiction that shouldn't go unnoticed."—**Books**, KCCK-FM, Cedar Rapids-Iowa City

"...Bilker shows the aspiring newshound how to be ready to roll into the action quickly and how to cover the greatest possible variety of angles...With its wealth of first person experience, Photojournalism: A Freelancer's Guide is essential reading for the would-be freelance news photographer."
—**Photographer's Market Newsletter**, by the Editors of Photographer's Market/Writer's Digest.

"The Extras Are Extra," a short story by Harvey & Audrey Bilker, adapted for the motion-picture screen.—**Winner of the Houston International Film Festival** (Sixteenth Annual Festival of the Americas) Bronze Award in Short-Subject.

"The clarity of the discussion throughout is admirable...the Bilkers have admirably packed a lot of information into a small compass for the beginner in the field...a first step for the fledgling writer...Libraries and individuals not owning (the s.f. books on writing by Ben Bova and L. Sprague deCamp)...may wish to begin with Bilker."—*Science Fiction & Fantasy Book Review*

"Adults (with a special interest in mystery writing) should turn to Harvey and Audrey Bilker's new book, 'Writing Mysteries That Sell.'"—**Ellery Queen's Mystery Magazine**

"Or the deadpan stuff the Realist has begun to use since they broke the s-f ice with Harvey Bilker's 'Genetic Faux Pas.'"—**Judith Merril**, Editor, THE YEAR'S BEST S-F

Chapter 1

It happened today, just this morning. For some reason I was unable to fathom, I reached a level in my daily involuntary meditation, fantasy, or whatever it is, when it took wing wildly in a new and extraordinary burst of imagination. And it's been that way since.

Is this what old age is all about?

I'm sitting in my wheelchair, as little interested in what's happening on the nursing home's TV screen as are the other dozen or so residents in this large, creaky room. I look around me. One is distracted by imaginary loose threads on her clothing. Another leans to the side, a few sleep. Others stare into space chewing their cud, fine hairs waving on their chins. They're all passing time, unaware of the bright television colors changing with each scene in the dimness of the room.

In the next moment, I see a vision of my father wagging a finger at me, saying 'Ochtzik', which in Yiddish means eighty. My father, at that time, was eight years younger than I am now—88.

I find that thought hard to believe. It seems barely possible that the years have gone by so fast. But here I am in a nursing home, surrounded by 'alter kockers', or 'A.K.s', literally 'old farts', another Yiddish term.

But am I really, myself, an A.K.?

I have to admit that for many, many years now, when I've viewed my face in the mirror, I've begun to realize that I do look like one, with the creases and smooth, drooping skin.

Well, yes, of course, I am one. What's there to admit? I mean, let's face it, at this age how can I deny it?

But, frankly, I don't feel I am. Most people my age, and even decades younger, seem to accept old age early.

But I can't.

I don't know why. Maybe it's because I have a brain left and they don't. Are they just tired of life, waiting for death? Is it that I'm truly alive, just hampered by occasional physical incapacity?

Now, again, my mind is flying like a blur back into my former years. And each time it's like never before. My thoughts are winging into what seems like eons past: my early childhood, my youth, my college days. Moving back and forth like an insect preparing to land here or there.

Or, you might say, scanning my mind's computer menu.

If only I had been able to bring all of these visions to my mind when I was younger—imaginatively, creatively. I could have used them in my writing. I might have been a successful writer.

My memory is a mixture of indistinguishable reality and fantasy—an unoriginal concept.

I recall a comment regarding that very point in one of W. Somerset

Maugham's autobiographical pieces. In it, Maugham said that he was unable in his later years to differentiate between fact and fiction in his life because he had imagined so much in order to write his short stories and novels. Maybe I'm able to be aware that much that I remember hasn't happened, to judge that flaw in myself, too, and not to be able to know which is which. But I also take advantage of that ability. Since I've been put in this nursing home, I use my imagination to envision scenes that I wish happened to me when I was young. I use the fiction writer's technique for my own personal pleasure. Such thoughts are what make literature, and I employ that poetic license for myself.

If only, though, I could have created genuine and lasting literature.

Well, maybe I'm doing it now, although I might not be around to see it acknowledged.

I continue to scrawl notes on the yellow pad resting on the lap of my untidy trousers. Yes, of course, they're untidy. I don't have the energy or time to have it otherwise. I have to accept, for the most part, what is done for me, being unable to do a great deal for myself.

"I was staring dejectedly out of the narrow passenger plane window," I'm writing, "at the Los Angeles airport. We were about to take off. Soon I'd be in New Jersey."

I'm thinking for a moment. Then I move my hand, on the back of which green veins stand out and work prominently while my squamous cells wrinkle finely—another situation I find difficult to accept.

But, I go on, "I was soon to discover, also, that I would be going into my first depression."

"I've always been manic-depressive," I continue, writing somewhat faster, but not fast enough for my thoughts.

"However, until that experience in Los Angeles, losing my job in advertising and being stranded out West, I had never before fallen into a deep, incapacitating depression that possessed me so powerfully both physically and mentally."

In an instant, my thoughts are again shifting drastically, as they began doing just earlier today, and again I'm experiencing a passing-by of selections about my experiences. It's as if I'm reading a restaurant menu and the words describing a dish paint a picture of food that's desirable to eat, yet upon looking at another item, that item replaces it in appeal.

Now, though, I'm forgetting about the passenger plane and Los Angeles.

She has come to mind and I'm selecting her from my mental computer menu—voluntarily or involuntarily, I'm not sure.

She has appeared in my memory as if she has been put there by a television or motion picture camera that has moved into a new setting and freeze-framed.

I see her, Melissa. As clearly as if today were the first time. She was a typical beautiful shiksa, slim, with blond hair and a ski-jump nose. Her jaw is almost square, determined, with neat teeth. She is laughing. She is young, as she was at the time—35. I am 45. I make a quick mental calculation. Now she's 78. God!

It's a backers' audition for a Broadway play.

If I may be so vain, she has spotted me. We had met each other before, been introduced here and there—at rehearsals, in theatrical offices, elsewhere, and we had barely exchanged words. But that had been all. I had never really taken careful notice of her at first.

I was feeling low that evening, when she appeared before me. Yet, at that time I still didn't see her as an incredibly beautiful vision. I was "down," as usual. Depressed.

She said, "You seem awfully quiet. How come?"

I never would have approached her. It had to be this way, with her initiating the 'Hello'. She was too overwhelmingly lovely, I would subsequently decide, for me to be the first one to start a conversation. Besides, if I had taken the initiative, my wife would have been right there. Anyway, women like that didn't happen to me. Although ordinary, average women did, occasionally—when I made a conscious effort. But as I later learned, Melissa was definitely about to happen to me—considerably. I was to find out that she was in love with me. Madly. Something that had never happened to me before, or after.

Did it happen to many people in life? Even in marriage?

Rarely, if ever, I would say. Yet, she would fulfill dreams for me that until that time seemed totally beyond anything I had ever imagined. Dreams of both love and sex, and of devotion and loyalty. Dreams of complete commitment, despite her life with her husband and children.

My thoughts are racing along.

Now I'm suddenly aware of my wheelchair.

Can I really be decrepit with these memories so vivid in my mind?

Melissa and I are sitting on the edge of a motel bed, in an embrace, kissing. I am tilting her body back dramatically, until her soft, golden hair touches the covers. She slowly lifts her feet from the floor, and her shapely form is supine.

"I've always been a manic-depressive," I scrawl. "But until that time, I didn't even know what that condition was. Although, when I began my affair with Melissa," I write, "I had already been over my first depression."

There were to be more depressions.

That depression, my first, had begun to precipitate when I knew that I would be catching the plane in California for New Jersey, but it didn't really hold me in its unyielding grasp until I started my new job back East.

I wouldn't find out what a deep depression was until at least a year after leaving Los Angeles—before seeing a number of psychiatrists and doing a bit of reading on the subject.

"I thought," I write, "that for the most part, my dour moods, which went back to college and high school days and even before, were the result of tiredness, or they were just normal lows that everybody had. But I didn't realize I was in the minority when I had my frequent moments of feeling 'down.'"

My wife, sitting next to me on the plane, was used to the vagaries of my career, so she was resolved to the changes that were taking place in our lives, financially and otherwise. Hadn't there always been such constant occupational chaos in the nine years I had known her (four of which were in marriage)?

I was to think, as I suffered through my depressions, that she was brave, weathering all we were going through with the soul of a survivor, without floundering hopelessly in the depths of despair, as I had always done. But any manic-depressive would think that any "normal" person who could adjust to changes wrought by fate was extraordinary.

The plane taxied, and I looked out of the small window at the other passenger planes and the dry bleached view of cement, distant palm trees, smog, highway, and traffic of Los Angeles.

When our plane's turn came and we were heavily pulled aloft and feeling the drag of gravity sucking at us, I felt as if I were being wrenched involuntarily from the earth, from California, where I had always wanted to live, having always resided in the East.

Age 35, in the prime of life, possibly at last about to have made headway in a field for which I had talent (one of many, that is, as a writer)—advertising—and then, bang, the agency going up in smoke, and with it my future.

Not that advertising was my main goal in life. It wasn't. Playwriting was.

I move my pencil aside and look at what I had put down.

Not bad.

Good feeling. Nice imagery. Catchy phrasing. "Wrenched from the earth." Then a lead-in with my manic-depression. Autobiographical. But what the hell. What's literature, anyway?

I read further. A good opening for a novel. Because it was true. Not that I preferred the novel form.

But a Broadway play? Today? At my age? Forget that!

I haven't worked on Broadway as a stage manager, playwright, or producer for how long now? About fifty years.

It was shocking just to think about all of that time behind me, not before me, to realize that those decades have slipped by.

So here I am, sitting in my wheelchair at a nursing home in New Jersey. Can you think of anything more ignominious?

But I'm putting this down on paper for my heirs and assigns. That's more than these slugs sitting here with me are doing. So I must have a brain. I mean, look at George Bernard Shaw. When he was in his 90s, he was still sharp, making pithy comments worthy of being published in newspapers around the world. And I'm not doing so badly myself.

I didn't retire years ago, like the alter kockers here. I didn't get tired of life. I'm not sitting around here waiting for the end.

Don't get me wrong. I realize that health determines lifestyle, one's quality of life. And that some people here might not have been that lucky. But more than a few of them must be in reasonable shape. As for myself, I fortunately have my health. To a reasonable extent, anyway.

I mentioned that I'm an unsuccessful writer.

That's why you haven't heard of me.

Have you ever read fiction about a writer, or seen a movie or TV show about one?

They're all successful, right? You never met an unsuccessful one in literature, yet, have you?

Well, here I am.

Mark Gessel: Failure. Glad to meet you.

Wait. Don't get me wrong. I've been published. But there are a million of us. Who do you think writes your magazines? Your newspapers? Your TV shows? Even your scholarly books for colleges? It's us, the fringe people. Some of us do well. Some don't. We come and go. Maybe it's luck. Maybe even talent. Most of us, though, make a buck here and there. But many of us support ourselves with any jobs we can get, or with financial help from others. We hold jobs that range from dishwashing to the academe. We're supported by rich relatives, grants, or slaving spouses.

So I've been published. So what? So have a million others.

I've written nonfiction, fiction—some short stories in the lesser men's magazines: erotica, you might call them.

Wrote them way back when.

But I was in the theater. Broadway. Yes, the real thing. I was actually a Broadway stage manager, and a member of Actors' Equity. Then, I was a writer, and, yes, a producer. But that was when tickets sold for ten bucks apiece, more or less.

I was one of the 99 and 44/100ths percent who didn't make it. For a while I did. That was when I met Melissa.

My goal in those days was to make a living as a playwright. I wrote. I was produced. And I produced. But I didn't really make a living at it. I mean, a really good living. I sort of bounced around from job to job and project to project, doing odd bits here and there. Reading scripts, raising money for producers, then finally getting produced and producing—with no really substantial success, where I'd be secure. The story of my life.

I've been an advertising copywriter and also written many articles that have appeared in local newspapers and magazines. Also, in a few national ones. Even the New York Times. But all of this didn't happen that often.

So, I've spent most of my life freelancing. Getting by. That's why I'm writing this. Force of habit. Many writers use a diary. I'm one of them. Always with the hope of using some of the material for a play. But now it has to be a short story or novel. I can't very well work in committee at this age.

So, why a novel? Because a novel is a solo affair.

Besides, I want to record what's been happening to me lately.

And while I'm at it, this might be my novel at last. Who knows? If I can organize it and get it on paper before they find me slumped down here at the nursing home with my blood circulation at a standstill.

I'm grateful to my son, Lewis, for buying me a computer and teaching me to use it many years ago. It's in my little room here with bed, bathroom and bureau. And I lose myself in this amazing gadget, transcribing my notes.

As far as putting all of this into a play, as I started to say, I think its a little bit too late for that, for me, anyway. Even if I were in physical shape, having been in the theater, I can tell you that getting your script produced depends on optimal circumstances, not just the writing. You've got to be in the right place at the right time—with the right people. And, naturally, with the right goods—the script.

You've got to be able to say, "Hey, Jim," to the producer, who's got to be a good friend of yours, "do you want to look at a play I've written?" Then he'll say, "Sure," and read it and consider it because he knows you. If he got your script through the mail and didn't know you, it would end up who knows where. If he had a secretary, it would get sent back to you months later, rejected.

But a novel; there's a possibility to that. There are more novels published than plays produced.

With plays, it's different. I know from experience, having been a script reader for Broadway producers. First of all, satisfying a producer with a first draft isn't easy. If you can get the script through to him, that is. Then, if you get him, or her, to read it, there are only so many Broadway theaters in New York. Let's face it, Broadway playwriting is a tough life. And it gets tougher every year.

But as for a novel, I may just have the goods right now. I may be writing the correct words down here.

Say, are you reading this in hardcover? Or even in paperback? If so, I made it! And while you're enjoying my life, I may just be six feet under.

(I've been re-reading my notes. Each time I write where I met Melissa, it seems to be a different place. So what do you want? I'm 88. That's a good excuse, isn't it? After all, this is autobiographical literature: AKA, fiction.)

Okay, so what about Melissa? If she ever existed.

Of course, she existed. Or there wouldn't be this novel. If it is a novel. If it really exists. Does it exist? Are you holding it?

Am I pulling your leg?

If I am or not, what difference does it make?

Never mind; let's get on with Melissa.

Chapter 2

Melissa was a bold young lady, and so beautiful. I considered myself fortunate that she actually fell in love with me.

Look, I don't want to brag. I'm no Clark Gable, but that's the way it was.

Do I sound vain? I don't want to. Really, I'm humble.

I was just lucky.

How many times in life does something like that happen, especially to someone like me? If it hadn't been for her, I never would have had that heavenly experience (and accompanying misery). As I said, I had rarely been successful with women, but the ones that came my way willingly, with a bit of effort on my part, weren't that exceptionally appealing or exciting.

And there was never really love—being loved, that is. Not as I finally came to know it with Melissa. Sure, we all love (or do we?), but that look on her face whenever she told me she loved me...and even when she didn't say those words, but when she wore a revealing look and blush on her face...

Melissa was remarkably pretty. But when I say "pretty," I don't mean everyday pretty. I mean that kind of prettiness that at first is subconsciously captivating: plain on the surface, yet with the potential of becoming otherworldly as it is constantly observed by the particularly vulnerable observer; fascinating, yet with the latent potential of becoming overwhelming. The kind of beauty that, each time it is seen, gradually becomes more intense until it builds to a crescendo and becomes devastating.

In addition, her personality and intelligence were beyond that of other women I had known. Her thoughts and the way she conveyed them verbally, and with her own personal attitude, was unique, unusual.

And we both, it turned out, had the same "brain waves," which accounted for total compatibility—at least, initially.

She was the type of person who was intellectual without having to be a heavy reader, although she did, of course, read. Evidently, through her discussions with thinking people, she gleaned rudiments of profound philosophy that gestated and fused in her subconscious contemplation, and, with her mental dexterity, became wisdom. She was brilliant, to put it mildly; highly perceptive, to put it plainly; and sexy, to put it properly. A rare combination of woman.

Her husband, Brent Lourdes, was a very successful producer. She had married him when she was only fifteen.

Brent was about thirty at the time, and had already put a couple of hits on the boards. Call it luck, brilliance, creativity or business sense; whatever it was, Brent evidently had it—or else he had accidentally put together the right theatrical chemistry: an unlikely coincidence. At any rate, the bucks had begun pouring into his pockets and he was already being quoted in The *New York Times*.

Melissa was the daughter of an actor whose wife was exhausted with his trying to make a name for himself in the theater and/or movies. The family lived in Manhattan in a run-down apartment on 52nd Street. Melissa's mother worked, and she and her husband waited for the 'day' to come. They were both exceptionally bright, so naturally their intelligence was passed down to their daughter.

Melissa, having traveled with her parents in intellectual circles, and having met successful men—who were quite interested in such a precocious and pretty young lady—would have been able at an early age to nab anyone she wanted.

Her parents, especially her father, desperate to make it in the big time, thought that by giving their daughter's hand in marriage to this 'young' producer on the way up, he would benefit as an actor.

When the possibility of Brent's marriage to Melissa became evident to all of them, Brent, at the last moment, gave her father an insignificant bit part in a one of his new plays; there had, at the last moment, been an opening.

The role could have gone to anyone with a minimum of talent. It required speaking only a few lines at the end of the third act. The man who was originally cast in it dropped out after realizing that the play was a bomb, (though it became an artistic success that added to Brent's prestige), and would never make it past the first few weeks. Besides, the actor's agent had arranged for a screen test for him: there had been some nibbles out West. Which, by the way, didn't work out.

But after Brent had wedded and bedded Melissa, he never gave her father another part.

Immediately after Melissa was married, she was pursued by just about every male associated with her husband, from stagehands to actors to investors of big money.

She innocently gave the impression of being a nymphomaniac because she was fifteen years old, overpoweringly attractive, and obviously made love. Enough to turn any man on.

But she was faithful.

Why she suddenly took a liking to me twenty years later, I'll never understand. I suppose it was part of the dynamics of the psyche that makes us all, at one time or another, fall in love with someone for no seemingly logical reason. I was a struggling writer. (Maybe that was the explanation. Her motives for finding a man appealing were somewhat perverse. A facial scar, she once told me, excited her.)

She hadn't been especially in love with Brent. But she had great respect for him—at first. And contrary to the impression she gave others, she wasn't open for any hanky-panky.

Until I came along.

So let me repeat, sitting here in this wheelchair, that it was all a phenomenon in my life as far as I'm concerned. I just don't want to sound egotistical. If I seem as if I'm apologizing for being so lucky, I am; and you understand exactly how I feel.

But it happened. And it was heaven (and torture) while it lasted, which was for about three years or so.

By the time all of this came about, her love for me, and my response: falling in love with her (if that's what I did)—she had already had three children. A daughter, six, and sons, ten and eleven.

If I remember correctly, the first time I saw her was at her husband's office in midtown. It was in one of the many business buildings along Broadway. Long, sterile, green halls filled with similar doors that have semi-opaque glass windows with the names of the companies in plain block letters on them. Most of these offices represented some area of show biz.

Through an acquaintance, I had just landed a job as an assistant stage manager for one of Brent's shows currently in rehearsal, and was delivering some rewrites to him. When I entered his office, I saw Melissa sitting in the small anteroom in a chair, reading a magazine.

I thought that she was an actress, friend, or businessperson. I wasn't particularly struck by her beauty at that time because I evidently knew better than to become interested in someone with looks as lovely (later, spectacular in my mind) as hers. My subconscious mind was most likely at work, protecting me from looking for rejection—my Achilles heel—so I hardly noticed her. In fact, I have to admit that she made no substantial impression on me at the time. Frankly, even when I subsequently saw her, I at first hardly remembered her. She was just a familiar face, until she initiated our friendship.

I would encounter her at rehearsals of her husband's shows, at parties, or at various other places. At the time, I was earning a living as a stage manager, whenever I could get such a job. I had made a lot of friends. So I got around.

But it was really Melissa who got our relationship going. She was, I came to learn, a very aggressive person. Especially sexually, well, to me anyway—to my delight.

The first time I really got to know her was at a backers' party for one of Brent's shows.

Producers of hit shows cultivated 'angels' to put up money, and for the most part could pick up the phone and get those people to buy shares in a show. However, most investors still insisted on seeing the script or had to be convinced that the show would make it. That's why there were backers' auditions.

Producers usually had some star at the party to impress the people who might put up the money. At that time, backers' auditions were extremely important. Just a decade or two later, shows cost about ten times the amount to produce and corporate investment and promotion had become involved. Still, even today, individuals are still behind some shows—usually put on by little-known producers. But the scene has changed considerably—as I've followed it in The New York Times, Variety, and other trade publications.

But let me get back to the first time I 'officially' met Melissa. I mentioned it briefly, but here are a few more details. This particular backers' audition was held at a sizable, well-furnished, outdated-in-decor apartment with large rooms, on Fifth Avenue, just across from Central Park. An oversized foyer was set up with a bar, and the place was packed.

Evan Cooper, the middle-aged Broadway and screen comedy star, who was known to be sleeping with many of his young co-stars, (when he wasn't at some bar drinking), was there to read the script aloud.

The potential backers' wives were all aglow to be able to actually go up to him and carry on a conversation. Evidently they didn't notice that he was bored with them.

The crowd, after about an hour of drinking and waiting for everyone to arrive, was silenced by Brent, who introduced Coop.

The famous Evan Cooper sat in a wood-framed, canvas director's chair and read the script, looking up occasionally when he expected a laugh. That was the cue to this well-dressed audience to give him what he silently requested, so they did. With the atmosphere electrified by his presence, they believed the lines were funny whether they found them so or not.

The playwright stood nearby, smoking one cigarette after another and taking sips of whisky, neat, between puffs.

Following the reading, Brent stood before the crowd.

"As you can tell, Art Lee has written another hit," he said. "I don't have to explain to you, or most of you who are my backers, that a hit comedy can pay off a show in a matter of three months, if we have packed houses."

Not too many years later, those figures changed. It would take many months, or years, or it never would happen.

"So let's get those checkbooks out, folks. Shares are $10,000 for five percent of the show. At this point, though, we're willing to sell smaller portions of that—as low as one percent—which will cost you only $2,000. But when we get rolling, that opportunity may no longer be available—if there are any shares left at all. So I say, invest big, profit big."

But there were no checks that night from backers. Show investors have to be convinced following backers' auditions. They have to be taken to lunch, engaged in long conversations, be barraged with phone calls, get news about who's being cast in the play, and even, in some cases, be shown script rewrites.

Following Brent's talk about the future success of Art Lee's play, there was more drinking and socializing.

That was when it happened.

Melissa and I were standing in the midst of the crowd, talking. It was she who had approached me. Of course, I was unaware of the significance of this at the time. It was just that another person in the large gathering who knew me had dropped over to converse. Melissa seemed so friendly—and lovely—and I had had a few drinks and was feeling somewhat uninhibited, so in the midst of our conversation, on impulse, having been enticed by her provocative red lips, I leaned forward and kissed her on those exciting rosebuds. Then my eyes automatically scanned the room to see if anyone had seen me do it. Her husband was nowhere to be seen, my wife was with a group of people in another part of the room, chatting, and everyone else was engaged in conversation, drinking, or pushing their way through the mob.

I expected a negative response from Melissa. Nothing seriously bad, such as a slap in the face, but a cold stare that said, 'You shouldn't have done that.' Or just a smile that told me that it was cute and all right.

Being under the influence of a second Double Martini by that time, I didn't really much care, anyway, how she reacted.

To my surprise, she said, "Do that again."

She later told me that she had purposely put her lipstick on crooked that evening, so that she would entice me.

That's how clever she was, how well she understood men. Even though, up until that time, twenty years after marrying at age 15, she had never had an affair.

I was to learn that Melissa had an instinct, an uncanny perception of people and male-female relationships that went beyond any I had ever observed in any other woman before. (However, it was to go awry, except, perhaps, from her point of view.)

Nevertheless, she was a gal who had everything.

"Can I call you?" I automatically asked.

"Yes," was her simple reply.

I could hardly believe it. She was so beautiful and so seemingly unapproachable, yet she was saying to me, "Yes, I'll make love with you." It was all so easy, there was nothing to it.

Inconceivable. Implausible. Incredible. Wonderful.

With lesser women, who appealed to me only because they had bodies that you could have sex with, it had often taken great effort to make out.

Why this?

I didn't ask questions. I accepted it gratefully.

Chapter 3

Despite the fact that getting Melissa into bed was going to be no problem at all, I had to follow certain precautions. I couldn't, of course, make her husband suspicious. And I knew, obviously, that she felt the same way regarding him, and about my wife.

At that time, I was thinking only of sex, but that was to change.

So I dropped by Brent's office on the pretext of getting some literature on the latest play for which he was raising money, and a copy of the backers' contract. His secretary put them into an envelope for me.

Brent's door was closed.

"Is Brent in today?" I asked casually.

"Yes," she replied. "Would you like to see him?"

"No, that's all right," I said. I looked at my watch. "I'm in a bit of a hurry. Perhaps later this afternoon. Will he be here then?"

"Yes," she answered. "He usually puts in a full day. If he isn't seeing people, he's reading scripts."

With my heart beating somewhat faster than normal and a strange excitement that I had never felt before, I left the office and headed for a pay phone.

I called information, got their home number, and dialed. I didn't recognize her voice, so I asked, "Is this Melissa?"

"Yes."

"This is Mark Gessel."

"How are you?"

"Fine."

I paused. Well, here goes, I thought. It all seemed so impossible. So strange. After all, I knew Brent. I was his stage manager. And she was most attractive.

"Can I see you?"

"Yes," was the simple answer.

Silence.

It was my move again.

"Where should we meet?" I asked.

"Where do you want to meet?" she asked back.

Our very first tryst was at a restaurant and bar across the street from Port Authority, not quite in the theater district, a semi-dump that catered to transients and local workers with a fast open-faced roast beef sandwich and beer. A clean place, where you looked through glass at the food counter behind which a man dressed in white and wearing a chef's hat held a scoop as he stood before steaming tureens of meats, fish, and vegetables. It was a seedy but fast and functional restaurant. And although it was just south of 42nd Street, on Eighth Avenue, it was the last place a theater person would go. So we were safe.

She was beautiful. I allowed myself to see that now as we stood at the bar having our drinks—a double martini for me, a bloody Mary for her.

I say she was beautiful because I could notice it now, could consciously admit it to myself. She was letting me be with her, not rejecting me.

I saw in her eyes what I had never seen in any other woman's eyes, ever in my life. Complete admiration. From the start, I had strongly sensed, unconsciously, that she more than liked me. Even before she told me how much she did. I had never observed such an expression on my wife's face or in her eyes, or in any other woman's attitude toward me.

Her blond hair in the brassy light of the bar took on a glowing quality. Her features seemed perfect. She was sweet, lovely, exciting.

"Mark," she said. "I was waiting for you to call me ever since I first met you. Did you perceive that? Didn't you feel an attraction between us?"

I didn't know what to reply. I didn't want to say the wrong thing, to let this potential for future joy be swept away. I felt that to be safe, I had to be honest. If I guessed wrong and ruined everything, I'd regret it forever. But if I said what I felt, I could only blame fate if it went wrong.

"Actually, you did appeal to me," I lied somewhat, after all. "But I wasn't sure that it worked the other way."

"Mark," she said, putting her hand on mine as I held my glass on the bar's counter. "The first time I saw you, I loved you. Since then, I've sat in the dark occasionally, but more and more lately, thinking about you. I've looked for you at parties, rehearsals, meetings. And when I saw you, I thought I'd die, just being in your presence." She took a sip from her glass. "Just seeing you somewhere was enough to make me feel weak."

What could I say? Those were strong words. It sounded like some line that I should be giving her. I couldn't believe what I was hearing, that this was happening to me.

I have to admit that although she was so pretty, so appealing, I wasn't in love with her at first. But it eventually happened, I think. Her love for me, her attention, her loyalty, beyond her allegiance to her husband and even her children, aroused in me a such a passion that I ultimately become almost madly insane for her. But probably the most dynamic influence was that she gave me sex not only when I wanted it, but when she wanted it with me—which was almost always. I had never had the experience before of a woman constantly initiating sex. It was a dream-come-true for the teenager in me. And it eventually became an integral part of our love—a natural happening, beyond just the erotic physical act it is commonly considered to be.

In time, we became almost inseparable.

But those beginning hours were so beautiful, and they became increasingly better—before everything got worse.

Where it got better was with our lovemaking. But not necessarily with our relationship. Although I came to love her—because of her love for me, I've often wondered, and I wonder even now, as I sit in this wheelchair, if it was, after all, only a dependence on my part, a love I returned because I was loved, a need that became so essential to my life that I found, in time, that I could hardly live without it.

And so, in those first enchanting moments at that bar on Eighth Avenue, our love affair began.

Shirley and I had been looking for an apartment in Newark. We always kept up with what was happening in real estate and rentals through The New York Times, and she had spotted an ad for a Mies Van der Rohe building just being constructed in an area of Newark. (Some years later, this area was made decrepit by the city's riots and subsequent neglect). It was a beautiful high-rise, but the surrounding terrain left much to be desired. The developers felt that the building would inspire transformation of the neighborhood.

At any rate, fate had worked out well for me because it was a reasonable drive from there to potential meeting points with Melissa—where we saw each other often during our few years together. From the New Jersey Turnpike I could easily get to the Garden State Parkway. And off of that well-traveled road, the availability of motels was infinite. Getting together in New York would have been just about impossible. You never knew when you'd be in some area where someone in the crowd would know you.

So Melissa and I had our first intimate rendezvous at the Paramus mall. She had given Brent some ridiculous, unbelievable excuse for visiting her parents, who were living in New Jersey. She brought her children to their place and asked them to take care of the kids for the day. Whatever reason she gave Brent for leaving and staying out late made no difference, because it was all so far removed from his concept of their relationship that he would never even have thought of looking into it.

It was evening when saw each other for the first time, alone together. She looked ravishing—and ready to be ravished. After all, although nothing had been agreed upon regarding our making love, it was certainly assumed by both of us that we would. We were obviously not getting together to talk about the theater. That was for sure.

She was wearing dungarees. It was the first time that I had ever not seen her in a dress. She also wore a white long-sleeved blouse with delicate blue ticking that had two full pockets over her less than fully generous, but pert, breasts.

We walked through the interior of the mall, one of the largest in New Jersey at that time, with two sparkling floors of shops, its polished brick walls and walkways decorated often with large leaves and an artificial fountain.

"Let's go to the liquor store," she said.

Melissa knew her way around the mall very well. She had obviously shopped there often since her parents lived not too far away.

I didn't question why she wanted to buy alcohol. The fewer

questions the better, I figured. I was, frankly, looking forward to getting laid.

She selected a bottle of wine, and I insisted on paying for it, although she certainly could have afforded it better than I. Considering the fact that her husband was a successful Broadway producer and I was a struggling freelance writer/playwright/et cetera.

The reason for the wine, I was soon to learn, was to lessen her inhibitions. It was her first infidelity, she would explain, and she felt that being even somewhat intoxicated would help her get through the initial stage of giving herself to me. She was that sober about her first affair.

She had also thought, I later learned, that I would take her to a motel. But stupid me, I had never considered that. I had sort of a high-school-days mentality about the whole situation. You know, get laid in the car —in the back seat, after it got dark.

When dusk arrived, we found ourselves walking in the woods behind one of the large department stores, handing the bottle back and forth and taking sips. We were hand in hand as it got darker. Then we had our arms around each other's shoulders. And only moments later, it seemed, her back was against a tree and we were embracing, kissing, the intensity of it all like none I'd ever experienced. It was, at first, both romantic and sensuous, but that would change.

She slowly lowered herself to her knees, opened my fly, found the object of her desires, and set upon me voraciously, like an animal in heat.

This was something new to me. I had had sex but never had experienced what she was doing. It was strictly straight sex with my wife— when I could get it—and the same with the others, whenever the rare opportunity happened. Who had time to experiment? Or, rather, who wanted to risk losing an opportunity by making such an attempt? And here Melissa was going down on me. And it wouldn't be the last time. I haven't since met any female who liked fellatio as much as she did.

She was to later brag to me that her husband had taught her the full gamut of sex. And, with regard to their age difference, rather brazenly, "His friends must have wondered what it was that he had in his pants that got him me."

We were pretty much in the thick of the woods and it was darkening fast. There was no one around. I could see the lights of the mall stores.

Then there was a slight rustle of leaves and a kitten appeared. It walked next to Melissa and, looking up curiously observed her as she sucked. The blank look on its face gave the appearance that it knew what was happening and was fascinated.

There would be times later when she would perform her delicious act on me and say of Shirley—whom she grew quickly to hate—"I can taste your wife's cunt! Did you take a shower this morning?"

Melissa made her way back up to my lips, but she still held me tightly in her fist.

She was still unaware of the kitten.

But when she matter-of-factly dropped her jeans, slipped off her panties, sat me on an oversized log, and straddled me, the kitten jumped up onto the log to observe further, and Melissa became aware of it.

But we both ignored the animal. This was our initial sex outing and neither of us wanted to destroy the mood.

It was somewhat awkward and uncomfortable making love on the log, so I maneuvered her down onto the leaves and, still kissing her, got myself into the missionary position.

We weren't exactly having our first love session under the best conditions, and I regretted more than ever not having taken Melissa to a motel. But to stop and make that suggestion would have been, I felt, the death of a beginning affair.

But no sooner had I begun my thrusts when the cat jumped onto my back, walked up its incline, and peered over my shoulder at the action taking place down below.

Melissa had been purely mechanical in all of her movements, in each aspect of sex, as if it were a task that was necessary to accomplish in order to initiate our relationship. The whole experience turned out to be, I felt, rather passionless. For someone who had confessed to being deeply in love with me, it was uninspired. But in time, under better conditions, it was to improve—considerably.

We saw each other regularly after that, and each time after we were ready to say good-bye, we would listen together to the latest popular songs on the radio in her car or mine.

It was through Melissa that I became aware of the lyrics of the current rock-and-roll hits and listened carefully to them. I had always liked the music (though my wife hated what she constantly told me sounded to her like a "washing machine"; for her, it was strictly classical music). Trite though the meanings of the songs' words were, I began to pay attention to them and found them filled with great significance.

As time went on, Melissa and I became closer and closer. We would call each other (a subsequent obsession which more than annoyed my wife). After Melissa's husband began producing my play, and sometimes just after our trysts, she would call to discuss the songs that had been played on the radio station that we were both listening to, since we parted just a short time before.

There was one song, she told me, that she associated with me from the start, with lyrics that spoke about someone not being able to live without the other—meaning her without me. It still rings in my mind today—decades later.

As I've said, it was her total love for me that moved me so much, I believe, that made me fall so deeply in love with her (if that was what I experienced). Otherwise, I doubt if I would have become so infatuated, as beautiful as she was. If that certain 'something' hadn't been there in the beginning, she certainly put it there, whatever it was. So, eventually, it did happen to me. It had to, under the circumstances. It was all of this: her loyalty to me, her hopelessly-in-love-with-me expression when she looked at me, everything that gave me feelings about her that I had never ever had for any other woman. Perhaps I hadn't even been meant to love her, yet she managed to bring out the elements in me that made it happen.

We became such a mutually enamored twosome that we were more inseparable than a madly in love, newly married couple.

In time, many on Broadway began to observe our close relationship —a famous producer's wife always with a lowly stage manager-potential playwright. They suspected that something was going on.

Naturally, my wife eventually found out, and so did Brent, but by then Melissa and I didn't give a damn about either of them. We even neglected our children to see each other. It was love, spiritually and physically. We seemed to fit together so perfectly. Even when we just took walks together, it was so right. We loved each other in the silence of our footsteps. Until it all finally ended.

Chapter 4

Mental depression.

In the late 1980s, the National Institute of Health estimated that 10 million Americans suffered from mental depression. That's one out of every 25.

Have you ever heard someone say, "I'm depressed?"

Most people who say that don't know what depression is. Believe me. They just happen to be a bit "down" at the moment, and eventually the feeling will pass.

True depression, however, is feeling so 'low' that much of the time you're affected not only mentally, but physically. You feel like a lump of lead. That's how I described it to my wife, when I was down. Her reply was always a cynical "Hmmmph," especially as my depression wore on for months.

When you're depressed, you can hardly get out of bed in the morning. In fact, you could stay in bed for 15 hours or more with the covers over your head and your wife saying, "You lazy bastard, get out of that bed and get dressed!"

If you've got a white-collar job, you're lucky, because you can drag yourself into the office and fake your way through the day by shuffling papers, be paid at the end of the week (while wondering how you're lasting on the payroll), and then drive home in the right lane at a ridiculously slow speed while the drivers behind you pull out, disgustedly, to pass.

You're tremendously sensitive to cold, yet hardly able to select the right clothing for changing weather: you don't have the mental energy to make decisions or the physical energy to carry them out.

Your thoughts are concentrated only on your miseries.

Depression, after you've lived with it for one or two years or more, can be not wanting to live anymore, because there's obviously no future for you. You wonder how people can say, "What a beautiful day it is today," when you know the sun is shining, it's comfortably warm, the grass is lushly verdant, and the world seems right for everyone else but you.

It's also not being interested in a damn thing. Going to the movies doesn't appeal to you; neither does TV. A newspaper? Forget it, you don't care. When I've slipped into my deep depressions, I continued buying newspapers for my wife—when I was able to drag myself out of the front door.

When I brought the papers back, I watched her read them, and couldn't understand why she was still interested in what was going on and I wasn't.

We had many shelves of books, which included plays—since that was my primary writing goal. Yet, when I was in one of my major depressions—and I've been through a good number of them—books, plays, or any other literature meant nothing to me. It went from a fantastic interest to blah.

And during those low times, I would pace through the house for hours (usually unemployed—and when you're depressed and unemployed, you're also unemployable), stopping occasionally to look at the rows of books, thinking, "That world is now closed to me," and, "Will it ever open again?"

When you're depressed, even writing a letter is a chore. I was pretty big with correspondence. But during depressions, I just dropped out, lost my epistolary connections. I stopped replying to my mail because it meant putting a sheet of paper into the typewriter and hitting the keys; and my arms, my hands, my fingers, were dead. But most importantly, it meant thinking, and when you're depressed, you just can't think—not for longer than a few seconds at a time. You've got a very short attention span. You lose track of what you're thinking about. You're dull. You're dead.

Of course, depression affects different people different ways. Some have panic attacks: moments when they think they're going to die, or when they're overwhelmed by anxiety. People who suffer from this don't often consider it a part of depression, but it is. I never had the kind of panic attack during which you feel that you're going to die—as it was explained to me by a woman in a hospital ward to which I had been sent for ECT (electroconvulsive therapy), better known as shock therapy (which, fortunately, I didn't get). She didn't consider herself depressed. I've had panic attacks, though, in which I suddenly felt lost, alone in the world, with the sun shining and people around me on the street going about their business knowing what had to be done in their lives, while I didn't know what move to make next. It was panicsville alright, petrifaction.

But I did know what to do about being cheap. Be cheaper. When you're in a deep state of depression, you know that you're unemployable. So if you're employed, you realize that if the axe falls, you'll probably never find another job.

What I did during my deepest depressions, for one thing, was use the same plastic cup for an entire day, for soda, milk, and other beverages. I rinsed it out each time, of course. My wife told me that these constantly used cups were disgusting. (There was, by evening, sort of a rainbow-colored ring at the bottom.) And years later, when I was out of the depression, I came to the same conclusion as she did. I didn't know how I managed to drink the guck that had settled on the bottom by the end of the day. Subsequently, I post-depressively took pride in tossing away one plastic cup after another.

At the time of my multi-used cup syndrome, my son, who was about 15 at the time, would often bring friends of his over. I would hear them go into the kitchen and use the cups freely, pouring the soda that had gone up in price by a big 10 cents or so per bottle. I would be tortured by the loss of the several cents the fluid ounces of soda cost me. So I would head for the kitchen when his friend arrived, and stand there, waiting for his desire for a cup of soda. And if he would finally want a drink, I would pour it, making sure that there wasn't too much soda in the cup. I realized that I had to forgo many 'expensive' cups, but at least I saved soda.

Still, I knew that I was acting irrationally. So, in those instances, I cynically called myself the 'Keeper-of-the-Soda'.

During those deep depressions, the living room couch looked forever inviting. I found myself constantly lying on it for hours, in an attempt to put myself into a dark, obliterated world without thought, often not wanting to live. Whenever I arrived home from work or anywhere else, I would head for the couch's softness and escape. I wore out its pillows. Shirley would stingingly criticize me for sacking out into oblivion, where I escaped from the material world.

When Shirley watched television, I'd lie on the couch and roll over and face the back. I wasn't interested in anything that was on the tube, no matter how interesting it may have been—but nothing was interesting to me when I was in that state.

I was a vegetable.

There are cases of agoraphobia, a condition in which people fear being in a open space. Actually, it usually resolves itself as a fear of going out of the house, mingling with others. Many people who have this problem think that it's a condition in itself, but it's a form of depression. I had such occasions during my depressions. It was a manifestation of them. My wife would say, "Go out and get the New York Times before they're all gone." I'd go to the door, and even though the sun was shining and it was a 'beautiful day', the thought of going out there into the world where there were people appeared to be a difficult task. But the way I sort of overcame those mental blocks was to set a time for carrying them out; then, when the time appeared on my watch, I'd charge out of the house against my will.

"All right," I'd say to myself. "I'm going to leave in twenty minutes." Then, as the time drew near, I'd fortify myself by preparing my thinking and muscles, and then, at that given moment, mechanically force my body into the outdoors to do the chore. I did other necessary duties that way, too, like making phone calls, or even engaging someone in conversation.

But, as I mentioned earlier, being deeply depressed was all new to me after I was 'wrenched' by that airliner from the soil of California. Up until that time, I thought that everyone had their share of depression, and that what I had was mine. For example, while I was attending college—for what I didn't want: pharmacy (at my parents' insistence, but that's another story)—I knew that at noon, when I had my break from classes, it was time to eat, although I didn't feel hungry. So I'd go with some other students to a restaurant across the street from Temple University Pharmacy School on Philadelphia's Broad Street, and order sandwiches along with them. And when I ate them, I began to feel a hunger I didn't totally sense, but that I was aware of, and was being satisfied. So I knew I was doing something right by eating. However, I didn't enjoy the food in the least.

So when I returned from the Coast, from my medical copywriter job at an advertising agency, I spoke to a cousin who had seen many psychiatrists, and told him about my problems. He insisted that what I needed was psychotherapy. I had had a friend or two who had been in analysis, but even though I was by that time a registered pharmacist—which is obviously the medical field—psychiatry was all a mystery to me, except for what I had read about it in Freud's writings. I doubted that another human being, though trained, could do anything for someone feeling as low as I was feeling, just by talking to them.

But Sidney insisted. My mother, who was his aunt, wasn't exactly for it, when I told her that I was thinking about seeing a shrink.

"Sidney is wasting his time," she told me. "He spends a lot of money on that and it doesn't do him any good. He says his problem is that he never speaks up and that the doctor told him that if he does, he'll feel better." She waited for the facts to sink into my clogged brain, then went on with her theory. My mother appraised herself as a woman of the world when she hardly ever left the house or store and barely spoke with other people about serious situations. "His problem is he takes crap from everybody. He's not really depressed like you. It's just that he gets the runs when he can't handle things, and sits on the pot all the time or he feels nauseous occasionally. He took phenobarbital for a while, but it didn't do him any good."

Well, anyway, I followed my cousin's advice. Let's face it, I was desperate. When you're feeling as low as I was, you'll try whatever might possibly help.

He recommended his own psychiatrist, naturally, who was nearby—in downtown Philly. I was living in Jersey at the time, but I was willing to travel over an hour and a half each way—and even pay money—for the relief. After all, who wants to mope around all day feeling miserable?

I had just started working as a medical writer at that time—upon my return from California—for Cary & Philips, one of the many large pharmaceutical manufacturers in New Jersey, and my medical plan paid half of any psychotherapy fees. So that alleviated some of the financial burden. Although my wife said that if the company ever found out that I had 'mental problems', they'd fire me.

As it turned out, Sidney's psychiatrist didn't want to take me on because Sidney was a close relative, and the psychiatrist thought that there would be a conflict. For example, if my cousin and I would talk about each other, the doctor felt it wouldn't be fair to either of us when it came time for him to analyze and speak to us individually about our problems. Of course, the analyst could afford to turn me down. He was making $50 for each fifty-minute hour and had a waiting list, so he could fit anybody into an open slot. And on top of that, he also taught at a Philadelphia medical school, and did some group therapy—which evidently gave him multiple fees.

What he did, though, was recommend someone he knew who practiced somewhat near me in New Jersey.

In a way—pharmacologically—I lucked out. Dr. Horowitz was just right for my problem. I appreciated him more later, when he was no longer available, during my subsequent depressions, when I had to go from psychiatrist to psychiatrist to find someone else who could do something for me. Good psychiatrists are not easy to find.

Yet, even Horowitz wasn't perfect, but he was better than most.

I came to the eventual conclusion through my experiences with psychotherapy that most psychiatrists are charlatans, or else they don't really know what they're doing, at least in dealing with depressions. I haven't had decent advice from one of them. What they tell you is bullshit. But what's good about them is that they have experience in prescribing drugs which affect the mind. Where a general practitioner wouldn't know how to prescribe drugs, switch them, or adjust dosage by just listening to what the patient has to say since the previous session; a psychiatrist can. Especially anti-depressant drugs, a class of medication which had, fortunately, come into existence perhaps only thirty years before, but was only presently being prescribed to a great many patients. Since then, of course, anti-depressants have become a multi-million dollar market.

I've gone through a good number of shrinks, and in my opinion, besides their prime goal being money, they're a bunch of nuts.

There was one who was extremely well dressed. I could see his Gucci boots shifting under his desk as he told me that if I ever came to his office feeling unbearably depressed and had to speak with him immediately—and that's what depression can be like—I should go around the side, through the anteroom, to behind his office, and wait for him there by his other door. "Just knock," he said. Well, forget it. He never answered the knocks. It was just a dishonest promise, made no doubt to all of his patients, to keep us paying him those $50 fees for additional sessions so he could buy more Gucci. Not only that, he always cut his sessions short. After about ten or fifteen minutes, he'd write a prescription like there was nothing more to discuss—all for the full $50 fee. With other patients sitting in the waiting room. Get it? Less psychotherapy time, more money. And if you were severely depressed, you didn't have the guts to complain. I dropped him after a few visits. He was a liar, a cheat and a thief. And his comments brought me no relief.

Another shrink, one who just sat there listening quietly to me but never commenting or answering my questions, once asked me, when I was speaking about my wife, "How come you got along so well with her when you were first married, but don't now (after six years)?"

What the hell was I paying *him* for? *He* was supposed to answer that question.

I was hospitalized once, by a Dr. Rose. He was very short, and his feet didn't touch the floor. He had a moustache and dressed well. As they all do, on their suckers' money.

When he suggested hospitalization during a session in his office, I asked him, "What can you do for me in the hospital?"

"Well," he said, swinging his swivel chair from his desk to face me, his feet swinging in the air. "We can find out what medication is best for you."

Dr. Rose was on the staff of the New Jersey Coast Hospital. So with a phone call, he was able to get a bed for me.

This was for my fourth depression, which lasted a couple of years. It was really a recurrence, though, of my third depression, which happened about eight years before—the result of a bad nonfiction book contract on photography on which the publisher jerked me around.

I was in and out of depressions at that time—within moments. Sometimes I'd take an anti-depressant tablet or capsule, and an hour later I'd be feeling really great: not high, just 'normal', not depressed. But it would last about five minutes and then I'd descend once more into the abyss of despair.

I remember the office of another psychiatrist, in New Brunswick—a lair no doubt for Rutgers University students with problems and money, whose door had about three locks and a bolt on it. Maybe some of his patients eventually wanted their dough back for poor diagnosis and treatment.

Even being a registered pharmacist, as I sat in Dr. Horowitz's living room (he worked out of his home—a lovely and large one), listening to his advice at my first psychotherapy session, I was skeptical when he told me that he could help me by giving me a drug. After all, I knew about drugs; that was my education and background. I had studied the gamut of drugs so that I could be licensed to dispense them properly, even advise the doctor when he was wrong, or help a patient who might have a drug interaction get the right medication or correct dose. I knew of the versatility of drug therapy: how drugs could effect physical changes; and some mental ones, by stimulating or deadening, so to speak, various centers of the brain. But a depression? When there were underlying experiences and pathological thoughts, and an outlook and distorted philosophy resulting from past life events? I couldn't see that. It made sense to me that drugs could be used for infection, visualization of X-rays, constipation, diarrhea, and the other usual physical ailments, or mental ones like sleeplessness. But as for actually getting rid of obsessive, self-deprecating thoughts, bringing a patient back from the throes of depressive anguish? I just couldn't believe that a drug could do that, not with my education and experience of medication.

After listening to a brief summary of my life, Dr. Horowitz put his evaluation of me this way (in his German accent): "You are a psychoneurrrotic!" His proposed therapy: "I vill be a krrrrotch under vun arm und der drrrrug vill be a krrrrotch under der udder."

I gave him my frank opinion. "Dr. Horowitz, I just can't believe that you can help me with words, and as for a drug, that's ridiculous. After all, I'm a pharmacist. I can't see how a drug can change a person's thoughts and outlook on life."

"First," he told me (continuing in his heavy German accent; but I won't bother to continue doing his dialogue that way for you, because you've got the point), "you have to forget you're a pharmacist, and just listen to what I say, and do what I tell you to do. I've helped in the research on this drug for the drug company that makes it. I used it on my patients when it was first being tested; I did clinical studies. This medication works by stopping secretion of a chemical by the hypothalamus gland in the brain. It's those secretions that cause depression. But," he went on, "you don't have to know about that. Just take this medication the way I prescribe it."

The drug was Tofranil, its generic name, imipramine. It was one of the first anti-depressants ever discovered (and, coincidentally, is used now in conditions of enuresis, or bed-wetting—an early problem of mine. So, looking back, its function and effect really makes sense to me, being that it's a psychotropic substance—a chemical that when put into the system goes to a specific location—in this case, the brain. You see, I feel that bed-wetting is parent-generated; but more of that type of evaluation later—if I ever do get to it).

Anti-depressants followed the class of drug called psychic energizers, which I had actually dispensed as a hospital pharmacist. Miltown was very popular at about that time, too. It supposedly worked by relaxing the muscular system.

As for all of these psychotropic drugs, for the most part, no one knows how or why they really work, but they do. But that's what pharmacy is all about. Centuries ago, certain drugs were used that are commonly prescribed today—and no one at that time knew why they worked. Now we know about them and how they work. Or, at least the drug companies theorize their mechanisms of action. Probably the ancients' research and development was hit and miss, as ours is today with more sophisticated drugs, such as those which are synthesized.

Subsequently, there were more anti-depressants: the MAO Inhibitors, which when taken by the patient did not allow the eating of certain foods, such as chocolate, some cheeses, wine and bananas—or high blood pressure and other problems might occur.

And then came the anti-depressants, which were not as prohibitive in use, such as the tricyclics.

Had Ernest Hemingway been given anti-depressants, he might have had a pleasant ending to his life—writing more novels and short stories that would have been classics today—instead of blowing his head off.

Shock therapy was used on Hemingway.

It was also used on Tennessee Williams.

Both became miserable and basically unproductive as writers.

As you can see, I'm concerned about the effect of shock therapy on writers, feeling akin to them (from an unsuccessful perspective, of course).

What shock therapy does, evidently, is make a person forget about past traumatic experiences. However, it unfortunately takes additional memory away with it. The medical literature notes that the good memory eventually comes back, but the impression that I get from my reading about the subject is that the memory is never really normal again.

So, Dr. Horowitz finally convinced me that I should give Tofranil a try. It was easy for him to persuade me, because I was sitting there with eyelids that were hanging down at 3 Gs.

I was also easily influenced. (Another one of my basic problems.)

So, what the hell, I thought, I have nothing to lose. I figured that if I can get any kind of palliation it's welcome.

He explained to me that the drug was 'cumulative', that it would have to build up in my system before it took effect, and that this usually takes from two to six weeks to happen.

I followed his regimen and only three days later, when I woke up in our tiny apartment, one of the most magical and magnificent experiences of my life occurred.

Chapter 5

I discovered that the depression that had plagued me for little over a year, that I thought would be with me forever, was completely gone!

I couldn't believe it.

The feeling of lethargy, the lack of confidence, the short attention span, and all of the other manifestations of depression were no longer with me. I didn't have to cringe under the bed covers. The world was beautiful. Not just again, but more beautiful than ever. I was alive—more alive, I was to discover, than I had ever been before. (Especially much later, after I started my affair with Melissa. Sex as she pointed out, is a great reliever of depression, if not just a physical narcotic to allow you to forget your problems. And, with her, there was also the friendship that came with it.)

I found myself actually looking forward at that moment—standing there in my underwear—to going to work at the job that I thought I had despised, that I considered was a dead end for me, that I thought would destroy my chances of having time to do my writing.

"Shirley!" I shouted, jumping out of bed. "My depression is gone!"

My wife rolled over, facing me with eyes wrapped shut by the deadly strain of living with someone who was in an abyss of grief without the slightest enthusiasm for being on this earth in the present or in the future.

It was just before dawn, and the darkness outside the windows was beginning to become light gray.

"Yeah, what is it?" she groaned.

I was stunned by the pleasantness of it all, amazed at how well I was feeling.

"My depression is gone!" I repeated.

"Yeah," she said, and rolled back over, exhausted, facing the other way, her eyes obviously still closed for continued sleep.

"But it is!" I repeated.

"Yeah, go to sleep."

"But, Shirley, I feel good. I feel great! Don't you understand? I'm not depressed anymore. Dr. Horowitz's drug worked!"

She stirred, as if pondering my words, then spun slowly back to face me again, this time parting her eyelids with difficulty. "Really? You're not kidding? You're not being sarcastic like you usually are?"

"No! It's really gone! And, believe it or not, I can't wait to get to work. I know I'll love the job. Isn't that crazy? Everything is terrific!"

She paused, looked at me with growing concentration. "That's fantastic," she finally said, seeming to come around to believing me. But then, again, not quite so sure. "It's really gone?"

"I'm taking Lewis to see the sun come up," I told her enthusiastically. I had always been an early riser; my creative juices flowed in the early a.m., when I usually wrote. But I had had up and down moods all my life, not knowing that it was my depression in mild form. There would be long periods of mania and enthusiastic writing periods, then the same time spans of depression and lack of productivity. But now I'd be back again to my usual abnormal manic schedule.

"That's crazy. Go back to bed."

"Who wants to go back to bed? That's for depressed people who can't get out from under the blankets and face the world. I love the world, and I want to share it with my son," who was then two years old.

I dashed to his room and scooped him out of his bed. "You're coming with me, pal," I told him. "We're going to watch the sun come up!"

We hopped into 'Goldie', the old yellow Corvette that we had bought in the Hollywood Hills, and I drove to the nearest highway, where I parked on a downward-sloping apartment driveway so we could view the horizon.

Early morning cars and trucks whirred over the asphalt, filling the fresh, early air with incipient, pungent, gray exhaust. I rolled down the windows and felt the chill of weather that would soon hot up when the sun broke through the horizon.

I hauled Lewis onto my lap and wedged his warm bulkiness between my gut and the steering wheel, and we waited. He was chubby then, but would in time become slim.

Soon the dull sky before and above us began to brighten, and a pinkish glow formed at the earth's horizon.

When the view turned a warmer white, a red sun slid gradually upward to burn off the coolness of the night and create a new day.

"Look, Lewis," I said to my son, all the while feeling goose bumps. "Look, the sun is coming up! It's beautiful, isn't it? Everything's beautiful! Life's beautiful!"

I looked down at his face. He was smiling.

This was one of the greatest joys I was to experience—at that time —until a few years later, after I met Melissa.

The second time Melissa and I made love, it was in a motel. I suppose it should have been that way the first time. But the other experiences I had had with women were essentially one-night stands, sudden moments at a gal's house when the carnal climate was right, or when a limited amount of time was available to me at the place of a friend who would be away.

But it was obvious to both Melissa and me that this was going to be a long-term affair. We knew that without even discussing it.

It was up to me to find a motel that was decent, and that didn't cost too much money. There was no doubt that we were going to meet often, and that I was going to have to be prepared to pay for it, despite the fact that her husband had money and I didn't.

I spent a day checking out the various motels around our meeting point in Paramus. There was a constant trafficking of human beings through the major motels, as well as minor ones, the run-down places where it was plainly apparent that trysts were held regularly. They had that look about them.

During my search, it quickly became discernable to the motel managers that I was looking for a meeting place with someone of the opposite sex. I was rather shy about it, so I guess my halting inquiries gave me away. Of course, *they* were frank about discussing it. After all, it was the business they were in, how they made part of their income: providing an arena for sex.

The going rate, I soon discovered, was $10 to rent a room for a couple of hours. After asking to see sample rooms, I found one motel that seemed clean and neat, appeared to be reasonably new, and had blankets that looked like they weren't infested with fleas.

The next time around for us wouldn't be in the grass behind a mall; it would be in a bed.

I thought that our second get-together, under those conditions, would be softly loving and warmly passionate. However, it was anything but. Not that it wasn't torrid. It turned out to be a horny encounter, something I least expected from Melissa.

Because we had this amazing understanding of each other from the start, after making love at the motel, we discussed our most intimate thoughts and, as she suggested, we ended up masturbating for each other.

Her sexual philosophy was that a woman should be a lady in the drawing room, and a whore in the bedroom. But Melissa always surprised me in one way or another. I could never anticipate her thinking. Sometimes when I'd meet her, she would be delighted at what I said; other times she would go into an angry tirade.

I had never thought of her as wildly sexy. Perhaps she didn't think of herself as such, either. This was her first infidelity. There would be more, I was soon to learn, not long after our blistering affair began to fall apart. Eventually, it would be with a number of others—making me tremendously jealous.

What happened was that Melissa discovered sex at age 35.

Chapter 6

My father.

One incident I remember, especially, about my father is when he caught me smoking. I was about 13.

Those were the days before the cancer scare was started by the famous Reader's Digest article, and Old Gold cigarettes were advertised on television by emcee Dennis James as not producing "a cough in a carload."

My brother, three years older than myself, was smoking pretty regularly, and he introduced me to a number of other things in life, too—when he had anything to do with me at all. He was busy with his contemporaries, having fun, and didn't particularly want to be with his younger brother. After all, a three-year age difference that early in life is a huge gap.

But I do remember one day when my brother Harold brought home a small tin and showed it secretly to me. It was a container of condoms—then better known as prophylactics—which had been thrown away in the street. He had figured out what they were.

Harold and I had the same bedroom. The room next to it was my parents'. The door that was between the two rooms was usually left open to air the place out.

This one evening the door was open and the other room was dark.

Harold came in and withdrew a pack of cigarettes from his pocket—there were no filters then. Smokers really 'lived'.

He offered me one, and though I hardly took a smoke up to that time, I accepted the offer.

As I put the cigarette to my lips, lit it, and took the first draw, I heard my father's voice coming from the blackness of the next room. "You too, eh?"

I was immediately in a state of shock. Somehow I had developed a fear of authority—which plagued me throughout life, even to the very end: sitting here in this wheelchair.

I feel that the way I was brought up was what gave me this phobia and that it, additionally, contributed to my states of depression. Of course, it could have been genetic. Science considers this possibility. In fact, I understand from one of my sisters that my father had depressions. Once during the country's economic depression in 1929, when he couldn't pay his bills, and he was driving his car over a bridge, he suddenly had a strong urge to stop, get out, and jump off.

But, believe me, no depressions could be as deep as the ones I believe he gave me. I think my mother helped, too.

But then, the old philosophy goes: Don't blame your problems on other people.

Talk about fear of authority, I remember once, as a very small child, being in my father's hardware store and being picked up by our local policeman. I fought to be put down. All I could see was his menacing dark blue uniform and shiny, silvery badge of authority. I was a captive and wanted to be free.

So that's the way it's been. With jobs. Writing. Everything. When people boss me, I cower. Of course, psychotherapy helped. And anti-depressant drugs did, also. Even self-help books, which I devoured after coming out of my early depressions. But all of those books eventually repeat themselves: there are certain standard philosophies that you should follow in life to maintain self-confidence.

Anti-depressants, primarily, gave me the capability of following those rules, and eventually I could deal reasonably well with other people. I became 'like everyone else' in that respect.

In other words, I could 'cope', as Dr. Horowitz insisted I would. (But no thanks to his psychotherapy—just his prescriptions.)

Other remembrances about my father:

As a very young child, his showing me pictures of himself and friends on a fishing trip, with fishing rods and fish, on a boat. He never took me.

Sundays. The hardware store closed. We went together to the American Legion, a cellar all lit, with a bar, and a one-armed bandit—which I later saw in multitudes in Atlantic City. Round wooden tables all around. (He took me there, I later learned, to get me out of my mother's way. She had to clean the house, cook, do the bills, and send checks out for merchandise for his hardware store. She also helped out in the store.) And he sat there, in the American Legion beer cellar with his brothers, drinking and discussing their philosophies. I was just an object to be moved around.

Strong memories. Riding in the car with him. He, joking, then his grasping one of my knees with his thumb and forefinger and squeezing mercilessly until pain clouded my eyes with tears. My fighting to get his locked fingers off, but the fear of being too drastic in response, since he was driving. I was in agony, and he was laughing. (At one point, Dr. Horowitz told me that my father was a sadist. I had to believe it.)

Am I, therefore, a masochist?

More of a confirmation of the sadism (or inadvertent sadism?... or interpreted sadism theory?): Atlantic City. Where we kids—I less than school age—went for occasional weeks to stay with our grandmother, my mother's mother. The old Steel Pier. Hamid's Pier: water shows with diving horses, black men pushing roller chairs along the Boardwalk, jitneys.

I hated the beach. When we came back to the house, we had to go up the back wooden steps, wash the sand off of our feet and legs by stepping into a metal bucket filled with cold water. Chilling. Horrible.

My father would come down on weekends, materialize on the scorching whiteness of the beach in his bathing suit, grab me up from the hot sand, and rush me to the ocean. I was a prisoner fastened onto his shoulders, my feet, secured under his arms, fettered by his tight hands, watched the cold, relentless, curling green waves rush toward me. I raised my hands high, trying to block the huge descending whirls of icy water that smashed into us, washed over us, then turned to white and green suds in frigid droplets. Converting the surface of my sun-hot skin to a freezing numbness as liquid filled my nostrils and choked me. Rocking, angular tunnels of roiling water rose above my hips, my shoulders, and up around my neck. I was a prisoner in a sea that threatened to drown me in coldness that contrasted with the fiery sun in which I had been baking only moments before.

And, finally, at last, at his decision, release, freedom, no longer the dreadful jeopardy of the wild sea observed by a child, I was brought back to the blazing beach in peace.

My first short-story sale, while in college: I opened the envelope. A contract!

"Look, Dad, I sold a story!"

My father: "You were lucky!"

My father and I were never close. When my mother died, I was shattered, sobbing. But when he died, there was nothing. I looked at him in the box, felt no emotion.

Cruel on my part?

I don't know. There have been many times when I've felt no emotion whatsoever toward people.

Sadism?

A Nazi Holocaust-type attitude?

I just don't know.

Chapter 7

Why did I become a pharmacist?

It was like this.

I was always interested in writing. I can remember putting out a family newspaper (as do the editors of the *New York Times*). Mine, though, was printed on 8 1/2 x 11 paper—by hand.

No, this isn't about pharmacy—so far. But I'll get to that.

I don't know how old I was when I wrote my newspaper, but I was obviously able to read and write at the time. And there wasn't a Sesame Street in those days, or even TV. So I had to be in one of the early grades.

I made my headlines by cutting letters out of cardboard, placing them on the floor, putting the sheet of paper that was going to be my newspaper's front page over them, and then rubbing over the letters with crayon or pencil. (Like gravestone rubbing.) I wrote my columns under that, put in squares for my pictures, and even drew the pictures.

I was interested in journalism at the time—and forever after.

My stories were family, not earth-shaking, items as: "Mother breaks glass in sink," or "Mr. Radolin gets sick at wedding."

My sister, Esther, inspired me to write. There was a children's column in the now defunct Philadelphia Bulletin, and one day she showed me a poem that she had written that had been published in it.

Eventually, at age 11, I wrote for that column.

And I was hooked.

Ever since then I've been thrilled by seeing my writing in print, and my name with it.

As for Esther's aspirations, they were short-lived.

She never did much writing after that—that I knew about, and eventually she married an orthopedist and found that it wasn't necessary to struggle with words to make a few bucks. Her husband's astronomical fees kept her busy buying clothes, the best food, homes, and trips two and three times a year around the world—most of them at tax-deductible medical conventions.

So she put her quill aside.

At any rate, the column that she had contributed to was a children's column called Heigh-De-Ho.

I don't know how many years after that it was, probably before age 11, I asked my sister, Zelda, to teach me how to type with ten fingers. Subsequently, she bought me a typing book with a keyboard on the cover and told me that to learn I had to look at the cover while I hit the keys. I was able to type with ten fingers after a matter of days, although efficiency required subsequent practice and constant use of the typewriter.

After that, I practiced and became faster. The desire to learn to type and eventually write was so great that I stuck with it.

(My son did the same later, also at age 11, and also in a matter of days.)

Pharmacy?

I'm getting to it. Have patience. There's a(n) (il)logical transition.

Eventually, I surpassed my sister in her one published piece in Heigh-De-Ho. Between the ages of 11 and 13, I really poured it on, sitting at the typewriter and doing something like ten 'articles' a day. These ranged from a paragraph of an interesting happening at school to a short poem. Many were accepted.

What really inspired me was that the editor mailed a clipping to each published little author so that it reached them on the day of publication. So sometimes, when the mail arrived before my mother bought the newspaper, I'd be overwhelmed by the receipt of a business-sized envelope with the return address of Heigh-De-Ho printed in blue. And inside there would be a Philadelphia Bulletin/Heigh-De-Ho letterhead in blue with my own words printed in black on newsprint taped onto it, which I would later know as a 'tear sheet'.

Wow!

I'd dash to my parents every time, saying, "Look, they printed it!"

And the inevitable response was always blasé. They were always busy with the hardware store, true. But their interest in their son's being published was the equivalent of Japan's desire today to have another atomic bomb blast on its soil.

I accumulated a stack of those letters, and pasted up a book with the actual clippings in it. God knows where it is today. It might be down in my son's basement—if he didn't have the sense to get rid of all of my odds and ends before he and his wife put me in this nursing home.

Pharmacy?

Give me a chance.

Now a word about my mother and journalism. Then my father and journalism.

But first, let me just tell you about when I became a Newshawk.

What's a Newshawk?

That was the kid who had the most pieces printed by Heigh-De-Ho in any monthly period.

I made it once. I received a press card, with the name of the now defunct paper on it: Philadelphia Bulletin, and an interview and picture-taking session—which consisted of one picture taken with a Speed Graphic by the Bulletin's photographer.

In the article about me, I was quoted as saying that my goal after high school was to go to college for journalism.

Now, to my parents, regarding my writing.

My mother first. After she asked me what I wanted to do for a living, when I was still in high school, I showed her the article with the quote about journalism and I told her that I wanted to be a journalist, which she knew I wanted to be all along. Her response: "All the kids your age know now what they want to take in college. But not you."

"But, mother, I want to be a journalist."

No answer. Just disgust at my aspirations.

Now, my father, calling me into the hallway by the stairs leading to the second floor of the hardware store building: our living quarters. "Look, I want to show you something," he said. He had just introduced me to the son of a friend of his. The father, by the way, was a pharmacist, and owned a drugstore a block away.

The beginning of this secret conversation had taken place in the store, when he told me that the young man was a journalist.

All right. Now we're in the hallway, and he's showing me this young man's by-line on a front-page article in The Philadelphia Inquirer. The young man had written an exposé. I don't remember what it was about. But I do remember my father excitedly holding the newspaper up to me and saying, "You see how dangerous this can be? Somebody's going to come and kill him, kill his family. This is what you want, journalism."

Many years later, after I had become a registered pharmacist and ended up sporadically in journalism anyway, I asked my father why he had opposed me in my goal of becoming a reporter. He was almost retired at the time, no longer the younger man that he was when I was just a kid. And his feelings were just as strong as ever about the subject. "Because," he said, "reporters are people who get thrown out of bars!"

Pharmacy?

My parents: "First, you'll get something to fall back on. Then you can do what you want."

There are some people who just can't take tests. They panic. They are so anxious to get every answer right that they read each question extra carefully. Then they forget what they read. Or fear that they don't understand, (and psychologically make sure that they don't). In my opinion, it has to do with upbringing. Their parents for some reason want them to fail, so they comply. Result: they have to the read questions over and over. By the time they're halfway through the test, they should actually be all the way through it. If they're taking a high school or college exam, they look up with sweat on their brows to discover, as expected, that confident students—not more intelligent or knowledgeable about the quiz's subject than they—have completed their tests and are on their way out of the classroom.

I'm the one still sitting there. The impotent test taker.

I have a hard-on, but I can't get my rocks off. (Still, it beats not being able to get an erection to begin with.)

When I took my college entrance exam, although I knew the subjects well on which I was examined, I failed them all. I had planned to take Liberal Arts and major in Journalism. Now, I was out. On the street. Not college material, I felt. My parents, my father especially, had succeeded.

How did I get hooked into it in the first place? Two of my friends, one of them especially (let's call him Izzy), had considered taking Pharmacy. Izzy had worked in a drug store throughout our high school years. And his outlook was: It's amazing how much this druggist makes! The profits are incredible! This is for me!

Izzy didn't do well in high school. He didn't do well in pharmacy school, either. But he passed, and after he graduated from college, he opened his own drug store and was very successful. He did a lot of traveling with the profits. Not much with his first wife, some with his second, but a lot with his third.

He certainly did better than one of the students we went to pharmacy school with, who did extremely well as a student, but not otherwise. George went to each class with a separate three-ring binder for that specific subject. And each of those were large and filled to maximum thickness with paper, about all of which he'd used by the end of the semester. As each professor dictated and wrote on the blackboard (now chalkboard), he studiously took notes. He kept his hand writing from the beginning of each class to its end.

He, too, opened a drug store. In later years, his wife cleaned out both their business and personal bank accounts—and took off.

The other friend, Max (I'll give you some more details on him shortly), just talked about becoming a pharmacist, because Izzy did. But he didn't really mean it. All of us were in the same grade, and were close, so when my father asked me what I was going to do now that I hadn't been accepted to college, I said, with my mind barely on the subject, "Well, I was thinking about pharmacy."

What a mistake!

We were in the hardware store at the time. I never had seen him become so animated. He was in some kind of ecstasy. Grabbing my hand, he rushed me out of the store (my mother was helping out and would take over as number one salesperson) and hurried me across the street to the corner drugstore. He halted at the fountain. All of the stools were filled with patrons eating their lunches. Family members of the owners were slaving away behind the counter. Orders were being yelled. "Eggs and bacon with toast!" "One Bromo Seltzer!" There was rushing back and forth to the kitchen by the owner's relatives who were dressed in whites.

"See how well they're doing?" my father told me, his face smiling at the prosperity that can result from being an educated man in the pharmaceutical field.

Then he pulled me to the prescription department. "Can I show Mark where you mix prescriptions?" he asked his friend, the owner-pharmacist.

I was taken back to the Rx room. It was filled with bottles of pills, different colored liquids, and other dusty containers. There was no activity.

I applied to both colleges of pharmacy in Philadelphia. And don't you know: I passed both exams with flying colors.

Chapter 8

I've seen a number of psychiatrists, some for just one visit, others for a short time, and a couple of others for a reasonable length of time, like Dr. Horowitz.

A few days after Dr. Horowitz brought me out of my depression with Tofranil, I went to visit him. I was excited about what I wanted to tell him. I had my story all set, as I usually do, and pictured his delight. In my mind, I often write future scenes of my life. I was certain he'd be pleased, perhaps overwhelmed. I'd describe how I got up that morning just a couple of days before, the depression gone. I'd describe how I felt, tell him that it was a miracle, heaven, a whole new world. He'd be all smiles, pleased with his accomplishment.

But he surprised me. I guess I should have known he'd be unimpressed. He no doubt had been through this before many times with patients.

"Yes," he said calmly, in a professional manner.

He'd had this experience before, all right. After all, depressives are a large part of a psychiatrist's practice.

Homosexuals, however, Dr. Horowitz told me during several sessions, were a problem. "They can't be cured." In fact, in interpreting a couple of my dreams, he hinted at the possibility of my having homosexual tendencies.

The asshole.

At any rate, when I gave him the news that I had come out of the depression, he told me, "I'm glad. I was afraid that I'd have to give you shock therapy."

I had been so depressed that I, of course, would have submitted to anything just to be relieved of my misery, including being put to death, literally, by auto accident, or any other way.

I was later to find out, though, about shock therapy by reading much about it. It was my son, Lewis, when he was about 21 years old, who gave me the words that made me change my mind—thank God! He had said, "Dad, the brain is a delicate organ, and you'd be putting so much electricity into it."

Let's skip to my third major depression, which occurred approximately 5 years after the first.

Dr. Horowitz had warned me, after I had come out of the first depression, "This may never happen again but, on the other hand," he went on, "it's possible that it might—maybe in 5 years, maybe 10."

He was exactly right the first time.

Why did it recur?

The chemicals were there in my brain ready to be secreted again; there was a build-up of problems that I couldn't handle, and the scale tipped once more.

Okay, so it's the third depression and this time it's the worst of all. I go back to Dr. Horowitz. But he's become much older and he's about to retire. He's hitting the nursing homes where he can make a few bucks without heavy involvement, with people who are too out-of-it to complain, especially when their children are handling the situation for them.

At any rate, I meet with Dr. Horowitz one blindingly sunny day, my wife with me. Despite my desire to divorce, I realized the necessity of staying together. Let's face it, I'd be helpless without her, just a pile of bones with skin on them, in a somewhat mobile heap.

(This was perfectly described in a cartoon I had seen in the New Yorker magazine. A husband is at the door of his home, speaking with a friend, and you can see his wife in the kitchen. She's a hen wearing an apron, and he's saying, "But I need the eggs.")

Horowitz wipes his brow in the nursing home driveway. He doesn't seem to be interested in having me back as a patient again, especially having to deal with my conversations about Shirley. At one point during my earlier therapy with him, he had given me an ultimatum—either I speak up to Shirley, or he'd drop me. But that was before the affair with Melissa.

He gives me a story about being very busy, unable to take me on.

I had to look around for another psychiatrist with a license to steal.

Chapter 9

I have often cried at my own funeral.

And there were real tears in my eyes.

I think it all goes back to when I was a child, circa age eight, lying in my bed in a room I shared with my brother on the third floor of our house. (The bottom floor was the store; the second floor was the living room, kitchen, den, and the other usual rooms of a residence.)

I remember it all clearly to this day, at age 88. My mother downstairs with my father, brother and sisters—and me, upstairs, in bed, crying. It happened often. I'd hear voices, and one of my sisters saying, "Don't go up. Let him cry himself to sleep."

Every time I'd hear that, I pictured myself dead and all of them mourning. Crying. Like I was. They'd be sorry that I was dead. They'd regret it.

Perhaps that was what lead to my wanting to write. I could create scenes in my mind and make my wishes come true. I could put it on paper, and it would be real in my life.

James Thurber's 'Walter Mitty'. That was me, I guess.

During my affair with Melissa, when I was driving alone, listening to music on my car radio, I'd often find myself sitting at a piano, playing away. Beautifully. She was there. Shades of Humphrey Bogart and Ingrid Bergman in 'Casablanca'.

Melissa would be enraptured, overwhelmed with my musical artistry, let's face it.

Play it again, Mark.

My fingers really gamboled over those keys.

Sometimes other people would gather around the piano along with her. They'd be in awe, too. I was the life of the party.

That mental process came in handy for self-eroticism, too. I had a friend who had to read pornography (which I later wrote and sold—under a pen name, of course) in order to arouse himself for solo flights. But reading about sex wasn't necessary for me—not by a long shot. This Walter Mitty performed some kinky scenes, believe me.

Actually, at about age 12 I put my first erotic paragraph down on paper, and when I re-read it, it was happening to someone else.

But Melissa was unpredictable in life and in love. What I foresaw in my imagination with her never happened. What did was always unexpected. I'd plan dialogue and action in advance, with her enraptured, flattered, enchanted and ecstatic at my words and performance, and it would actually turn out that she'd be angry and at first unresponsive, and I'd hardly know where to go from there. Or my expectation and her reaction would all be just the opposite.

So this plotting of my own life scenes worked out to my advantage —on paper or in my mind, that was it. Not in my life.

I'd plan love scenes with Melissa, but in those instances when they happened, they turned out better than I had envisioned. When they became actuality, she'd thrill me with more than I ever imagined.

Her philosophy was a woman should be a lady in the drawing room and a whore in the bedroom. And she lived up to it.

When she taught me to eat her (the first time I ate any woman—do Jewish lovers go down on each other? Definitely not Jewish husbands and wives, you can bet. It wouldn't be kosher. If Jewish wives screwed more than annually or even semi-annually, it would be a miracle), it was a whole new realistic physical thing to me, if you know what I mean.

At any rate, when I finally made a meal of Melissa for the first time, and I choked momentarily, she said to me angrily, "You gag at my cunt? You son of a bitch!"

As I say, she was unpredictable.

Funereal tears. Example.

One day I go shopping, thinking about the local newspaper I work at, where I'm loved by the entire staff—even though some of them really secretly—or not so secretly—hate me, but put on the love performance because we all have to work together, often under stressful conditions. One day, I'm sitting at my desk and I get a call from Hollywood. Joe Blow, one of the biggest producers at the most important studio there, is on the phone.

"Mark," he says. "I read the screenplay you mailed to my office. We don't know you, but this property is a sure-fire blockbuster. Get out here fast. We need rewrites immediately. We'll wire your expenses and there'll be a room waiting for you at the Beverly-Hilton. We're giving you an advance of a quarter of a million. When you get off the plane, look for a stretch limo with a TV a bar."

The staff of the newspaper senses what my conversation was all about, either by ESP or osmosis, and organizes a quick going-away party for me.

Cut to:

Five minutes later: The grand occasion at the newspaper.

While we're all gathered together in the newsroom eating a layout of food ordered on the spot and delivered within 20 seconds, and polishing off a few bottles of champagne, and they're all looking at me in awe, surprise! They show me a layout of my photo and an article about my success that they've quickly thrown together to put on the front page. My picture was taken, developed, printed and engraved, and an article was written about me, set it in type and laid out in less than two minutes. They had to tear the news out of the front page to put it in.

Cut to:

I'm on the Coast, in the middle of the rewriting of the screenplay (at poolside), and for some reason I have to fly back East. (Any reason: Maybe to pick up a tie that matches a fancy shirt I bought at the hotel in order to attend a formal orgy the next evening.)

The plane crashes.

Shirley calls the newspaper. I was killed.

The editor, in her office, puts the phone down slowly. She goes into the newsroom.

Naturally, everyone is there (from day side and night side, for the convenience of my fantasy).

She tells them that I died in a plane crash.

The place goes into a funk. It's like the typical office in New York the day Kennedy was assassinated.

No one can work. The mass sobbing is overwhelming. The editor finally concedes to the expected lethargy and dismisses the entire newspaper staff for the day. "Fuck the deadline," she says.

Dissolve.

The funeral parlor. The newspaper staff members are slowly filing by my coffin, looking lovingly at me. I'm lying there, arms folded, wearing a yarmulke.

(My body survived the crash intact.)

There are tears in everyone's eyes.

There are tears in my eyes as I go through the aisles of the supermarket, shopping and thinking about the incident, feeling sorry for the staff members feeling sorry for me.

Despite the differences I may have had with each of them from time to time, they now regret the hard times they gave me. They realize that they should have always been nice to me. But it's too late.

Now they have regrets.

Lots of tears.

I wipe my eyes, take a bottle of liquid detergent from the shelf, and put it into the shopping cart.

Chapter 10

My relationship with my wife started out with sex almost immediately. In fact, soon after we met. It continued throughout a courtship that lasted about four years. Then, less than six months after we were married, it petered out, so to speak.

The cause? A number of reasons.

One somewhat basic one was that she tried so hard to change me that she quickly became my mother. And intercourse with one's son, obviously, is incest.

Being Jewish, she eventually turned out to be a typical Jewish mother, and, to a good extent, a JAP (Jewish American Princess).

Her reading interests were primarily mystery and science fiction. Genre literature in which the characters, for the most part, don't have opposing genitals.

Only six months after we were married, we'd be in bed and when I'd put a hard-on into her hand, she'd fall asleep.

She developed an overpowering disinterest in sex.

That was my cue for eventual sexual freedom.

Still, strangely enough, the marriage was functional. In a way, she was good for me. She kept the house neat, handled family finances, and did my income tax. I could never make decisions on how to budget. So, with that out of my hands, I could take just enough money—when it was occasionally available—and use it to do my own thing.

Actually, she was good for me at the time.

You must be aware of the situation in which a spouse outgrows a marriage. Well, that's what happened to me. But the reason why it happened to me is explainable.

I was a depressive. I needed a mother. But at the beginning, it was more subtle than that. At that time, the problem of my not being self-sufficient was resolved.

But at the same time, I needed a woman.

Unfortunately, she wasn't both.

Later, when I thought back to our premarital lovemaking, I began to see reasons for her reluctance to perform the act as well as her lack of physiological lubrication and her constant need for Vaseline, as well as sexual disinterest in me. It was then that I realized she had forced herself to take part in coitus because of her need to be married.

Every Jewish woman has to be married.

We had had mutual interests: classical music, reading (which I was later to evaluate, as I've mentioned, to be monumentally different—genre [formula plots] for her, mainstream [which is about "life"] for me. But we both liked plays—which she went to constantly before we were married, when she also lived in Philadelphia.

In fact, we had met at a little theater there. She was running lights, and I was directing.

One incident in our pre-courtship days was often brought up in times of marital stress: the time we actually met. It was during a rehearsal, and we were down in the basement of the theater, which had been converted from an old, abandoned movie house. The large, dank, cardboard-box-filled room was crowded with props, racks of clothing, and crude dressing rooms. She had accidentally bumped into a low pipe and was holding her head in pain. I went to her immediately to see what I could do. Her answer to my offer of aid was, "Go away!" It was that brief conversation that started our friendship. To get to the point, she often referred to it by saying that she wished the whole thing hadn't happened. Or that I, at least, would have accepted her demand and gone away. We would never have dated and been married. I agreed.

Oh yes, one other important factor in our relationship: years later, when I had fallen into deep depressions. While keeping me in that state in order to control me, she was also the person who regulated my dose of anti-depressant. That's right, not any psychiatrist. So she actually pulled me out of it. (Ironically, however, she might possibly have been the person who triggered those traumatic depressive incidents from my subconscious time bomb of depression.)

After all, what do psychiatrists do but prescribe medication, listen, and talk (very occasionally, if ever, if they're Freudian)—poorly guessing whether there should be a change of medication or an increase or decrease in the dosage of a currently prescribed drug.

Do most psychiatrists really listen to what their patients say? As far as paying attention to a patient's statements, I've seen many psychiatrists—at my expense—hide a yawn behind a fist. As for their advice, it's primarily of textbook quality, mainly based on pure conjecture. Bull, to put it pithily.

Shirley knew my psyche so well after so many years of courtship and marriage (and suffering through my depressions), that she was able to evaluate my conversation and attitude (as the doctors should have) and suggest increases or decreases of the drugs that had been prescribed. Most of the psychiatrists I'd seen didn't really seem to comprehend whether their drugs were actually working or not. I doubted that they really knew what a depression really was. They sort of played around with different medications, judging by my conversation, or bursts of verbiage, whether I should stay with that drug or not, or whether the dose should be raised or lowered. But most shrinks—in my experience, at least—can't judge the import of a patient's verbiage based on a total of a couple of hours a week. They're just not that perceptive or interested.

After a Dr. Schwartz had given up on Adapin (generic name: doxepin) and switched me to different medications, one after another, and I had given up on him, and, finally, psychiatrists, in general, Shirley told me she had noticed that Adapin had been somewhat effective while I had taken it. Of course, being depressed, I told her that I didn't think that particular anti-depressant had any affect on me. I hadn't felt it. But being anxious to be rid of my despair, as usual, I said all right, let's try it, and got some from a pharmacist-friend.

When I had worked for Carey & Philips in their Drug Regulatory Affairs department as a medical writer, my job included evaluating clinical reports on doses, and deciding which were most effective. Following that, I had those doses I determined—which included those I ascertained through college clinical studies and other outside sources—approved by the company's staff physicians, through memos.

So, in a combined effort, Shirley and I started me off with massive doses of Adapin, and I began to come out of the depression for minutes at a time. And those few minutes were pure joy, with the depression totally gone. I could envision, in those quickly passing moments of being lifted from the doldrums, a future life of enthusiasm once again. But when the drug's effects faded away, and hope with it, I descended back into hell. Shirley regulated the dose daily, telling me to take so many milligrams, changing the dose regularly after we conversed.

Dr. Schwartz, my final psychiatrist had prescribed for me the limit in outpatient dosage: 150 milligrams in divided doses over a period of each day.

When I had asked him if he would increase the dose, he said I needed a blood test to evaluate whether I was absorbing it properly.

The stupid ass. If my physiology wasn't accepting the prescribed dose, then, I felt, I should be given a more potent quantity. Although I requested it, he told me that if I took that amount, the excess would go out the 'therapeutic window'. Which it obviously didn't. I should have thrown him out of the therapeutic window!

So when I quit Dr. Schwartz, and decided to go along with Shirley's idea, I suggested to her that I begin with doses of 400 mg per day, which, according to the Physician's Desk Reference—the doctor's bible—was 100 mg over the suggested maximum dose for in-patients.

Then she recommended that I alternate doses daily, of 400 mg and 300 mg. And I continued on that for a few weeks.

Slowly and surely, as she regulated the dosage, gradually lowering it, my depression evaporated—completely. And finally, I put myself on a maintenance dose of 25 mg per day, sticking with it as a diabetic would stay with insulin. And I've remained out of the depression since. Totally and permanently. Without a shrink. Even now, sitting in this wheelchair. (I had my son insist that the doctor at this nursing home keep me on it.)

So I learned, by experience, that anti-depressant drugs, prescribed properly, could affect depression for the better.

I have a theory about depression, at least regarding Jewish families. Dominant Jewish mothers make their sons extremely dependent on them. For example, mine, when I was at Columbia University taking writing courses one summer, insisted that I mail my laundry to her in Philadelphia to wash and mail back. (Of course, the condition might possibly be inherited through genes.)

I didn't.

So, with the confidence I should have had at the start of life, I began my first full-time affair. Thanks to Melissa—and the anti-depressant. And, ironically, Shirley.

I was free, at last, with Shirley left behind at the starting gate.

Chapter 11

My other women... my other loves... my sex life?

It goes back to my childhood.

I had my first orgasm while I was climbing a pole and my little female playmate from across the street was standing on the pavement below, shouting something at me. But I was glazed over. I really didn't hear her, and didn't want to. The experience was too physically engrossing.

I hadn't as yet associated the orgasm and the little girl, although I was always excited when there was some opportunity to see some of her bare tush.

I sensed at that age that there was something electrifying (which I would later call 'sensuous') about the body of someone of the opposite sex.

My hormones were already at work. In fact, a number of times I managed to get one of the neighborhood girls to lie face down on the couch in my parents' living room. While no one was around, I would lift her dress, pull down her panties, and look at that lovely landscape: two voluptuous hemispheres of baby skin.

Stupid me. That's all I did.

If porn videos, which I felt, many years later, had been on the market then, and were used for sex education, and I had seen them, I wouldn't have wasted my time feasting just my eyes. Had I been an informed child... But no such luck. Oh, well, what the hell, live and learn.

However, when I reached about fifth grade in grammar school, I became buddies with Max, another student, who *was* well informed on he subject of sex. His brother, who was quite hip, and who later became a gynecologist, provided him with the proper information and, as a result, Max developed—beginning at age 11—a proclivity for seducing little girls.

For me, as the years went on, getting females to go along with my little experiments, and some more developed ideas I had, became more difficult and complicated.

My friendship with Max blossomed, and by the time we reached high school, he had became more and more successful with girls. Finally, his advice to me about how to make out finally paid off.

"Girls are as interested in sex as we are," was his trite, age-old philosophy. It was new to him, of course, and me.

At last, I scored.

Until then I had bungled almost every opportunity.

My first victory, though, was with was with a classic nymphomaniac I had met at a party. Her 'condition' was written all over her.

She was somewhat heavy and not at all attractive, but quite torrid. When I picked her up at her parents' house for the date, I asked her if she wanted to go to the movies or for a drive. The ride interested her.

I followed all of Max's instructions.

I pulled the car into Lover's Lane after dusk—in Fairmount Park

"Do you want to go into the back seat?" I asked, according to my instructions, yet expecting resistance.

Sure enough she did. His advice was working! I was overwhelmed!

I kissed her for a while, anxious to get down to business. Then, I put my hand under her skirt and grasped my way around unfamiliar territory—with no opposition on her part.

Next step according to Max, panty removal.

No problem.

Remember, these were the days before heavy drug distribution and casual teenage sex. It was when most of the girls claimed that they were 'saving' it for their husbands, although Kinsey had reported otherwise. It was before seduction of one's willing partner was called 'date rape'.

I pushed her knees apart, at the same time complicatedly maneuvering a prophylactic into its proper position. This device later became more known, during the AIDS crisis, as a condom. I had been carrying one in my wallet for years. Then I groped with her flesh and mine. But my search of her topography was to no avail. I was going nowhere. Or, rather, everywhere but the right place. Then my fingers found the object of my pursuit. Nevertheless, I kept constantly finding myself a step away from my functional goal; that is, I was not quite able to accomplish it.

It was anatomical ignorance, which as I pointed out, could have been wiped away with the study of porno tapes.

But then she helped.

"Up the middle!" she groaned, and came to my aid with her hand.

My total blunders?

One was...

During the time I was attending high school, I often looked out of the front window of our living room where I had for months, or perhaps years, observed the bedroom window of the once-little girl across the street. The one, by the way, who had quizzically observed me many years before when I had an orgasm climbing the pole. She was quite rotund, but full of personality.

One day she invited me to keep her company while she baby-sat for her brother at his apartment. She was in high school at the time; I was in college.

I showed up, hot-blooded.

Full of spunk, I immediately sat down next to her on the couch, put my arm around her and kissed her easily for the first time. No resistance. (Great!) So I reached over and wrapped my palm around her fat, voluptuous thigh.

Still no problem.

Then I slid my hand upward immediately to her crotch and, according to Max's guidelines, rubbed.

It did not seem erotic at all.

But, surprisingly, she said. "That does it. Let's go into the bedroom."

Holy shit!

She had her panties off in an instant and was handing me a palm-sized tin-foil package she had taken from a drawer. "My brother has lots of these," she told me. "He won't miss them." And she was on her back in bed in the dimness, obese knees spread wide and drawn back.

I got my pants halfway down, and was over her, nervously trying to find the way to pathway of ecstasy for my already physiologically prepared counterpart—when the doorbell rang.

We quickly gathered ourselves together, tugging at snarled attire. Then she rushed to the door, as I frantically followed, evidently wearing a sheepish expression.

It was her aunt, also rotund (whom I now judge to have been between 35 and 40 at the time, and who later, when she married for the first time, wedded an Irishman, driving her relatives up he wall because they were Jewish). She looked back-and-forth from my almost-seduced childhood companion to me, her face showing that she questioned circumstances.

I felt all sorts of guilt. I imagined that my friend's aunt guessed, in detail, what had so far happened.

The aunt left almost immediately, and my young neighbor, still radiant with exuberance and vivacity, led me back to the bedroom.

"Okay, let's go!" she said, getting herself back to her previous state of semi-dress and positioning herself as before.

"We'd better not," I told her nervously and in shock. I was seeing white. "I think I'd better leave," I said in the midst of that mental explosion: a blast of worry about what her aunt would think and imagined possibilities of word of my despicable attempt being passed along to the girl's family.

"That's all right," she said, attempting to calm me with a smile. "She won't be back."

But I had already reached a state of hyper-anxiety and was out of there, fast.

When I think back to that moment, that opportunity, that memory of potential sex, I could kick myself. Except that, now, at this point in life, I could hardly lift a leg on this wheelchair to do it.

I was later informed that the girl was secretly married only weeks later, and the news didn't come out for some time. I learned about it from, of all people, my mother.

The young lady had obviously been quite experienced—and was looking forward to getting a little on the side with me.

Shit!

Another time, I was dating a really beautiful young lady. I was in my first year of college and she was a sophomore in high school. A relative had arranged our introduction. After only a few dates, we began to talk a lot about sex, but she seemed rather prim in her outlook. (After having been around for 88 years, however, and spent a great deal of that time observing the psychology of females, many of whom are prim on the surface, but not underneath, I now realize, too late, that my conclusion at the time was without basis.)

After parking with her, kissing her, and running my tongue as far as possible into her décolletage, she frankly stated, "Let's go to a motel."

I was surprised, but before considering making such an investment, I informed her that, "you have to prove yourself first."

Of course, she didn't.

Another occasion to think back on.

Hmmmmm... I'm thinking back on it...

My conclusion?

Mark, you schmuck!

But there were successes, too. Some, anyway. Somewhat?

Wait.

You're wondering why I'm digressing in this novel from getting to the plot. Right?

In fiction, you see, a writer has to develop the characters. And since the protagonist in this novel is me, rearranged so that "All of the characters in this book are fictitious, and any resemblance to actual persons, living or dead, is purely coincidental," I'm giving you 'my' experiences and thoughts so that you can see me three-dimensionally. Get it? But the disclaimer points out that it's not really me.

So, is it me? Did what I'm writing about really happen?

That's for me to wonder, and you to guess.

Have patience, (as they say) 'Dear Reader'.

Now I'll tell you all about Melissa. The only woman I ever really loved (if I did love her, that is—and if she really existed). All of this I'm informing you about now only concerns sex: the basic development of my protagonist.

And I'll also tell you about how I almost made it as a writer. Maybe I did make it. I don't know. You can be the judge.

You're judging me now, aren't you?

So there was Marsha Katz.

I met her while doing medical research at a college of medicine in Philadelphia.

After I graduated from pharmacy school—I worked one day in a drugstore (arranged by my father, who said, "You'll see, you'll like it"). I quit the job at the end of that day. I never worked in a drugstore again. By the way, the pharmacist, a friend of my father, told me at the start of the day, when he saw me smoking, that I couldn't smoke there. "I'll end your smoking habit," he insisted with strained determination, as his own cigarettes, during the day, added burned holes in the counter where he compounded his prescriptions.

So I got a job at a medical school doing medical research. I was an assistant to a physician-instructor at the highest salary he could afford with a grant from NIH, the National Institute of Health. It was, of course, quite low. But the work was considerably more pleasant than dusting off bottles in a drugstore and taking crap from a druggist.

I found myself investigating the uptake of radioactive iodine in the rat stomach. Dr. Brown, my new boss, who was one of the instructors at the college, was a specialist in the thyroid, about which he had published numerous papers.

Marsha was rather thin, but quite appealing, with a rosy face. And super-friendly. We met in the halls of research at the college, where she was a lab technician.

I dated her almost immediately.

And, of course, at the end of the first date, again following Max's advice, I drove to Fairmount Park and pulled into the darkness.

She was absolutely unresponsive. So I figured that it was the usual reaction that occurred so often—with me: Mark Gessel, official turnoff.

I turned on the ignition, pulled out, and drove her home, discouraged once more as a lover.

When we arrived at her street and I was about to pull up to her house, she said, "Park here," just before the row home in which she lived. We were a few doors down.

I shut off the motor and turned to her and she quietly leaned toward me and brought her lips to mine.

She was butter in my hands. How rare. And wonderful.

After a while, she said, as she stood, "Sit over here," indicating the passenger side of the front seat where she had been sitting.

As I slipped over to her side, she turned and stood in the small space, arching over me and moving her legs so that they were on each side of mine.

Physiologically prepared, I zipped, or ripped, my fly open.

She moved the crotch of her panties aside, descended, and slid me into the warm, silky interior of her nubile body.

There was no kissing as she arose and descended, until in seconds, my body and brain exploded. It was the shortest time that it ever took me to come or ever would.

"Okay," she said, "let's go in."

We then preened ourselves, got out of the car and went to her house, where her mother was waiting for her.

We sat at the kitchen table in lively conversation.

Two more almosts and then I'll get into the crux of the story. Skip ahead if you want to. Press I for Index.

The following will give you license to do so:

Norman Mailer once wrote that if the manuscript pages of William S. Burroughs' novel, Naked Lunch, had been thrown into the air and then picked up in a different order, it still would have been the same work of genius.

And William Saroyan has written that he 'reads around' in books. After coming across that comment, I was abruptly given permission not to have to read novels linearly from beginning to end. And I appreciated it. It has made a difference in my reading since, changing occasional boredom to pleasure—by my being able to skip parts that were dull to me; also not feeling the obligation to complete the reading of a book if it doesn't appeal to me.

Therefore, as I said, feel free to jump ahead here.

Otherwise, just continue.

Or, of course, quit or exit.

(You pays yer money and you takes yer cherce.)

While Max and I had been in high school, he had been steadily dating Vicki, one of the students, while carrying on with others, of course, on the side.

Vicki was a highly intelligent young lady, who went on to become a heart surgeon. Her family was well-heeled, and there was no doubt among their friends that she and Max were making it together. Vicki seemed, to me, to be strictly his girl.

She was somewhat-broadly built, big-boned, and had sort of a subtle toughness about her.

One day, when I had gone over to her house to drop off some pictures—my hobby; I had a darkroom—I found her home alone. Max wasn't there; neither were her parents.

She led me into the study and told me to make myself comfortable while she looked the pictures over.

I settled myself on the side of the couch, sinking into its softness.

Vicki then sat next to me, very closely, her leg against mine. I tried to move away, not wanting to appear to be intimate, in the event that she thought I was the one doing the touching, but was stopped by the arm of the couch. Nevertheless, I had managed to move away from the physical contact.

I looked at her face in an attempt to discern whether she might be giving me a sign of sexual interest. (I can dream, can't I?) But she seemed to be concentrating on the pictures. I was certain that the touching was accidental.

Then she looked up from the photos and her face seemed very close to mine. In addition, the expression on her face seemed extremely warm, and her eyes looked directly at me.

She handed the pictures back by placing her hand on my lap, with them in her fingers.

"These are excellent," she smiled. "You're a wonderful photographer," she added, her hand still resting there.

I felt no erotic response in myself. All I could think of was the possibility of my betrayal of Max. But there was again the feel of her leg against mine. This time much more firmly.

I was unable to move away again. It was impossible. I couldn't slide any further in the opposite direction. At that point, I sensed that she wanted me to make a pass at her. I felt that I had the obligation; after all, we were friends. But if I was guessing wrong, I worried, I'd be terribly embarrassed. But my hormonal blood level won out.

So I leaned over and kissed her. She reacted positively, passionately, putting her hands behind my head so that our lips were tightly together.

What the hell, I thought. Max had other girls; he didn't own Vicki. So while we kissed, I unbuttoned her blouse.

I was reaching both arms around her, inside of her blouse, to unhook her bra, when we heard the front door open.

Vicki quickly broke away and buttoned her blouse while I wiped the back of my hand along my lips to remove any lipstick that was possibly there, and flattened my hair with a palm.

"Could that be Max?" I asked anxiously.

"No," she replied with calm. "He doesn't have a key."

It was her parents, home early from a trip.

We greeted them pleasantly, and they happily stated how delighted they were to be back home again.

I never tried with Vicki again.

Stupid. Right?

Yes, stupid, I've thought many times over the years.

Are you beginning to assess the personality of the main character of this book written in the first person?

One more incident, and I'll let you go. All right?

This is about an older woman.

Interested?

She was the mother, in fact, of one of the little neighborhood girls who would never even let me touch her from the time I first knew her, when I was at about age eight. The daughter had been brought up to be prim and proper. But her mother...

I think I was about 21 when this situation happened, the girl just a few years younger. And I knew for a good many years that her mother was a hot cookie, because I came upon my brother and some of his friends late one night, years before, as they were huddled together on our roof, peering down at her window, with its shade up. It faced a brick alleyway wall, which deceptively promised privacy.

Mrs. Courtney and her husband were both bare; he was lying on his back, she was sitting up, chatting, and casually stimulating him.

He was obviously aroused. And arousable under her eager hands.

They were both laughing. I remembered how often he would brag about her legs when neighbors were visiting them. And I noted in that, to me, very exciting moment of voyeurism, he had good reason for boasting.

All right, so now I'm visiting their house to say hello to their daughter who was to return from college that day for the summer holidays. She had grown up.

Mrs. Courtney was home alone. She had just returned from a party where she had obviously belted a few. It was late in the evening and she had changed into her nightgown, having prepared to turn in.

She eyed me with a strange look on her face, one that I'd never seen before. I nervously suspected that it was sexual, yet hoped that it wasn't, because I had been for years trying to make it with her daughter, unsuccessfully. I just felt plain uncomfortable. Although she looked beautiful, I felt a wall of inhibition, on my part, between us.

"I'm really knocked out," she said. "Why don't you tell me a bedtime story when I get under the covers?" She laughed, as she led the way to her bedroom.

I followed, meekly.

She got into bed, briefly exposing her lovely legs, and, I could swear, a flash of crotch, and pulled the blanket up, just below her generous cleavage.

She reached over and took my hand.

I felt that it would be improper, under the circumstances, to remove it, so I just let her continue to hold my limp fingers. "Sit down," she told me invitingly, patting the bed with her other hand.

"Do you expect Helene to be here soon?" I asked.

"Charles just called a few minutes ago," she told me with a cozy smile. "He's still at the airport. The plane is about two hours late."

I felt a subtle tug at my hand.

"Maybe I should come back tomorrow," I said.

My hand seemed to come back to me involuntarily.

She lifted her shoulders, pale flesh moving under her silky nightgown.

"All right," she replied with another smile, not looking at me.

I rushed out in an anxious state.

Subsequently, after thinking this situation over, I returned numerous times on various excuses to see her. I did find her alone a few of those times, but she never broadcast those intentions again. That magic moment was lost forever.

When I think back to all of that, you can imagine what goes through my mind. And how I often kick the shit out of myself.

I thought that would be the last story, but just one more, okay? And if you're not interested, just go to the next chapter. I told you, you have my approval. But before you consider that, this next—and last—incident is about Barbara. The sister of one of the male kids from my neighborhood. And this took place after I had become engaged to Shirley. It's about my inability to undress a girl.

Interested?

I hope so. Don't go to the next chapter, then.

Here it is. I'll give it to you in swift prose.

I had been trying to make Barbara on the side.

I had graduated from college, pharmacy school, about four years before.

She was a year out of high school, and had just broken away from her parents, had two jobs and just moved into her own apartment.

When I arrived, she was wearing a bathrobe. Had she "changed into something comfortable" for me?

I had been trying, futilely, to score with her in my father's car, since I was still living at home.

Now we were alone in her apartment.

And she was ready to go.

She put out the light.

"I think men's things are ugly," she said in the dark, speaking, I guessed, from theory rather than experience.

Barbara was stockily built.

I had her bathrobe off in an instant.

I could feel that she was wearing a bra and women's briefs that were tight around her waist and hefty thighs.

I tugged mightily at the waistband from one point unsuccessfully, forcing my fingers between it and her skin. Yet, with my fingers inside, all of my yanking was fruitless.

Then I tried pulling at the leg bands in my attempt to remove the cloth obstacle from her torso.

I struggled with great difficulty. Shirley wore silk panties that slid down easily. But Barbara's seemed ironclad.

Barbara's thoughts about my incompetence were summed up with her statement: "Get them off, and you can do it to me."

She laughed.

After almost a half-hour, with her tightening up her midriff at each of my attempts, she pulled away, and put on the lights and her bathrobe.

"I guess I'll be a virgin for a while longer," she giggled.

Again, over the years, I thought considerably about that situation, and figured out how I could have accomplished my goal: by simply moving my fingers around under the circumference of her tight waistband maneuvering the rigidly immobile underwear down slowly.

But the opportunity to get together with her never arose again.

Now you've obviously pinpointed 'Mark's' personality and understand my concept of the protagonist of this piece of fiction—whether it's my creation, or me.

Chapter 12

My mother.

Although my father dominated my mother, she actually ruled the roost.

Dr. Horowitz, during one session in which I discussed my parents, told me that my father (who had diabetes) would die first, and when he did, he said, my mother would be happy for the first time.

He was wrong, as usual.

My mother died first, of a heart condition.

My father was finally put into a nursing home. My mother had taken care of him in a small apartment to which they had retired, but my brother and sisters were busy with their families and earning a living, so they had no choice. Since I lived quite far away and worked in New York, Shirley and I visited him as regularly as we could.

My parents had claimed to be religious Jews: especially my father. They went to synagogue—an orthodox temple—on the major holidays, where the men and women were separated.

I had to sit next to my father for the entire day, dressed stiffly in a suit and tie that they had selected for me, and follow the services. He leaned over me from time to time, licked his forefinger, turned pages in his and my siddurim and, for my edification, pointed out the words that the cantor was ringing out throughout the temple.

Flashback.

My mother is dressing me for school in the kitchen above our hardware store. She's pulling on my knickers. I hated them and the long stockings I had to wear with them. I'm fighting her every inch of the way.

"I'll call your father on the pipe," she tells me, "if you don't put these on!" The pipe was a vertical water pipe, about an inch and a half in diameter, with elbows at each end, that you yelled into, either from the kitchen, or the back of the store, downstairs, to get the attention of someone at the other end to speak with them. I break away, run to the door between the kitchen and dining room. "I'll put them on myself!" I tell her.

"You'd better!" she replies emphatically.

"Mmm hmm, yeah, yeah, mmm hmm," I say. (My usual sarcastic reply to her.)

"You're the black sheep of the family!" she returns: her usual comment to me during moments that I put her under stress.

Now I'm sitting on her lap in the kitchen. We have company, and they're having a Jewish conversation—everyone's speaking at the same time. My mother is bouncing her knee up and down impatiently. She really doesn't want me on her lap. I'm a nuisance.

She takes me shopping with her, to the grocery store, the

delicatessen. It's only a short walk on our north central Philadelphia street — just a few blocks. I watch her as she searches through the vegetables and fruits and makes her selections. She goes to the counter and buys rolls, cans of food and sliced cheese and meat. The slices are wrapped in brown paper by the grocer. He totals the purchases on a brown paper bag with a thick lead pencil.

We're walking home. She meets a friend on the way. I tug at her hand. I want to continue going home. She ignores me.

Next scene.

A typical occasional morning.

"I have to go downtown shopping," my mother tells me.

"Bring me something?" I plead.

"Okay," she agrees.

I spend the day upstairs alone, passing the time, as I usually do, by going from room to room and looking into drawers. I know everything that is in each drawer, from those in the large bureaus and kitchen cabinets to the little pull out drawers with the big inset knobs in the Singer sewing machine. Buttons, pins, screwdrivers, folded notes, nuts, bolts, washers, thimbles, odds and ends of all kinds. If asked, I could have gotten to any item in an instant.

Hours later, which seems like ages later, I hear footsteps on the stairs. I run to the door with the glass window.

Mother's home!

She'll have something for me!

I pull open the door and watch her trudge up the steps burdened with bags and packages.

I stand back hopefully and she enters the hall.

What will it be? What kind of toy?

"Did you bring me something?" I ask, my mind brimming with ideas of what my surprise will be.

"Oh," she answers. "I forgot."

Time after time. Forever the same reply.

I remember standing at the toy counter of the five-and-dime, looking at all of the toys. I would go there often to enjoy seeing them after school.

One day, I stand there before this vision of paradise, delighted by the sight, when the saleslady comes up to me on the other side of the counter. She looks at me angrily. "You want to steal something, don't you?" she announces accusingly.

I leave and never return to look at the toys.

Which probably explains why I always brought my son some kind of a toy every day, even if it was a ten-cent nothing: which annoyed Shirley to no end.

An incident that stands out vividly in my mind happened one day when I had come home from grammar school. I went into my father's hardware store, and one of my sisters took me by the hand and whisked me off to the five-and-dime, where she bought me a hot dog. I don't remember why this sudden event took place in my life. All I remember is that I ate it slowly on the way home, savoring each bite.

I had no male friends my age in the neighborhood. It was a rundown area with mostly blacks, then called negroes. My brother, however, three years older than I, had found friends his age. When I went out, I usually got held up for my pennies by black kids. I'd complain at home, to no avail.

My mother would always say to me, "Why don't you go out and play like the other kids?" Perceptive, right?

So I read, wrote little stories, and listened to music.

I remember at age 11 winning the summer library contest for having read the most books. I walked miles there and back each weekday to exchange books. I had discovered the joy of reading later than most kids, but better late than never.

My mother's reaction?

"Why don't you stop reading all those books, and go out?"

When I was in high school, I became hooked on classical music through friends, and bought hi-fi components when they were first becoming popular.

I was in the 'den' listening to a new set of LP's of Handel's Messiah one day, when my mother came in and looked at the cover of the album. "Is that what you're listening to?" she asked, shocked. "Church music?"

Another time, she burst in as I was listening to classical music and shouted, "Boom boom, boom boom. Is that all you're interested in?"

Such was my relationship with my mother.

Chapter 13

I had moved to New York from Philadelphia on the promise of a job as a Broadway stage manager.

After obtaining the representation of an agent (who never sold anything I wrote, and whom I later dropped for another years later), I learned, through him, of a young producer, Marty Bernstein, who was looking to raise money for a play.

I got together with Marty and he told me that he would give me a piece of the show on a percentage basis—a finder's fee—depending upon how much of the $100,000 capitalization I raised, as well as a job with the production.

I went to work on relatives and friends in Philadelphia, and brought in over ten grand.

Shortly after, I was living in New York in a fourth-floor walk-up on West 82nd Street, and working in Marty's temporary office while he put the show together.

We opened in Baltimore, continued in New Haven, and closed in New York after a six-week Manhattan run.

After having, at last, made contact in the theater, I then landed a job as a secretary and script reader for Robert Kempton, a very successful elderly producer (for little pay). I tried to worm my way into his world with a play I had written—The Wrecker's Ball, an autobiographical account of my childhood that opened with a house being demolished—actually the fictional home of my childhood. And the main characters of the play, a reflection of my wife and myself, visiting the scene and recalling the past just before the building was totally destroyed. Other roles included montages of friends and relatives.

After working for Kempton for a few months, I gathered the strength to submit the script to him, personally. As I handed it to him, he looked at me with a jaundiced eye, and grew even more suspicious when I pitched the story and then related it to my life. He promised to read it, and gave it back to me the next day, saying it wasn't right for him. I doubt that he even looked at a page of it. I think his opinion of me, which seemed obviously not to be a high one, (formed day by day as he passed my desk in his anteroom), prejudiced him against me, and I don't think he would have been interested even if I had handed him the script of Hamlet.

But I finally did get a break with that play.

My first and last produced on The Great White Way.

It happened a couple of years later, after I had met Melissa and we had become lovers.

I gave the manuscript to her one afternoon after a few kisses. We were lying next to each other on a motel room bed, our clothes on the floor, our love and lust for each other satisfied.

"I just happen to have this with me," I told her in a tone of voice purposely intended to have a ring of irony to it, as I rolled to the side and reached down to the floor and into my briefcase. I brought up my script of The Wrecker's Ball, with a matching ironic smile.

She sat up, her back against the headboard, drew her knees back, rested the bound typescript against her legs, and opened its pages. As I situated myself next to her to follow her reading of my lines and simultaneously observe her reaction, my eyes went to the blond pelt at the bottom of the manuscript.

"Is it good?" she asked.

"Naturally," I said, slipping my hand through the space between the back of her neck and headboard, curving my arm around her, and enclosing her arm with my fingers.

"Should I have Brent produce it?" she said in mock seriousness.

"If he likes it," I said. "And if you like it," I added.

She turned her head and kissed my neck. "If you say it's good, then I like it."

"But he has to like it, too," I said. "Doesn't he?"

"He will, if I want him to."

"Do you really think he'll like it?" I asked.

"He may not, but after I'm finished with him, he will."

"And you haven't even read it yet," I laughed.

"Don't worry," she assured me, putting the script aside, placing her hands to my cheeks and bringing me face to face with her. She pressed her lips to mine. With the wet sound of our kiss, I tasted the heat of her body in her mouth, and smelled the subtle combined odor of her flesh and perfume. I felt her hand touch the inner part of my thigh, then move upward. When she reached her goal, there was a shock of pleasure.

"Don't worry, darling," she promised me, kissing my arm. "You'll be in, I can promise you that."

She kissed me aggressively, bringing her weight onto me until I was on my back again and ready for more love.

Chapter 14

Let's go back a bit in time.

Melissa and I became inseparable.

After we had first made love in the woods behind the shopping center, enveloped in the decaying fragrance of leaves that saturated the warm, potent air, we took a walk. The distant lights of the mall across the way sparkled in the autumn night.

Our arms were around each other.

"We'll have to be discreet," she told me. Then she turned her face to mine and said, "I have a feeling, though, that one of us is going to get hurt."

That was putting it mildly. And I should have wondered whom she had in mind.

"I can't imagine how," I replied. "If we're discreet."

We had stopped walking in the deepening darkness, and she looked directly into my eyes without embarrassment. She reached her arms gently around me, placed her hands on my buttocks, and pressed my body lightly against hers. I was startled, even though we had just made love moments before. I had never thought of Melissa as sensuous. She had seemed, until that moment, like Brent's one-man woman who had had his children by some form of immaculate conception. Then, even with our first erotic encounter, she had conducted herself as someone who had to get past the preliminaries by rote in order to make our companionship work.

She slid her hands under my shirt and up above my waist to the small of my back and down again, with the experience gained only in her marriage, into my pants, beneath my shorts. I felt the warmth of her palms on the skin of my buttocks, put my arms around her, and tightened them as if in a contraction of orgasm.

Then came the words that I would hear over and over, that combined her feelings for me with the overwhelming eroticism that I had least expected from her. It was new in my life, having any woman say it to me with such depth and sincerity. I had never known such ecstasy, nor would I ever know it again.

She breathed, "I love you," in a tone that swept my senses into a galaxy of sparkling lights. "I fell in love with you the first time I saw you. At the rehearsal of To be Forgotten."

How wonderfully elating those words were, as well as the expression of love and admiration in her facial expression. I was already, at that moment, feeling an initial surge of love for her. This was my first really genuine such experience with her, and I was already beginning to fall very hard for her, as I would later realize. And my love for her (which I always doubted) would continue growing and become an obsession. I was never able to be certain—and I'm not sure, even to this day—if it was real love, or a spell, which she cast by giving herself to me with such overwhelming passion. Not only every time I desired her body, but by constantly initiating sex that unabashedly showed her need for me.

I wanted to ask why she had this compelling desire for me, but I was afraid to inquire, because I feared that if I did, she might explore her thoughts and discover that her infatuation didn't really exist at all. It all seemed to be a miracle that had been created by some unknown force which favored me, a radiance in my life that might turn to a fading shadow as quickly as it had materialized.

Perhaps she suspected the same possibility in her life.

And now that all this was mine, I wanted never to lose it.

Then, surprisingly, as all coincidences occur, she answered my question as if she had heard me through mental telepathy.

"I don't know why I feel this way, Mark. There's something about you that excites me. I don't know what it is. And, frankly, I don't care. All I know is that it's the way it is. That I want to see you again—and again and again." She kissed my lips.

Melissa was mine. This beautiful, highly intelligent, exciting creature was mine, and I was soon to learn that she would sacrifice anything just to be with me. Unfortunately, even to the point where it might interfere with my life. Our wanting to have each other all the time was to become an obsession.

I had no desire to have complete control over Melissa, but nevertheless that power was there. I didn't want to feel it, because it seemed cruel and unkind to possess it. Nevertheless, it gave me a feeling of extraordinary virility, which evidently was necessary because I had been put down continually by my parents, and never felt like a 'mensch', or man, in their presence, even past my twenties. And that had led to my unconsciously developing pattern for accepting others masochistically. Not to mention my depressions.

"You know," Melissa told me sometime later, following a session of almost perfect, no-holds barred lovemaking, "I can understand why sex is so popular. It lets you forget all of your problems."

That comment was a portent of what was to come.

Eventually, it wasn't to be just me. Or anyone else special.

Just sex.

Chapter 15

So the play did, eventually, get produced.

Melissa put pressure on Brent, as she had promised. Not that the script wasn't good. Any play had to be at least competent before a producer would consider putting it on. But the determining factors for obtaining money to get a play on the boards could be anything—star or casting appeal to the money people, director, a respected person's belief in it, the words of a wife, the words of a mistress.

Brent had managed to get interest in the play from one of Hollywood's brightest young directors, Lester Hopkins. He had flown into New York and would be there for its four-week rehearsal, then through try-outs in New Haven and Baltimore, and finally through the first week previews, its opening on Broadway, and a week or so of its run—if it passed the test of the critics.

We all met for the first day of rehearsal in a hall above an Italian restaurant on 42nd Street.

Lester was a tall, intense, good-looking man. He was pale and highly intelligent, probably the result of sitting at home reading scripts, or, concentrating on show business as a career from his childhood. Or just keying up on literature.

Having obtained Lester Hopkins to do the play, it had opened the doors to Brent for a Hollywood star. A successful motion picture director was a pipeline through to the right movie people—top talent and the agents who represented it. Which Lester was pleased to use to Brent's advantage.

Despite the fact that most well-known screen actors look good when their image is blown up to two-dimensional oversize, because of the film editor's timed-with-feeling cuts, they are conditioned to doing three, four, or more takes until they get their gestures and dialogue right. Most screen actors are not experienced in being onstage, developing in depth the proper mannerisms for their characters, carrying dialogue through when they are cued by an incorrect line, and concentratively interacting with other actors, come what may, from an intransigent starting point: the moment the curtain goes up. But most importantly, they don't always have the capability of ignoring their mistakes and going on.

The theater requires actors with stage presence and a knack for remembering lines and blocking, who, once a play begins, can sustain a mood. For live theater, an actor must be a fascinating moving statuette in a distant world, which can capture the imagination of an audience.

Lester's first words to me at that initial meeting, when we sat down together on folding chairs in the large bare room were, "I'm looking forward to working with Brenda Williams." What he should have said was, I later learned, "I'm looking forward to getting into Brenda Williams' pants, in addition to enjoying the favors of my homosexual friends."

"I went over your script on the plane," he told me next, showing pain in his facial expression—purposely, I suspected.

"What changes do you want?"

"Well, first of all," he told me still looking blankly at the first page of my script, "I don't think it opens with enough impact."

"What do you mean?" I asked politely. This was my 'first' play, since it was the first to be put on the boards (I had written others and packed them away. The learning process...). A play is not a novel, I thought. It's the work of a committee, so why be vain and risk this opportunity. The main goal is to have my play produced. Then, later, with my next play, I can have a bit more power. Of course, I didn't realize at the time that the same power plays continue, whether you're successful or not. I should have been unyielding. But live and learn.

"I think the wife should come onstage first," Lester advised, "look around, then beckon to her husband. Then he enters."

"All right," I agreed courteously.

Actually, I felt that Hopkins should leave the script as it was. After all, the main character was the protagonist—me, incarnate, and it was his former home that he was coming back to, so he should come onstage first. My play, The Wrecker's Ball, which, as I mentioned earlier, was a good deal autobiographical, was about a man who visits his childhood home in downtown Philadelphia. The set is the rooms above his father's hardware store. By coincidence, he has arrived on the day that the building is being demolished. Throughout the drama, the lights dim, scenes of his past life take place, with the lights coming up subsequently at the end of each, and on the present. The other roles are of his parents, who have passed away, and additional characters who represent people who played important parts in his life.

"Now, on page three," he went on, having found me docile, and, as a consequence, continuing with the same strategy, "when they take a long look around, music comes up."

Error number two, music.

He was bringing Hollywood to Broadway. The first sign—to me—that he was already totally on the wrong track.

Not only do many movie and television actors often have problems on the stage, so do inexperienced theatrical directors, despite being experienced in movies. A play is a compact package of dramaturgy. A movie is loose and flexible and doesn't require, at least in minds like Hopkins, concentrated thinking and effort.

I continued to note his suggested changes (errors number three to infinity) that he wanted me to make that evening and have ready for him the next day.

Other members of the cast began arriving. The stage manager and his assistant had been there from the start, unobtrusively arranging chairs on a chalk-marked floor and noting cues in their black plastic-covered manuscripts.

While were making notes in our respective scripts, Lester suddenly looked up. I raised my eyes to him in order to ascertain the reason for his sudden reaction. His expression, a smile aimed at the doorway, was nothing less than dynamic.

I shifted my glance in that direction. It was Brenda Williams. She had just walked in the door.

Brenda was wearing a very obviously expensive black fur coat. Her face was immaculately made-up with colors right out of the paint box. She looked magnificently beautiful, though much smaller than she appeared to be on the screen. Still, she bore the same glow of charisma that surrounded her in her movies.

Brenda had worked her way up from television sitcoms, in which, over a period of about five short years, she had gained overwhelming popularity. Her picture had been on the cover of TV Guide, as well as on the covers of a good number of women and teenager magazines.

A number of articles about her had appeared in The *New York Times*.

The TV series that she had stepped into, just out of a communications curriculum at Oklahoma University, had taken off like a rocket. With just the right lack of talent to make her appear naive, she had captured the heart of America.

Two years later, she was cast in the leading role of *Battered Bride*, a message movie with a so-so script which, by some sort of mass hypnosis, attracted major moviegoers of all ages (most of whom had been her television fans). This wide interest in her included a great deal of acclaim from movie critics and moguls, and it brought her a nomination for an Academy Award.

No one could really analyze the success of the movie. It just took the country by storm.

She stepped over to where we were sitting, and not knowing either of us yet, immediately looked directly at the handsome young man.

She reached out a gloved hand, which was dipped down. "Lester Hopkins?" she asked.

"That's me," he replied with a sensual smile that he bore into her eyes. He took her limp fingers.

"I'm delighted to meet you," she said in a well-acted outgoing manner.

"My pleasure," Lester replied. "Have you had a chance to look at the last revision of the script?"

"Yes. It needs a bit of work."

Evidently the proper comments for both silver and small screen productions.

Her comment was Lester's cue for a smug introduction of me.

"This is Mark Gessel," he said with a grin. "The author. I mean, playwright," he corrected, widening his lips into a smile.

"Oh, I'm awfully sorry," Brenda apologized. "I didn't mean it that way."

I wanted to say, "What way?" But I didn't.

"It just needs a few changes," she amended, hesitating momentarily before she added. "Nothing serious." She was obviously an expert on Broadway plays, never having been in any. Not, in fact, having seen any, either. Perhaps, I thought, she was used to being asked subserviently for her opinion by television non-directors who were impressed by the aura of glamour in which she glowed.

From the start, I could see that I was flanked by two know-it-alls on ego trips. I had the feeling that there would soon be sparks between them, and I don't mean sparks of fondness. There eventually were—as I forecast to myself at this, their first meeting.

Within the next ten minutes, the rest of the cast arrived.

Most were bit characters who had also flown in from the Coast.

Brent, who was purposely not in attendance, had been quite proud of his accomplishment in securing Lester, and had let him do all of the casting. Which was why Brent wasn't there. Having given Lester full rein over the production, Brent's absence symbolized the fact that he was true to his word to Lester, that the Hollywood director had full control. So we ended up with a stage full of beautiful, not very stage-talented people—male and female. They had been hanging around the Hollywood Hills waiting to be cast in any kind of movie role, and suddenly found themselves, through the random fortunes of show biz, about to get that big break on Broadway. Any or all of them, I sensed, might have been to bed with Lester, except for Brenda Williams.

Now, after doing 'respectable' acting (appearing on Broadway), these pseudo-thespians no doubt figured that they could go back to the motion-picture cameras able to hold their noses high above actor-friends who hadn't performed on the New York stage. I was to find true my speculation that they were all one big, happy family of incompetent bit players.

Still, I had to be grateful. Without them and the circumstances that brought us all together, my play would never be seen.

After preliminary introductions, we set our metal folding chairs in a circle and had our first reading. It went fairly smoothly for Lester, though not for my play. But he needn't have been critical about my story line and dialogue. The atmosphere was all fun and games.

At the end of the first week, not one member of the cast knew all of their lines perfectly. True 'troupers' would have memorized their dialogue, or at least been confidently familiar with the gist of it by the second day.

"Take seven," Lester would say, as one of his friends blustered his or her way through my dialogue, prompted by the assistant stage manager. And everyone would laugh.

I had a few serious chats with Brent the first few days, away from the rehearsal hall, warning him of impending problems—and probably, disaster.

"The ball is in Lester's court," he told me on the fifth afternoon of rehearsals as we sat drinking coffee at Howard Johnson's on Broadway. "I trust the man. He's accomplished a lot for his age. I'm going along with his decisions. After all, he knows all of the people he's working with. If I interfered, they'd all resent it, and you'd no longer have that harmony you now have that Lester has been telling me about."

Brent was a heavyset man, who gave the impression of being snobbish, but really wasn't. His thoughts were so totally on his theatrical productions that he seemed barely interested in his own life. Which probably explained why he was completely oblivious to the affair I was having with his wife.

"I'll be very honest, Brent," I told him. "This play is not as good as it was when I first gave it to you. In a matter of days, Lester has made mincemeat out of it. Why don't you go to a rehearsal and take a look for yourself?"

"That's the worst thing I could do, Mark. It would make him and the cast nervous and untrusting. Let them do it the way they want. I just have a feeling that the chemistry is right. After all, Lester has done some brilliant work in films. He's known as a boy-wonder."

"Most actors know their lines," I reminded him, "by the end of the first week, especially small parts. But this is ridiculous, and Lester has me rewriting regularly. They don't even know the old lines or what they really meant, and he has me giving them new ones. They're all confused. I don't think they even remember what the story is all about—or was all about."

But Brent was inexorably trusting to his intuition, which in this case wasn't too discerning. He was under the impression that rehearsals were going well, and he didn't want to interfere.

By the middle of the second week of rehearsals (there would be four before we headed to New Haven), Lester's thespian-lovers were still struggling with their lines and blocking.

A typical question Lester would be asked by a cast member during rehearsal would be: "Was I standing over here when I gave that line last time?"

And the director's characteristic reply would be something like, "It really doesn't make that much difference. Just do it the way you feel it."

Hollywood.

Actually, a good director doesn't have to direct that well. A director who casts well will get talented actors who creatively develop their characters.

In Lester's case, his direction evidently worked well for movies, but not on a stage.

As for the major conflict of personality of the cast and crew, and contrary to Lester's hopes, Brenda took a liking to the brush-mustachioed stage manager, Stanley DeVeccio.

Stanley was a horny stud who directed occasionally at an off-the-wall

Off-Broadway theater. He had little money and survived in a basement apartment in Greenwich Village (which was, nevertheless, expensive) with cast-off furniture. Whenever he landed a Broadway stage-managing job, considering his personal wealth—or, rather, lack of it—he was in the chips.

Women flocked to Stanley because of his erotic magnetism, high intelligence, or both. In less than 10 days, Brenda was leaving rehearsals with him every night—after humbly waiting around for him to make changes in his and his assistant's scripts, re-mark the floor, and take care of other incidentals—while he ignored her.

This irked Lester to no end. Not just because he wasn't making out with the star he signed—which was obviously why he signed her—but because he knew that his seven homosexual actors, (two of them female, and most, if not all, also his lovers), were talking humorously among themselves about his inability to obtain this erotic goal. Lester constantly made a point of announcing his goal repeatedly during our bar sessions after rehearsal—to lay Brenda.

The accomplishment would give him something to brag about back in California, he told us all proudly.

While we sipped our beers or tossed down our drinks, they teased him with lines like, "Do you think you should give Brenda more lines?" or, "Do you think that you should give Stanley your job and become stage manager yourself?" Which he didn't exactly appreciate. But they were all close friends.

Some nights, toward the end of rehearsals, after hitting a bar—where he went heavily into alcohol—we had to help Lester into a cab after convincing him to leave. At least two of us would have to go with him to make sure that he got back safely to his room at the Algonquin Hotel.

Chapter 16

I woke up in Brent's bed. Melissa was still sleeping. I had slept over.

Brent had taken the kids to Chicago, to visit his relatives. He was so confident about the show that he felt no need to stay in town. Melissa told him she just didn't feel like going.

It was Sunday.

Friday night I made most of the changes Lester had requested for the weekend and dropped them off at the Algonquin. There was no use making more. The cast wasn't catching on anyway. It looked like disaster. And our first out-of-town opening was just around the corner.

I slipped my arm around Melissa. Her body was extremely warm from being under the covers, and her heat and the sweet, raw odor of her body, and pale makeup-less face, brought blood to my loins.

She stirred, slowly opened her eyes, and realized that we were at her apartment.

Her voice was weak at first. "I wish we were any place but here," she said. "It just doesn't feel right."

I expected to feel her hands moving onto me. But I was wrong.

"You're being ridiculous," I told her. "It doesn't really make any difference."

"It does to me."

I passed it off. "Melissa, what are we going to do about the play? I just know it's going to close out of town. You've got to talk to Brent. When it's reviewed in New Haven, it'll be the kiss of death. We'll never make it."

"Yes, you will. In the worst case, Brent will use the sinking fund."

"One hundred thousand bucks down the drain," I said. "And my career. I slaved over that script. My first break."

She touched her fingers to my face. Finally, contact. I felt relief.

"I appreciate what you've done for me, Melissa," I went on. "But just the same, it was all for nothing."

"All right," she replied, resigned, taking her hand away. "When he gets back Wednesday, I'll have a talk with him."

Suddenly it all seemed hopeless. "Maybe it won't do any good. Maybe the play is too far gone."

Melissa got on her knees, and leaned her face over mine, the blanket falling from her shoulders. Her expression was suddenly so full of love that I forgot all about the production for an instant. Until she spoke, reminding me.

"Everything will be all right, Mark. Don't worry."

I stewed. "I finally get a play on the boards, and a goddamn Hollywood director screws it up. No producer will look at anything of mine for another ten years. They'd sooner produce a play by a newcomer than one by a produced playwright who had a bomb on Broadway."

"Maybe everything is all right. You never know. Maybe Brent knows what he's doing. Maybe Lester knows what he's doing."

"Unlikely," I said.

"Audiences and critics are unpredictable," she insisted, and gave me a warm kiss.

I put my arms around the bare skin of her back. Touching her was comforting. I felt the beginning of an erection.

I embraced her more tightly, and her smooth flesh reminded me that I hadn't shaved. I reached to my cheek and felt the fine bristles. "I think I'll shave."

I slipped out of the bed and went into the bathroom with my shaving kit. The room was shiny clean, gleaming. Their live-in maid took good care of their large Fifth Avenue apartment. After I had persuaded Melissa that I should stay there, she had given the maid off for the weekend.

Brent's shaving cream and razor were lying on the shelf above the sink. Next to them were several bottles of after-shave lotion and various bottles and tubes of medication.

Suddenly it all hit me with stunning impact. I had been making love to Brent's wife in their bed. In a flash I realized what Melissa had been talking about, why she hadn't wanted me there. But it was too late. The deed was done and would forever be etched in our memories. And at moments in the future, during times together, when words would become tense about our individual marital relationships, as well as our own relationship, I was certain I could see this day in her eyes.

Chapter 17

It was already the third week of rehearsals.

I had become friendly with Tom Decker, a gay friend of Lester's who had the role of a cousin in the play.

Even when Tom invited me to his hotel room at the Algonquin, and we put away almost a half bottle of Jack Daniels—with him guzzling most of it—he didn't admit, directly, being one of Lester's lovers. But it could be perceived by what he said and how he said it.

It wasn't that he was feeling me out (pardon the pun) as a possibility for a sexual relationship, either. I could tell that he sensed that I was 'straight'. But we both wanted to be friends. I could sense that there was a bond between us the first time I spoke with Tom. And we were close friends, at least for as long as he was with the production.

After several shots of straight booze, Tom, who was short and stocky, about 35, opened up about Lester.

"Lester looks like a conventional sort of guy, but he's weird, as kinky as they come. I've seen him in action, if you know what I mean. Both AC and DC. He's the best performer of us all." He wiped his mouth with the back of his hand. "Anyway," he rattled on, "when he got your script out in LA, he was immediately sold on the main role for Brenda. He had been an admirer of hers from the first time he saw her on the TV screen." He paused, took another sip, smacked his sensuous lips, and continued. "He's absolutely overwhelmed by her. He even joined her fan club—would you believe? And he carries pictures of her around with him in his wallet."

"Had he ever met her?" I asked.

"Never. When he read your script, he was clobbered, not with the script as it was—but as he saw it rewritten for her. He had her unlisted number. Didn't even have to go through the usual procedure of getting a play to her through her agent. He just picked up the phone and called her directly."

"That explains all of the script changes he wants me to make," I said, not too happily.

"He had been passively hot for her. He talked about her all the time. He was actually keeping an eye out for a vehicle for her. Now he's actively hot."

Great! I thought. My play was a means to his end—or, better put, her end.

"I'm going to be brutally frank with you, Mark," Tom told me. "She wasn't as excited by the script as she was in getting on Broadway. You know, for prestige."

Strike two! I thought. And Brent's trust in the production makes it strike three. I'm out!

"You can imagine Lester's anger at Stanley running off with her."

"What's happening with them, anyway?" I asked.

Tom gave me the facts about Stanley and Brenda in such detail that it made me wonder whether Stanley, like Lester, swung both ways. I guess Tom had also made friends with Stanley because Tom was the type in whom almost everyone confides from the start. He was that kind of a warm person.

The first day of rehearsals, as Stanley had put it to Tom—according to Tom's intricate verbal rendering—Brenda and Stanley just looked at each other and 'signals' gleamed in their eyes." Stanley looked very much like the actor Tom Selleck—same build, same face, same brush moustache.

Stanley had told Tom that he "worried about having a job problem because of Lester's interest in Brenda and her interest in me," but not, of course, a relationship problem regarding Brenda. "So I played it cool like I always do—on both ends," he had informed Tom.

Tom reminded me about the day we started rehearsals.

"Remember when we all sat in a circle on those folding chairs, doing our first reading?"

Stanley, he recalled, purposely ignored Brenda and noticed that she kept looking directly at him throughout the reading. Finally, by about page 13, Brenda asked Stanley, "Would this be a line that I'd deliver as I walk toward the front of the stage?" A stupid question, just to get a conversation up with Stanley. Then, apologetically, "This is really my first time working in the theater."

Stanley responded coldly, not even looking up from his pages. "Lester's the director."

Lester hesitated. He was being put to a test. He could either make a strong statement and take control—and have power over the both of them from that time on—or be meek and let them step all over him.

He chose the latter strategy, which he ordinarily would not have done, only because of his interest in Brenda. He was willing to give up any authority he had in the production because he was so desperate for his star's body. He had no real interest in my play, other than to have the credit of having directed on Broadway. The money that he'd receive for just being there, even with the large royalty percentage deal he got with Brent, wasn't that important to him, where it might have appealed to a Broadway director who relied on such income and credits. If the play ran, he'd only get a couple of thousand a week, which compared only slightly to his Hollywood income. After taxes, he'd end up in an even higher bracket, anyway, and have to pay most of his theatrical income to the government. So it all was a lark to him. An opportunity to pursue a woman whom he lusted for so madly.

He was wise enough, even at his age, to know that a bomb on Broadway means nothing. If a director fails on a major theatrical production, it can be blamed on anyone, and that flop fades away the same as does a president's mistakes. All that's remembered of a well-known director who has made it to the professional boards is the credit. And he's wanted again, some years later. Sometimes, even sooner.

As it turned out with Lester, by the way, many years later he had a Broadway hit—because there was no Brenda.

But I'm jumping ahead.

So, Brenda left rehearsals with Stanley that first night, according to Tom's detailed verbal coverage. She asked him if she could come back to his place and go over the script. She said that she didn't trust Lester, and that although she had respect for her director, she felt that with Stanley's experience in theater (as if she knew what it was), she could get better advice from him on her role. She made it all seem very businesslike.

Stanley didn't want her to see his meager apartment, so he said it would be best to go back to her room at the Algonquin. Which they did.

Stanley said that Brenda was his easiest seduction. In fact, he described it as her seduction of him.

"She ordered drinks from room service, and—after they'd had a few —while he sat on the bed seriously going over the lines with her, she slowly and lasciviously took off articles of clothing one at a time, until she was down to her panties, and then just stood there, until he finally impatiently removed them."

"She was a torrid animal," Tom quoted Stanley as saying.

"You wouldn't think so to look at her," Tom analyzed, "especially after seeing her on the little or big screen. She was sort of like a Doris Day gone wild. I wouldn't say she's exactly a nymphomaniac. It's just that she's highly successful and famous and can have all the men she wants, so she can pick and choose physical or cerebral men, or the combination, and let the rumors fly."

What she liked most about her newfound show-business prominence, she told Stanley later, was that people gossiped anyway, so she could always easily deny any affairs. And if nobody believed her, it made her all the more interesting. Besides, she didn't plan to get married for some time, she had told Stanley.

She was an average good-looking girl-next door type who, because of sudden fame, had found herself unshackled from the conventions with which her friends had to contend. Her unconscious licentiousness had become liberated.

"She really threw herself into the sex act," Stanley said. "If Lester could have observed her making love with me, he would have rushed down to the Brooklyn Bridge and jumped off."

According to Stanley, Brenda didn't consider Lester a man. She had figured him out from his first words and physical manner, she said. And, besides, she was unimpressed with him. "I've seen better directors than Lester," she told Stanley. "There are lots of guys younger than he is who are production assistants in TV and have fire and personality and could make it one day and do better than Lester. But most of them will never get the breaks that Lester did. Lester is a nothing, a nobody who had some luck, the asshole. And the way he walks and talks, you can see that he really likes boys. He probably couldn't even get it up with me, anyway."

"Stanley banged her regularly through rehearsals," Tom went on, "and Lester ate his heart out every evening following rehearsals, when Tom and Brenda went off together into the night. Finally, toward the end, when Lester realized that he'd never make it with her, he began putting his foot down with the cast. But it was too late for him to insinuate that he might replace Brenda."

By that time they were all out of control at rehearsals, sloppily giving their lines, doing their blocking differently at every rehearsal, and generally ruining what little was left of my play.

Chapter 18

The set designer, Christopher Thomas, lived at the Dakota, the overpowering brown stone building on Central Park West where, many years later, John Lennon, of the Beatles, subsequently lived with his family; it was where he was shot. Christopher's studio apartment, with unexpected rooms, was impressive.

I went to one of the meetings there with Brent, where I saw the in-progress model for The Wrecker's Ball. It was damned good. Brent had signed one of the best set designers in the business.

The miniature three-wall prototype was sitting on Christopher's desk when we arrived for a final discussion about the set decorations. The actual set was being built at a studio across town. It was almost done, and would reach New Haven a week before we did, for setting up. It was planned that by the time we arrived at the theater there, we'd find the lighting designer adjusting the spotlights, gels, fresnels and inkie dinkies.

While Brent and Christopher discussed the furniture and props that we'd be using, I looked the tiny set over. I was overcome by the experience. The effort of my imagination had created a reality of its own. Before my eyes was the arena I had conceived, a physically rearranged vehicle of the original. A version mutated from the house in which I had grown up, in which would be re-enacted a literary variation of my childhood in Philadelphia, above a hardware store. And the story was to take place there in this replica modified to appear half torn-down.

But I was later to be even more overwhelmed, when I would first walk into the set itself, onstage, in New Haven.

After leaving Christopher's apartment at the Dakota, Brent and I went back to his office.

Melissa was there, working at the desk of his receptionist, Pat, a bright, young girl who had recently graduated from Bennington. She also screened unsolicited scripts, but was now in Brent's office answering the phone for him.

Melissa and I had just made love that morning at a motel in north Jersey for almost three hours. I always found it inconceivable when the three of us were together that Brent had no inkling of what was going on.

Melissa was casual to me, almost cold. She acted as if we were just impersonal acquaintances, as if we had never been lovers and weren't at that moment.

Brent went directly into his office, put down his brief case, hung his coat, and returned. During this time, I waited by the desk where Melissa was sitting, wanting to connect with her through eye contact, to break through even momentarily to the warmth of our relationship, but she was reading a letter seemingly intently and didn't look up at me. Brent, distracted, began going through papers on Pat's desk. He was getting another production together, a musical that would be capitalized at $400,000. He had optioned a novel and was having it adapted to a play by a Broadway book-and-lyrics writer with a series of hit shows behind him and a composer who had also seen a fair amount of success himself in the musical theater.

"Did I get a call from Basil Worthe?" he asked Melissa. "He's the agent for the Killington book. We're supposed to work out additional terms on less of an advance against an escalation arrangement."

"No," she answered. "But Killington, himself, called. He said that Basil is out of town and will call you next week." Then she turned to me and said impassionately, "Hello, Mark. How's the play going?"

It felt strange carrying on such a chilly conversation after a morning of such flaming amorousness. Her acting could have brought her the Academy Award.

"I'm not that pleased," I replied.

"Why?"

"Frankly, it's gotten far from what I originally wrote."

"I should think it would be improved after all this time."

"To be honest," I said, "it seems to be going downhill."

Brent was still occupied with the papers, but he was listening to everything we said. "Still dissatisfied, Mark?" He continued shuffling the sheets he was reading.

Melissa gave me a meaningful glance. I suddenly felt our closeness again. But then the look faded from her face as quickly as it had materialized, and she gazed downward again.

"What's your opinion of Mark's play, Brent?" she asked, twirling a pencil as she seemingly concentrated on the page in front of her. He was always too busy to fill her in on all of his theatrical activities, so he hadn't told her that he was leaving Lester to his own devices.

"I haven't seen any of the rehearsals," Brent said, still partially distracted.

Melissa's acting became even more exceptional. She looked at him. "Do you mean that you don't know how the production is going?" she questioned with what only I new was artificial surprise. "You always go to rehearsals as often as you can."

Brent looked at her. "I trust Lester. He's highly respected, and he's had five very successful movies—especially his first. Five films. Five hits."

"But that doesn't mean that he knows what he's doing in the theater," she said.

"I have a feeling he does."

"Brent, I'm surprised at you. You always say that everyone right down to the prop man has to be watched by the producer."

"This is a special situation—with a special director."

"It's so unlike you. I think you should stick to your principles."

Brent looked at Melissa, then me. For a moment I felt that he had caught on to our affair. But then he said, "Well, all right. It won't hurt. I promised Lester that I wouldn't interfere. But I could just be paying a visit."

When Brent went back to his papers, Melissa flashed me a half-smile.

The next day Brent showed up at the rehearsal hall immaculately dressed in suit and tie, carrying a brief case.

I was going over some script changes with Lester, and Brent came directly over.

"Lester," he said in a businesslike manner. "Here is the final draft of your contract that I worked out with the William Morris Agency. It winds up the loose ends that we agreed to work out. We came to a compromise."

"Yes," Lester replied. "They called me about it yesterday."

Brent handed him a brown manila envelope. "How are you progressing?" he asked nonchalantly.

"It's beautiful so far."

"Glad to hear that."

"Yes," was Lester's non sequitur.

"I'm so anxious to see all of the progress you've made. Do you mind if I stay during your next run-through?"

"Not at all," Lester said proudly.

"Great," Brent returned, removing his coat.

Brent sat unobtrusively in a corner to watch.

The cast seemed suddenly tense at the prospect of being observed by their producer. But Lester was laid-back, as usual.

"Okay," Lester announced. "Let's take it from the top."

The first-act people took positions in the 'wings'.

Stanley rubbed his moustache with a finger and said, "Stand by." He paused, then, "Curtain!"

Brenda walked onto the 'spiked' floor, and stood on the 'X' chalk mark. She looked around at imaginary crumbling walls. "Irv!" she called offstage. Her voice was louder, more resonant, than it had ever been before. She was obviously thinking 'theater' because Brent was there.

The thin, Jewish-looking actor playing the lead—my alter ego— quietly entered the 'room' and slowly beheld the surroundings.

"Music up, slowly," Stanley said. A scratchy record was played.

What corny shit! I thought to myself. Hollywood. TV. I glanced at Brent. He was sitting there impassively. I hoped that he had the same feeling as I did.

The cast made it through the first act with fewer mistakes than usual. Stanley avoided prompting any of them on errors, unless he had no alternative, such as when they forgot a line and stood there mentally groping for words. If they faked a line, he let it go. Usually, he was a tough stage manager, making them repeat a line if just one word was wrong. Except, of course, with Brenda. He told her about her slip-ups after rehearsal. In bed, that night.

We took a break to have coffee and doughnuts that had been

brought by our gopher, a very young homosexual aspiring-actor Lester had picked up at a bar somewhere.

I was anxious to get Brent's opinion, but he avoided me. I couldn't interpret his evaluation by his facial expression. It was, as usual, neutral.

Brenda spent the break time next to Lester. Obviously, she felt it was the thing to do. Brent went over and sat with them, chatting. I could tell that they were discussing everything but the play.

Lester seemed more confident than ever, because Brent hadn't made any complaints. Brenda, for some reason, seemed worried. Perhaps it was because this was her first time out in the really big time—the high-class big time, that is. A failure on the boards would still be a good credit, of course. She could blame it on the script or the director. But a hit play would really put her on top. With that, she could write her own ticket when it came to parts and advances in theater and movies. As for TV, she would just drop out of that altogether, according to Stanley's knowledge, which I received from Tom.

They went through the second act, rested again, then hit the third act.

After Stanley said, "Curtain, slowly," Brent put on his coat, picked up his briefcase, shook Lester's hand, and smiled. Then he waved goodbye to the cast and left.

After he had been gone long enough to get back to his office, I ran down 42nd Street to the nearest pay phone and called Brent's office.

Pat answered. "He has an appointment with Christopher Thomas. They're at the shop checking on the construction of the set."

"Is Melissa there?"

"Yes, I'll get her for you."

I waited.

But Pat was on the phone again. "She said she's too busy to speak with you now."

Overly cautious, I thought.

I went directly to the office.

When I got there, Melissa was gone.

I was so tense, so desperate for Brent's opinion, that I didn't feel the warmth of Pat's friendliness until she had spoken enough to get through my anxieties. Then I heard her words fading in...

"It must be so exciting having a play produced. I took drama at Bennington, you know."

"No, I didn't."

"You really shouldn't be so tense, Mr. Gessel," she advised me. "You got this far. And your play is being produced by one of the biggest producers on Broadway, Mr. Lourdes. Everything is in your favor." Then she added, "It's such a thrill to be working with all of you. I mean, I've seen all of Lester Hopkins' movies, and I even met Brenda Williams the other day, when she came by to pick up some of her mail that was forwarded here." She took a deep breath and released it. "It's all so exciting," she said, raising her shoulders.

It was the first time I had really noticed her. She was pretty, bookish with her black, thin, horn-rimmed glasses, and she had full breasts. She looked no older than 23.

"You know, Mr. Gessel," she went on, "I'm working on a play myself, right now. And I want to show it to Mr. Lourdes when I finish it. I mean, I hope he'll look at it. I mean, my drama teacher got me this job." She drew herself up slightly, as if preparing her strength. "I know you're busy, but if you ever have the time, I'd appreciate it if you'd give it a little glance-over. I'd like to have your opinion before I finish it and try to get Mr. Lourdes to read it."

"Please don't call me Mr. Gessel," I said. "Just call me Mark." She had become very appealing. And I was feeling upset that Melissa had left.

I sensed the admiration that comes with 'success'. By 'success', I'm talking not about the fame of an Academy award-winning male movie star who turns housewives on, but the literary accomplishment that turns some young intelligent women on because what you've done seems so glamorous —such as publishing a short story or novel, or having a play produced on Broadway. Something they'd love to do."

"Sure, Pat, I'd love to read your play and give my opinion of it."

She scrunched her shoulders up and clasped her hands together. "Oh, Mr. Gessel!" She paused, re-thought, then corrected. "I mean, Mark! It's so kind of you."

I was feeling the anxiety that comes with horniness. "When would you like to have me read it?"

"Oh!" she exclaimed with delight. "I know you're so busy." The dark eyes in her pale face were larger than usual. They blinked like an owl's behind the magnification. "Any time you have a chance."

"I have a chance right now," I told her, suddenly feeling a strong desire for her that momentarily relieved me of the tensions of my play-production problems.

She opened a drawer of her desk. "Here's what I've written so far: the first two acts."

"Can I take them with me? Do you have a copy?"

"Oh, yes. I've made carbons. It's so kind of you...Mark."

"I'll read it tonight," I said.

"Oh, it's so kind of you," she repeated. "I appreciate it so much. I think I'm in trouble in the second act. You see, the protagonist got rid of his main problem and I have to come up with another one."

"Maybe you should find some way of continuing the first problem," I advised, being the wise elder.

"That's right!" she almost screamed in her naivete. "I never thought of that!"

"Well, let me take a look and see," I advised.

Pat's admiration for me was irresistible to my ego. Nevertheless, she turned out to be a one-night stand. Call it one-time payment for my reading her script, or her loss of interest after her 'conquest'. Still, it was a purely physical situation, nothing like my first experience of being loved—by Melissa—which had never happened before, and never would again.

At any rate, Pat soon left Brent's employ, and with that, she was no longer a part of my life, only a memory.

To be honest, I don't think I would have appealed to Pat in the least had it not been for the literary aura she saw glowing around me. It has always amazed me, and always will, that pretty, intellectual women went for men who often had no great surface appeal. (Shades of Melissa.)

Melissa didn't find out about Pat, or a few other quickies, until much later, when she questioned me intensively at great length and I stupidly gave in. She became upset if I even looked at another woman. She thought that she had found love with me, and was, in time, disillusioned. Perhaps that was what started her on the road to promiscuity. Although, no doubt, it would have inevitably occurred.

Chapter 19

The next day, I found myself sitting opposite Brent in his office. He was formal, as usual—with jacket and tie, toying with his pen, looking at a page of my current script.

"Yes, it does seem to need some rewriting," he told me. "But so did the original script."

"But this is not even near my original concept," I said. "The story has been changed considerably. And so have my characters. Frankly, Brent, it's Hollywood."

"What's wrong with that?" he asked, eyeing me directly. "We're dealing with a different kind of situation, different thinking. Lester's Hollywood might be right for Broadway. You never know what the public wants. No producer ever discovers that. It's always a guess."

"Well, I'll tell you what my guess is," I informed him confidently. "It's that my play is going to be a bomb."

"Mark, you could be wrong."

"Not likely."

"It's my opinion that your play, as directed by Lester, has something. I don't know what it is. But with my experience in the theater, I'd say that it's got a certain theatrical magic about it."

"Where?" I questioned.

"I can't pinpoint it." Brent shifted in his swivel chair. "Perhaps it's the whole concept of the main character's early life being snuffed out with the demolishing of his childhood home, and the way it's done, with lighting, fades, timing..." He moved his head slowly from side to side, wearing a strained expression on his face. "I can't find that much fault. There's a certain mood to the entire piece."

I leaned forward. "Yes, but that was my idea." I tapped my chest with a forefinger. "I'm the one who came up with the plot and characters. Even the mood—right on paper. And now it's gone."

Brent put his jacketed elbows on the desk, slumping down on them. "Mark, you're like any other creative person. And I can understand your outlook. Sure, you, the writer, are the one who conceived the story and put it down on paper. But now there are other people contributing to your script, too. I'll bet if you asked Brenda who was the most important person involved with this play, she'd say she is. Or Lester—he would say he is. That's the way it has to be in the theater. Once that script leaves the playwright's hands, it's a committee effort. It's right that everyone should feel that they're the most important individual in the entire production. What about me? I'm the person who believed in your play in the first place, raised money for it and put my time into it, and am now risking my reputation on it."

All right, he had a point. "But nevertheless," I told him, "you can see that my script has gone downhill."

"That's your own personal viewpoint, Mark, and you have a right to it. But everyone else has a right to their own opinion, too." He clasped his fingers together in a tight knot in front of him and gently banged the mass of flesh and bone on the desk. "But you could be wrong, too, you know."

I evidently acceded momentarily in my attitude, because he jumped at the opportunity to win the debate. "Your play might be going in just the right direction. I don't see anything terribly bad at this point. You've still got another week of rehearsal and a lot can happen during that time. In addition, we'll be making changes in New Haven and Baltimore—and that will be after the audience's reaction. This is your first time out, Mark. You have a great chance for this play to be a success. We're all working hard together."

There was no use arguing further. He did make his case, I thought, but not convincingly enough for me. I'd seen many Broadway plays. Yet, I had to concede: Brent had not only seen many, too, but had produced a good number of them—which I hadn't.

"Lester has put some fine touches into your play. He has taste and artistry. And I think he cast the play very well." Brent was obviously intransigent. And he was right to be so hard and fast in his belief. He was, as he had pointed out, the one who was really taking the gamble.

"Okay," I said. "I'll just do what has to be done. I'll go along with it."

Brent reached a hand across the desk. I took it.

"Good," he said. "Most importantly, we need harmony. That's what every play that goes into production requires to be successful."

So, that was it. I decided that there was no use fighting city hall. I'd have to play the game, like everybody else, and hope for the best.

Chapter 20

New Haven, Monday morning.

I arrived at the Taft Hotel and began to unpack. The Shubert Theatre was just nearby. I was so anxious to get there that I left my still half-full bags open on the bed and headed over.

As I approached the building where my first play was to have its world premiere that night, I saw the marquee. It read, in black letters against white glass:

Brent Lourdes
presents
BRENDA WILLIAMS
in
The Wrecker's Ball
by Mark Gessel

I paused in the street almost involuntarily for a moment, consumed by the sight.

It all seemed so unreal, so like a dream, like standing in the midst of a movie set as a part of all that was going on. The theater, the surroundings, everything I had imagined as an aspiring playwright as I slid each blank sheet of paper into my typewriter, had led to this fantasy-come-true. I had made it.

This far, anyway.

As I continued walking, I noticed the huge poster behind glass on the wall. It showed a black-and-white photograph of Brenda's face. Her famous visage, bearing a demeanor of seriousness that I had never seen on it, that I doubted she could ever attain, was large, graphically altered to appear as a charcoal drawing. Superimposed over that, also in white but screened to be almost invisible, was a wrecker's ball swinging against a house that could only partially be seen. But the little of it that appeared had already been half bombarded.

How ironic, I thought, that in a mammoth work of art, in which many creative people are eventually involved, so much happens, unbeknownst to the original creator, that builds toward your goal, as you work so tightly on your own part of it. Other people have been working, simultaneously, to bring the fruits of your imagination to life, not only for your benefit, but for theirs too.

I now understood how, when dealing in large creative terms, I had given up full ownership of my idea, in some instances for the better, in others, not. The main character of my play—me—had been predominant. But now everything had all been considerably changed; the subject of my story line had become the wife's life. All because of Lester's obsession for Brenda. It seems that writers have to pay their dues. But it was a high price for the accomplishment that I was seeing before me.

Well, that's life, I thought, shrugging it off. I went into the theater.

Emmett Dawson, the lighting director, and Stanley, were the only people in sight. Emmett was onstage, and Stanley was on a tall ladder that leaned against a box at stage right. He was adjusting the position of a fresnel and focusing its lens. The house lights were out, and only the stage was lit— by the spots that ran in a curve under the balcony, the footers along the front of the stage, and the lights that funneled their beams from poles on the sides by the boxes. As I walked down the raked aisle, along the empty cushioned folding seats, smelling the dank moldiness of the auditorium, my peripheral vision caught the varied colors of the gels that created the dramatic lighting rimming the men who were lighting the set.

Dawson's voice echoed in the huge, empty auditorium. "This way, this way...good...keep going." There was the squeak of metal. "Now, just a little more...stop!"

I reached the stage, and stood before the orchestra pit, dwarfed by the life-sized duplicate of the miniature Christopher Thomas set that I had seen at his Dakota apartment. It was beautiful, overpowering to me. I felt almost intoxicated by the sight of it. For a moment, I no longer cared about how the play would go, whether it would be a success or failure, whether it would represent what I had wanted it to or not. This moment was worth all of the torture and struggle I had been through and what I knew I had yet to endure. It was there. My life in a theatrical vision that I would remember forever. It was an experience that only a rare few enjoyed. I considered myself fortunate to be among them.

I heard footsteps and looked behind me.

It was Lester, dressed casually in loose trousers and a white shirt that was open at the neck.

He had appeared out of the darkness with a smile and a friendly hand reaching toward me to shake. I took it and felt his confident grip.

"Well, this is it, Mark. I wish you lots of luck. In fact, I wish everyone lots of luck. Including myself. We open tonight."

I felt a warmness toward him that I never thought I would. It was as if we had forgotten our differences. His attitude caused my previous anger with him and Brent to dissolve. At least, for those few seconds.

Maybe it was because there was little more we could do to the general plot of the play now. We had to face the inevitable as we were all to begin weaving the fabric of the show together—a literary, theatrical montage of not just my life, but of all our lives. I began to understand even more about the combination of playwriting and production, that the roles were no longer completely mine, that Lester, Brenda, Tom, and all of the others, would help shape the people of my imagination, too. For a moment I could envision Brent telling me, "You see, you can never tell how it will all work out. It could be a good play, with all of us pitching in."

In a dazzling moment I felt an overpowering love for Melissa, although I didn't know why. Perhaps it was because her inexorable passion for me had made all of this possible.

Our work on the production was practically done, except for modifications here and there, good or bad, successful or unsuccessful. We had only to wait to see what would happen when the critics made their first comments. Thanks to her. I could see her sitting on the bed next to me, naked, reading my script for the first time. I had the desire at that very instant, standing in the Shubert Theater, to possess her in every way possible —forever. I realized all that she had sacrificed for me, and realized that she would have not done it for anyone else. I also thought about her coming up with Brent for the preview, and that she and I would have to show disinterest in each other at this most important moment in my life—and hers, as she had assured me it would be. When I had seen her last, almost a week before, she told me how excited she became every time she thought about the opening of my show, that it meant more to her than anything else ever did before.

Lester and I released our grips on the handshake.

"We're having a dress rehearsal this afternoon," Lester said. "Then tonight is it."

Brenda appeared out of the black auditorium space behind us, her face lit by the reflected stage lights. Two other members of the cast were behind her.

"Hi, Mark!" she said. "Sweating it out?"

Actually, I wasn't. I was resolved that the play would fail. I'd already accepted what I was certain would be the inevitable. But with Brenda's unusual friendliness, perplexity shot through my subconscious.

"Rehearsals went well," Lester went on. "Didn't they?" he asked Brenda rhetorically.

"Yes," she said. "Mark, if you would have been here over the weekend, you would have seen us give a run-through without one mistake."

I found that hard to believe, but she was convincing. Maybe she was at least becoming a better actress. "Glad to hear that," I replied, probably not too enthusiastically.

"But," she commented. "I did have a question about the character I'm playing. I'd like to discuss it with you, if you have the time. Could we have a drink together when we take a break after the rehearsal?"

"I guess so," I said. It was so unlike her to be so friendly to me. I thought that it was probably just a natural reaction to the elation we all felt just before the first opening night.

She apologized for me. "Of course, you might be busy with last minute things," she said. "At worst, we could get together at the hotel in my room or yours. But it would really help me understand the role better."

"Okay," I agreed.

Lester looked from her to me with cold, staring eyes. He was wearing either a questioning demeanor or a face of anger.

I later found out that it was anger.

Brenda had had a falling out with Stanley. She had visited his apartment unscheduled and discovered another young lady there. Evidently, Brenda felt that she owned him, at least for the run of the show. But Stanley could take or leave Brenda, or any other woman, for that matter. And gossip being rampant among the cast, Lester had quickly learned about the incident and felt that now was his opportune time to strike with Brenda.

Brenda's outrage over the happening left her with a need to put Stanley down, as well as, she correctly reasoned, to keep Lester at a distance. So her best gambit, she had decided, was to make a move toward me. Even if it was just verbally in front of Lester.

But all that was on my mind at that very moment was Melissa—driving up with Brent to see the opening night performance. They planned to stay over to read the reviews the next day. New Haven was known to have the toughest newspaper critics of all, and we had all agreed that when we saw the comments, we'd have a reasonably objective view of how the production stood and what changes might have to be made.

I seemed to awaken from a transitory trance when I heard the next words, Brenda saying, "Let's meet in the hotel lobby. What's a good time?"

"Oh," I replied, startled, aware again of where I was. "We should probably make it just after the dress rehearsal." I asked Lester, "Would that be late afternoon?"

"Yes," he answered coldly. "About one-thirty or so."

Brenda left us and went backstage, where she emerged from the wings into the set's lights. She made a production of looking the set over, her back to the theater seats, purposely not saying a word to Stanley, who went about his work oblivious to her being there, when obviously he was quite aware of her presence. Then she disappeared back into the wings.

The dress rehearsal went surprisingly smoothly. I have to admit that I was amazed at the highly moving and emotional performance. But I wondered if it just looked good to me because there was little else more we could do with the production, or if I was seeing it freshly as would a paying member of the audience.

Chapter 21

After shaving, I came down to the lobby before the arranged time and found Brenda already there. It was unlike her to be early. She was sitting on a couch, looking over her copy of the script. She had changed into leisurely apparel: a short black skirt and a blue-and-red flowered print blouse.

When I looked at her, I felt no desire at all. I was under stress, with the play opening in only a few hours, and Melissa and Brent about to arrive very shortly, if they weren't already in their room.

I had had a break from looking at the script, and dreaded the thought of seeing my words again before the next day after the reviews came in. But Brenda made a point of being quite serious, and appeared deeply determined to go over the lines with me, despite my suspicions about her motive.

She was wearing glasses that I had never seen before. The large lenses were almost completely circular. They made her look quite intellectual, a female characteristic that ordinarily turned me on, although I knew her to be far from intellectual. Still, I also knew that those glasses resting on her nose had struck a cord in my subconscious because I was believing my eyes.

I went over and sat down next to her. She didn't notice me, but before I could speak, she looked up.

Startled, her lips, as they came apart, reminded me of ripe fruit.

"Oh, you surprised me," she said, removing her glasses. "I guess I was really concentrating on this."

"If you'd like, we could probably go over it right here," I suggested.

"Oh, no," she replied, looking around the lobby at the people sitting here and there and others wandering or at the desk. "We need privacy for this," she said with a determined expression. "What do you say we go up to my suite, and I'll order some drinks."

I wasn't in the mood for complications, especially with a leading lady, but I told her, "Fine with me." I certainly felt the need for a drink.

She stood and led me to the elevator.

As it hummed quietly, rising to her floor, she faced forward, not speaking.

I observed her. She seemed to be smaller than she appeared on the stage, or even in the rehearsal hall. And standing next to this delicate little creature, I sensed a vulnerability that I had been unaware of before. Here was a young woman whom millions of people had seen on television and in the movies, and yet, now that she wasn't bigger than life, but just a passenger in an elevator, seemed to have the same emotions and fears as any other female. She was, of course, hoping, as I was, that The Wrecker's Ball would greatly enhance her career, her life, that tomorrow the world would know of this success and that she would be headed toward even greater triumphs.

I would have been glad just to have minor success.

She was worried, just as I was worried.

We got off of the elevator and walked quietly along the hall.

Brenda put her key in the lock, turned it, and swung her door open.

Her contract called for a comfortable suite, and it was almost that. There were three rooms, with somewhat worn carpets, and the walls needed a bit of painting. The large space in which she was temporarily living was somewhat moldy smelling, except for the fragrance of the flowers that had begun arriving from her friends, relatives and fans. But it was spacious enough for her to retreat to for study and apprehensive pacing. It was certainly the best quarters that Brent could get for her out of town.

"Make yourself comfortable," she said with a generous smile.

I sank into a small, plush, comfortable chair.

Brenda went to the phone. "Room Service? I'd like to order...What'll you have, Mark?"

"Make that a Vodka Collins."

"A Vodka Collins," she ordered, "and a Bloody Mary for me." She paused a moment. "And make that two of each."

Remembering that this was our most important day in New Haven, I almost unconsciously, but instinctively, held up a warning forefinger. "I think you'd better just make that one each," I quickly counseled. "We open this evening, remember?"

"That's right," she said, somewhat astonished that she had momentarily forgotten. "Just make that one Vodka Collins."

She hung up, sat on the chair across from me in front of the roll-top desk, and opened her script. "Now, these lines on page 78. His wife tells him to forget the past, that she hopes this experience will end it forever, that seeing the house demolished will put it out of his mind for good." She put the script down. "But does she sense that she's asking for the impossible? I mean, did you intend for her to give that impression with her voice and the way she looks at him?"

"Yes," I said. "That's exactly right." I was surprised at her perception. Maybe she had some idea of what acting was, after all, how to interpret dialogue that a playwright has put down on paper. "She realizes that," I explained, "because ever since they met and married, he has always been replaying the past over and over in his mind, and letting her know about it. And the audience is aware that such is the case, because the scenes have been dissolving back and forth from past to present."

Brenda leaned back, relieved. "That's primarily what I wanted to know. That's what I thought, and it's the way I've been playing it." She paused a moment. "I'll bet this is very much autobiographical, isn't it?"

The warmth and understanding of that statement touched me. I began to talk about my experiences in life and how they related to the play, and her interest was so honest that I got to like her immediately after all the time that we had been friends yet strangers.

Our conversation began to turn around to Brenda's life when my drink arrived.

I reached for my wallet.

"Please, no," she insisted. "I'll just sign for it."

I settled back with my glass.

"So tell me, Brenda," I asked, "were you driven to be an actress?"

"Not really," she answered. "But everything seemed to go my way. Smoothly. It was sort of like someone who makes all the right moves in the stock market, or in real estate. No matter what they do, they're successful. According to odds, some people in every industry have to have that kind of luck. In the acting field, I was one of them."

I was surprised at her humility. I didn't really know this gal so well, after all, except that what she said was exactly how I had interpreted her rise to fame and fortune. I had thought that she would talk about her talent, and how hard she had pursued her goals, perhaps even about a stage mother.

But her family didn't care one way or the other, she told me. "They figured that in time I'd be married, and that my pursuit of an acting career would be brief. And, frankly, I didn't really care one way or another, myself, about being on television or in the movies. I just didn't chase after success with a vengeance like other hopefuls I went to school with. It was just that every little effort I made came through. If it hadn't been that easy, I would probably have given up after the first failure."

She was putting herself down so strongly, I felt obligated to balance the conversation more in her favor. "But obviously," I said, "there had to be talent there."

"I guess so," she replied modestly.

I was even more impressed.

Now I understood. She had wisely developed an outer shell of confidence—or had it to begin with—with which she demonstrated brashness and audacity. She was a not quite perfect actress with a mass of jelly inside; however, part of it was guts. She had my respect.

"There's one question on my mind," I said, feeling at home between the drink, which was now affecting me, and her hospitality. I hung a knee over my chair.

"Shoot."

"If you frankly don't give a damn, my dear, why all the worry about the characterization of your role in my play?"

"Second of all," Brenda replied, "after this fame and prosperity that I've acquired, I've sort of become accustomed to a plushy way of living. And freedom." She smiled. "I like it. And I'd sure as hell hate to lose it." She tilted her head slightly to the side. "Sure, at first I didn't give a damn, but now I do. Now, because this lifestyle suits me, I often wonder if my luck is going to continue. I constantly ask myself if I made the right decision about going on Broadway, or if I took one step too far. And," she added. "First of all, I believe in giving someone who bought a ticket their money's worth."

"You're being very honest, aren't you?"

"Yes," she said. "I have a feeling that I can tell you the truth."

"You can. Be assured. I'll say nothing about it to anyone. I see the reasons for your trepidation. We all have them. But we don't all show it. Even Lester has it."

Brenda gave a slight snort that was completely out of character for her as I knew her, but not as Tom described Stanley's knowledge of her. "That fag?"

"Well, we all have our suspicions, but no one really knows."

"Believe me," she said, "I know." She stood, went to the bed across from me, and sat again. "Mind if I just lie down while we talk? I'm suddenly feeling tired. Maybe I'll nap after you leave."

"Go right ahead."

She slid into a supine position, her short skirt riding above one knee, and put the back of a hand tiredly over one eye. "There, that's better," she sighed. "So what are your plans if your play goes bust?"

"I may very well produce a show. I've been in practically every area of the theater, from raising money to stage-managing. There's a playwright I know who's had two successes Off-Broadway. And when I say successes, I mean both financial and artistic. He just finished another play, but he doesn't want to deal with the producers who did his first ones. He's had artistic differences with them. And he doesn't trust the big boys. He's even thought about putting on his new play himself, but he doesn't know the first thing about producing."

"So that's where you come in?"

"Exactly."

"You know, Mark," Brenda said. "I like you. It's too bad we didn't get to know each other sooner. I think we'd have been very good friends by now."

I was feeling the drink slightly. "Say, Brenda, is this honesty day? I mean, are we confessing everything to each other just prior to the most important night in both of our lives?"

She laughed. If her waist hadn't been so lean, I was certain I would have seen her tummy bounce up and down a few times. She rolled toward me and a thigh gleamed. "Now its your turn to be really honest. This time about me."

"In what way?" I asked.

"First, how do you think I'm doing with your play? And remember, it's honesty day."

I hesitated. "I think you're acting is excellent (I was careful not to praise her too much, since, considering my true opinion, I didn't want to be too honest), that you're getting all the points across that I intended for your role." Of course, maybe I had weakened and given up altogether on the production.

But she picked up some feelings of doubt in the tone of my voice; I hadn't been too successful in suppressing how I really felt.

"Mark, tell me the truth. Am I doing well as a theatrical actress, or do I need considerable improvement?" She paused, and the way she looked at me made me fidget. "Come on, Mark. Let's have it."

"Okay, I won't lie. You don't need considerable improvement." I waited for the right words to come to mind.

"Yes...?"

"As far as this play goes, you need to strengthen your character. She doesn't have—complete stage presence." I hesitated, though. "She does—to some extent," I apologized. "But not enough."

"What do you mean by that?"

I tried to think of words that would be inspiring rather than critical. "The only way I can put it is this: There's a tremendous difference between movies and TV, and the theater. I'm not trying to be snobbish. But on the stage, characters have to be bigger than life. Take Shakespearean actors, for example. Their actions, their voices, are strong, almost grandiose. Do you know what I mean? They're belting out their personalities to every seat in that large theater. And they're doing it without microphones and sound engineers."

"Do you mean I'm sort of..." She thought for a moment, and spoke apprehensively, as if she didn't really want to use the word, "...mushy?"

"Brenda, you're being a little tough on yourself to put it that way. I'm saying that you just have to play the part a little more strongly." Hearing my own words of criticism seemed to make my thoughts shrivel up. No other suggestions came to mind. "But that's not my job. I have no right to even say that to you. That's what Lester is here for."

"What the hell does he know?" she asked with a forceful voice.

"That's exactly what I mean," I said. "The way you put that statement. You really meant it."

"I think I know what you mean," she said. "Do you feel that there's time for me to change my acting style?"

"Why not? It's just a matter of thinking a new way. Sure, you can do it. If you really want to."

"Then I will," she said with determination.

"But remember," I cautioned her, "Lester and the rest of the cast will notice it immediately. The other actors have to play their parts against yours, and you may just screw them up when they find that your character has changed—considerably."

"I don't think that'll be too much of a problem. I'm sure that they'll accept me and just automatically alter their styles, too."

"All I can say, Brenda, is that what you do is up to you. I've never mentioned this to you before, but, to put it mildly, I don't totally agree with Lester's concept of my play."

"That's pretty obvious, Mark. Not only to me, but to the rest of the cast."

"Still, to suggest any changes in your part, even in the personality of your character, I should really go through channels. In other words, I should really go directly to the director of my play."

"I wouldn't let it worry you. I won't say anything."

She was determined to make the change. I could see that.

And I could also sense that she was extremely grateful for the help I'd given her, that I'd taken a sincere and undesigning interest in her and her career.

"Mark," she said, "you've been so nice. I'd do anything for you."

I could hardly believe the offer. If it was that. Maybe it wasn't, though. It was hard to tell. But if this had happened to someone else, I'd be sure that the whole incident had culminated in her offering herself in appreciation. A rare moment that happens in very few people's lives. But whatever my psychological makeup, I evidently just didn't think enough of myself to believe that this opportunity had presented itself. Brenda Williams, star. And Mark Gessel, failure.

"Do you like me?" she added. Let's face it, could she throw any more of a hint? Yet, I still had doubts about myself—and everything else.

"Of course," I told her. "Why shouldn't I?"

"I mean, really like me?" She was totally still, her head turned fully toward me as she lay on the bed, awaiting my reply.

"Yes, I do." I waited for a response.

She, too, waited for more words.

"Okay," I told her. "We might have been very good friends, but Stanley got in the way," I lied. I felt that I should tell her generally what she wanted to hear. I, frankly, felt confused. It was everything.

She chuckled. "But he's not in the way now."

"He isn't?"

Under other circumstances, I was certain, I would have been raring to go. But I was under pressure and suspected that she was looking for recreational sex as a tension-reliever, which, as I say, would have been all right —I mean, great, with me. But I was afraid that Melissa would read me instantly if I got involved, and the last thing I ever wanted to do was throw Melissa away. I had learned that the combination of love and sex was better than passing moments of willing flesh alone. If my play ran and Brenda and I got involved, it could be a continuing situation, a problem that would come between Melissa and me.

Damn it, I was always looking for ways to avoid opportunities, giving myself excuses, finding ways to fail.

"Come here," she said softly, lying there motionless, wearing a slight smile.

I didn't know what to do. It was a decision of importance. Would I ruin everything I had with Melissa? Would there be other complications when the cast found out, when Brent found out? She may not have been his wife, but she was his leading lady. Nevertheless, if I didn't go along with Brenda's momentary whim, would it cause problems with her and me?

The slight dizziness produced by the drink was gone, and I was left stone cold sober.

The eyes of Brenda's horizontal face stared straight into mine, awaiting an answer. I had to give it. And now.

"Well," I said, the words coming out without my even knowing what I was going to say, "I think this is something that should happen after the strain of tonight is over, when we're both totally relaxed and everything is going well."

She was flat on her back again, but now she was looking up at the ceiling. In a bored tone of voice, she said, "Why don't I get some rest so that I can give my best at the theater tonight. And good luck, Mark."

I had the feeling that I might have embarrassed her—and that I would never have the same opportunity again.

Well, I was definitely right about never having the same opportunity!

Years later, I evaluated my actions of that afternoon in that weak moment alone with the famous Brenda Williams.

And my verdict was: Mark, you asshole!

Chapter 22

I'm typing "Fuck it!" onto the screen of my computer in my little room at the nursing home.

I'm 88 again. It's now.

The goddamn patterns we develop; we don't see them until it's too late. Shit, I'm growling to myself, as I paw my way through the yellow sheets from the legal pads I worked with in the community room, where I could either take or leave what was on TV.

Well, anyway, what do you think of this novel so far?

I mean, it bounces around a bit, but I'm getting the plot more in order, right? You have to admit, don't you, that a lot of what you've read so far is the result of more than just the short attention span of an octogenarian, almost nonagenarian?

Thank God for computers, and my son for giving me this one and setting up the hard disk for me. If I had to type this on my old Underwood, I'd never make it. As far as adding words or sentences here and there, forget it! I'd have to retype all of the pages. But with my trusty little computer, once I get it all together for a section of the book, I just add words, sentences, punctuation, and print it out with the touch of a key on my keyboard. I can even take a nap while it's printing.

Believe me, organizing these notes is tough enough in itself. But I'm getting more into my affair with Melissa, so please don't mind if I flash back and forth. Okay? I mean, thinking ahead, I just know that's what I have to do. So you'll have to put up with it. But there's a reason. Continuity. Sometimes in real life, there's no continuity. We break off in the middle of situations in our lives and come back to them again months or even years later. But in a novel, you can connect all of the pieces together. Do you know what I mean?

All right, let's settle this 'novel' business once and for all.

You think that if this book is partly autobiographical, it's the truth and not fiction, right?

Well, not really.

You've read nonfiction novels and nonfiction that must definitely be fiction.

It's all mixed up.

Literature, being a mixture of fact and fiction, sometimes leaves the person writing it not sure which is which. And as the years go by, an author remembers which is which, less and less. Except that with me now, it's as the minutes go by.

All right. Now I have to smooth things out, polish the rough edges. You know what I mean, don't you?

Didn't I tell you that The Wrecker's Ball would fail?

But I want you to know what happened, anyway. It was all part of my life.

My real life?

My fictionalized life?

What difference does it make, anyway?

Now wait. Let me find where this continues. I have to go through these papers...

Just a second...

Ah, here it is. The first opening night of The Wrecker's Ball—out of town. New Haven.

I'll type it in from my rough notes and straighten out the grammar and syntax as I go along.

Okay, it goes like this:

(By the way, this is the final draft. I wouldn't put you through reading it until it was completely rewritten.)

Chapter 23

Shirley was in New Haven for the opening of my play. She didn't, of course, have any idea of what was going on in my life, because I told her as little as possible about everything. I kept my personal life to myself as far as she was concerned, and my professional life too, as much as possible.

Tonight would be the first time that she and Melissa met formally, although they had been at a few theatrical occasions at the same time.

I would rather not have had Shirley there, but I'd have to come up with a hell of an excuse not to invite my wife.

Shirley had no interest in my theatrical ambitions. She appeared to, before we were married. But after I put the ring on her finger, she became interested in my using my pharmacy license to earn a "decent living."

Within a year, she had practically shut off sex completely, reading mysteries and science fiction far into the night. My amorous approaches were met with, "We'll have fun tonight!" but we never did. I'd eventually fall asleep —sometimes with the help of a double—or triple martini. Which helped me subdue my depressive tendencies, although I didn't know it at the time. Love, of course, would have been better therapy. But now I had that with Melissa.

It wasn't long before I began to hear the comment from Shirley that she would increasingly assault me with: "Why don't you get a job, you lazy bastard!" while she sat in our apartment and played solitaire. Of course, I was employed as a stage manager occasionally, but that wasn't steady work. My theatrical 'jobs' were really temporary, depending on the critics.

In between, I wrote freelance articles for local newspapers and sold short stories and articles to the lesser men's magazines, primarily to an editor in downtown Manhattan.

But now she was on my side, because I was employed, so to speak. I had received an advance from Brent through the Dramatists Guild, a standard procedure. And, if the play ran, I would be getting a percentage of the gross, plus an additional sum above the weekly break-even point, or *nut*. If the play sold that many tickets, of course. I had married a fair-weather non-intimate friend who was quite possessive, to boot, as I was soon to learn.

Shirley arrived at my hotel room just a couple of hours after Brenda had propositioned me. At the time I thought I had handled the situation correctly and that everything had worked out for the best. As I mentioned, I was under too much strain heading into the opening of the play to have to deal with personal problems of my own creation. I had enough troubles as it was.

Shirley was dressed to the hilt in a black caftan to conceal the weight that she had recently put on and, in addition, she had decorated herself with gross trinket jewelry—somewhat overdoing it, I thought. And she went straight to the bathroom to work on her face.

After she had spent a half-hour in front of the mirror, as usual attempting to paint the Mona Lisa on her face, I said, "We'd better get going. I want to be there a bit ahead of time." I was dressed, and looked at my watch. "At this rate, we'll get there after curtain time," I added as politely as possible. After all, she was under a strain, too. The money that she had hoped I would finally earn, that I had promised her came along with success in writing—that I had a short while before told her I would have—might at last be forthcoming with a hit show.

I hadn't informed her about the problems with the production. If I had, I'd never hear the end of it. She'd throw it back in my face, and give me ridiculous advice on how to handle Brent, Lester, and the cast. She always had all the answers.

At last she was finished with her living self-portrait, and we rushed over to the theater, arriving just ten minutes before the curtain was to go up. I seated her and started to go off backstage.

"Aren't you going to sit with me?" she called after me with her darkly painted lips.

"I'm too nervous," I said. "I'll be pacing around in the back listening to the audience reaction."

"Okay," she replied with obvious disappointment.

I stopped briefly at each of the dressing rooms to wish the cast members luck, then went to the wings where Stanley and his assistant stage manager were checking final notations in the typescript by the bare light at the switchboard.

I could hear the murmur of the audience grow on the other side of the curtain as more and more people were seated.

"What does the house look like?" I asked Stanley.

He went to a peephole and looked out at the auditorium. "Might be a full house," he said. "It's filling up. At this rate, you might even have standing room only."

I couldn't credit myself for that. Obviously, Brenda Williams was responsible for the draw.

But this was the first night, and the play hadn't been reviewed anywhere yet. Tomorrow we'd know the real answer. Even with Brenda's popularity, a pan by the critics could cut off ticket sales.

And that, I was certain, was how it would be. But the theater is unpredictable. Maybe Brenda could carry the play, after all. Who could tell?

But there were so many factors involved. In the end, out-of-town reviews might not be the same as New York reviews. Ditto for audiences. Then there was always word of mouth, if we had a good solid production.

I heard movement behind me, the sound of a costume moving and shoes walking nearby, and then I felt the touch of a hand on my shoulder.

I turned. It was Brenda. "Nervous?" she asked.

"I don't know," I replied. "I guess I'm just numb. What about you?"

"Me? Nervous? No, not really. I'm used to it. I've been in front of enough cameras. And each time I always think, millions of people are going to see what I'm about to do right now. The way I see tonight is that it's just a handful of people who will be watching."

"Good philosophy," I said.

The actor who was playing the role of the husband came up behind her.

"Okay, you two," I said, "break a leg."

I heard Stanley's voice. "House lights down, slowly."

The assistant stage manager took hold of levers on the switchboard and gradually pulled them toward him in an arc.

The mass of voices beyond the curtain began to attenuate.

Stanley waited momentarily.

"Ready, curtain!" he commanded, then turned to the two actors. "Okay, you're about to go on."

Brenda passed me, stood by the backstage curtains, and looked out at the darkness. The other actor, my alter ego, went up behind her.

Stanley raised an arm, pointing upward. "Go, curtain!"

A switch was hit, and there was the creaking of rope and the rustling of heavy cloth.

"Ready, cue one!" Stanley whispered loudly.

The sound of the audience diminished to a few coughs.

"Go, cue one!" Stanley directed quietly, emphatically.

Faint illumination began to obliterate the blackness onstage. It grew semi-bright, then stopped. Christopher Thomas's set could be seen in the glowing dimness.

There was a ragged applause.

From our dark wing we could partially see rows of faces barely lit by the faintly reflected stage lighting.

"Brenda," Stanley said, "it's yours. Take it!"

Brenda walked slowly onto the stage, her hands clasped before her, eyes searching the set's representation of a partially demolished building. She walked in a purposely-halting step to center stage and paused to set a tone that matched the emptiness of the world she had entered. The audience was silent. Its tenseness and anticipation could easily be sensed.

"Ready, cue two!"

Brenda turned to face the audience.

"Go, cue two!"

A spotlight under the balcony grew to a hot white, bathing Brenda in its radiance.

A roar of applause and voices greeted the star.

She stood immobile until the chaos died down. Then she turned to look offstage at us.

"Ready, cues three, four, five and six!"

Stanley grasped the actor's arm, waited, and gave him a slight push. "Okay, it's yours!"

Brenda's stage husband walked into the half-lighted setting with meticulous, painstaking steps as she, with an attitude of understanding, watched his approach.

"Go, cue three!"

Music arose to fill the silence.

When he reached her on the vast stage, he gently began to raise his fingers toward her.

She reached slowly toward him and took his hand in hers.

"Go, cues four, five and six!"

A balcony spotlight came up on the second character, then the lights for the entire stage increased to full capacity, bathing the set in blinding brightness.

The result of all of our efforts had become reality.

Chapter 24

I learned later that evening that the theater was Standing Room Only on opening night, and that the first few days of the week's run were almost sold out. All of the ticket sales were obviously because of Brenda.

There were few tickets sold after the reviews came out the next day.

Brent, Melissa, Lester, Shirley and I were sitting in the hotel's restaurant reading what the critics had to say.

We had ordered breakfast and were awaiting its arrival. There was little conversation at first, as we passed the newspapers around and read them quietly.

Lester was the one who finally spoke up. "It can be fixed easily," he told us, putting on a conspicuous air of confidence.

My intuition had evidently been right from the start, confirmed not only by the reviews, but also by the opening night audience, which laughed in some of the wrong places.

Brent hadn't said a word about a decision to close the show out of town or chance it in Baltimore. He just silently pondered the reviews.

Shirley was caught up in the excitement of the occasion, not really being aware of the intricacies involved regarding personality differences and the actual problems with the production. To her, seeing the reality of my play onstage and reviews in the newspapers, assumed that it would continue running. Our generally abject dispositions didn't seem to register with her.

Melissa was very cold to me. I had interpreted her temperament (mistakenly, I later learned) to be guilt-related; after meeting Shirley, I thought Melissa was extremely uncomfortable not just for being an adulteress as far a Brent went, but because she was a husband-stealer.

After the group had broken up, and we were in the hotel lobby, I had an opportunity to chat briefly with Melissa alone, she told me very frankly what really bothered her. It was my excessive attention—as she saw it—to my wife.

She asked me to take a hotel room for the two of us so that we could make love. It was one of her many tests of my 'fidelity' to her, I later came to learn.

"Shirley's only going to stay here overnight," I explained. "She'll be leaving tomorrow afternoon. Why don't you stay over for a few days?"

"I can't. I have to help Brent out in the office tomorrow. He's got three more plays in the works."

"But I can't just not sleep with her tonight. If I don't show up, or just disappear, she'll be suspicious."

Melissa was extremely angry. I had never seen her like that before. "Sleep with her!" she grumbled with a cynical smile—another emotion that she had never shown me.

I had made the mistake, during our trysts, of telling her about my non-intimate life with Shirley.

"Why are you going to sleep with her?" she went on. "She doesn't give you any sex. But I do." Her comment was, at first, an amazing surprise to me, unexpected, seemingly out of character. But then, in an explosive flash, I glimpsed a facet of Melissa's psyche that I had never seen before, that I seemed to understand only subconsciously.

I was at a loss of words, so I took another tack. "You heard Brent say that he plans to be up all night with Lester in Lester's room discussing the situation without me around, and that Lester will let me know tomorrow afternoon about any changes they might want in the script."

"Since the start of our affair," she said, directly, "I've gone out of my way for you. I've neglected my husband and kids just to get together with you. And I expect some loyalty in return!"

Could this be Melissa speaking? I tried to reason with her. "But with Brent away, you have no worries, no reason for him to be suspicious."

"I don't care whether Brent is away or not. I live my life the way I want to, and he has to accept it. If he comes back to his room and I'm not there, he'll know that I went somewhere that I wanted to go."

"But it's not quite the same with me as it is with you."

"Do you love me or not?"

"Of course, I do, Melissa, but you're asking an awful lot of me. We've got things going discreetly. Or as discreetly as possible. Don't you think we should keep it that way?"

"I want you to get a room and let me know the number," she insisted.

"This is insane!"

Naturally, I didn't get a room. Why ask for trouble?

But it made no difference. Nothing could, at that time, change Melissa's feelings for me.

At first, anyway.

Chapter 25

Baltimore.

Despite the little success we had during our week in New Haven, convinced by Lester that the play could be improved with some rewriting, Brent had decided that we continue our schedule to play our second week out of town, to see how it worked out. I steeled myself for seven more days of tension. I had no complaints, though. After all, it would mean a continuation of income for me as playwright, with a base payment and percentage of the gross, and there was always the possibility, though bizarre, that the play might make it after all. We did have Brenda Williams in the lead. I felt that if despite the New Haven newspaper critics, who, besides finding many faults with my play, weren't too kind to her, the young lady might have enough talent and professional perseverance to eventually overcome her weaknesses onstage. But in those days, theater people looked down on television people the way that Broadway looked down on movie actors and actresses during Hollywood's early days. Only a couple of decades after my play was produced, did show business attitudes change considerably, and television was eventually considered a stepping-stone to the movies and somewhat so to the professional theater. In fact, community theater came into its own and also followed that trend.

Melissa had stopped calling me.

During the tryout in New Haven, she had phoned at least once a day, or even more.

I didn't want to call her from Baltimore because it might raise suspicions, although I missed speaking with her and thought about her often.

During the first week, I had made some major changes in the play, and we incorporated them into the production throughout the rest of the run at the Shubert. Lester and I worked at tightening scenes by getting rid of excessive dialogue, creating more mood with pacing and slower fades, and inserting a new scene in the third act that we felt would create tension so that the climax would build more suspense. Surprisingly enough, as a result, by the end of the first week, audiences had begun reacting differently—for the better.

Just the same, I didn't want to give myself the illusion that we could turn everything around, and end up greatly disappointed. Making it on Broadway with The Wrecker's Ball still seemed an impossibility. To me, at least.

Ticket sales, as expected, were brisk at Ford's Theatre in Baltimore, even better than for our opening week in New Haven. The audience wasn't made up of the Harvard-type intellectual crowd; more the kind of family individuals who spent most of their non-job time watching TV.

But after we opened that Monday, the reviews didn't seem too promising. They generally reflected the opinions of the New Haven critics.

Brent showed up alone on Saturday night, after the last performance. I found Melissa's absence almost unbearable.

We met with Lester at a bar near the theater. There was silence all around, until we got our drinks.

Brent was the first to speak. "It's possible that we could bomb in New York," he said. "However, if we quit now, we can still return about fifty percent of the backers' money. And there's always amateur rights, and movie rights—which just might be sold. They could eventually recoup the other fifty percent."

We were sitting at a table, and Lester leaned forward over his drink. "I know we're going to make it, Brent. Out-of-town critics don't mean a thing." Evidently, a newly learned, or read-about, second-hand statement. "This production is a solid candidate for a Broadway hit. I believe in Mark's play."

Brent turned to me. "What do you think?"

I just didn't know what to say. "I'm confused, to tell you the truth, Brent. I think I've worked on the script and seen it performed so many times that I'm not able to see the forest for the trees anymore." Of course, I wanted the play to go on, but at the same time I felt that I should be honest.

We watched Brent's face as he rubbed his chin. "Then I guess it's up to me," he said. We could tell that behind his poker expression, he was totaling up the pros and cons, the financial pluses and minuses, about to make an important choice that would profoundly affect all of our lives.

I looked at Lester. His posture revealed anxiety. He'd never have Brenda, so all that was left of his efforts in New York was the play. Obviously, he didn't now, at the eleventh hour, want to abandon the little that he had remaining.

Brent pressed his lips tightly together until there was a bulge of skin under his nose. Lester and I waited for his decision.

New York or not? The big step, or surrender?

Brent looked at Lester, then at me.

"All right," he said, "let's take it to New York."

Lester leaned back with relief and took a sip of his drink, then tossed himself forward with his hand out.

Brent took it in a handshake, then reached out toward me. I shook his hand, too.

"Well, that's it!" Brent said courageously, now that he had made up his mind.

The three of us raised our glasses and toasted the play.

I went back to the hotel alone, thinking about Melissa. I was wondering if I should call her, since Brent was down in Baltimore with us. But her absence from my life, which must have been an obvious choice on her part, was one I felt I should respect.

As I crossed the lobby, I noticed Brenda sitting alone, looking at a local newspaper, a drink in her hand.

I went over to her and saw that she was reading an article about herself. It was accompanied by a large portrait that was obviously a movie studio handout.

"Brenda," I said.

She looked up.

"I've got news for you," I told her. "We're going to open in New York."

She took in the news, and appeared to wait while it registered in her brain. After poised thought, she smiled. "Thank God!" She put the glass to her lips and tilted her head back until only the tinkling ice was left.

"Are you alone tonight?" I asked. Melissa wasn't there. My wife was back home, and some of my tension had been relieved, not because my rearranged play was going to have its chance, but because I knew what the future was going to be—for at least a week. Brenda suddenly looked extremely appealing to me and happy at the news—two elements, I felt, confidently, that would easily lead to a special feeling of warmness in a leading lady for her playwright, especially since she had volunteered previously to give herself to me. Now seemed like the perfect time to strike.

Even so, I had to muster my strength.

"Can I take you up on your previous offer?" I asked boldly, getting right to the point.

Brenda grinned. "No, thanks," she replied, then went back to her reading.

I've since wondered if I should have been more subtle or if I had stacked the cards against myself when we were alone in her room.

Well, what the hell. I'd blown it again, as usual.

Chapter 26

New York.

As soon as the last curtain had come down in Baltimore, the cast took off, and the stagehands began striking the set. Two trucks were loaded with the flats, props, electrics, wardrobe, and other production furnishings, and driven through the night.

I arrived at the Longacre Theater as they were unloading and setting up.

The marquee was lettered, with Brenda's charcoaled face behind the words, and two large posters advertising the show were on sandwich-board frames set open on the sidewalk. Pictures taken of various scenes were behind glass on the wall.

I walked into the lobby. Only three people were in line buying tickets. New York theatergoers are always aware of out-of-town reviews.

I went through one set of rear mirror-paneled double doors into the dark theater.

Stanley was on the stage, his hands on his hips, directing three stagehands as they set flats into place. The fantasy of my childhood was becoming artificial reality again.

I walked down the aisle to the front row, found a seat in the center, dropped the cushion down, and sank into it to watch what was happening. I felt relaxed. There would be no more changes in the script. It stood as played on the last night in Baltimore. The New York critics would judge the show the Monday night following a week of previews, at the premiere, with our final Baltimore changes, and it would either run or close. It was up to the fates.

I watched the goings-on, high on the excitement of the theater, knowing that I should enjoy the experience to the fullest, since it would be years before I'd have a similar one. I felt someone sit down next to me and turned. It was Melissa.

My placidity was somewhat jarred. "What are you doing here?" I asked.

She put her arm through mine. "I haven't seen or talked with you for a whole week."

I looked around into the darkness behind us, then took a chance. I kissed her on the cheek.

"Thanks," she smiled, tightening her arm against mine. "You look very good."

"You look beautiful. Even more than before."

Her face, lit by the reflected stage light, showed deep appreciation for my mere comment.

"How has your play ultimately shaped up?" she asked me.

"I still have my doubts."

"There's a chance, though, isn't there, that you'll get good reviews? Brent said there was. And I understand that Lester is optimistic."

"They both feel that there's a very good possibility for it to succeed. But, in my opinion, there's lot going against it."

"All plays have that. But there have been many that got bad reviews out of town and raves here."

"The shortcomings of this production, though, are obvious. And I just know they'll be obvious to the critics."

"Is any of the cast here?" Melissa asked.

"I doubt if any would show up this far ahead of curtain time."

"Good! Let's go up to Brenda's dressing room."

"Why?"

"We can't talk here," she replied, rising and lifting my arm with her. "But we can talk there." I stood, physically compelled by her upward pull, and followed.

We went up the backstage stairs, stopped at the first room—the star's —and entered.

Melissa closed the door and locked it, then put her arms around me passionately and kissed me.

"This isn't exactly the best place for us to get together," I said.

"But it's exciting, isn't it?" She seemed to glow with a mystic, inexplicable aura. In all the time I had known her, I always found her to be unpredictable. Or have I said that before?

"We'd better get out of here," I advised her. "What if Brenda shows up?"

"You said no one will be here this early."

"That's true. It's most likely. But you never can tell. Suppose, for some reason, somebody does show up? I mean, what if Brent or anybody else should decide to get here early?" I regretted that my worry and panic were exceptionally evident. It seemed so in contrast with her calm and mood. But perhaps my basic naivete was one of the components of my personality that intrigued Melissa, my tendency to panic, my not being particularly assertive with women. That could have been what brought out her sexual aggressiveness toward me in the first place. She had been used to constant pursuit by males. It seemed to be kind of a reversal that she enjoyed.

She said, "Sit down on that chair." With a half-smile, looking directly into my eyes, she reached under her dress from the sides, and tugged, and a delicate pink garment with lace fell to gather around her ankles.

I was sitting in the chair, feeling uncomfortable. "Not here, Melissa. Really. You shouldn't even be at the theater."

She stepped out of the ring of silk and walked to me with the half-smile frozen on her face, stood astride the chair, lowered herself onto my lap, and embraced and kissed me.

So my affair with Melissa continued when I got back to the city almost as if there had been no interruption. Seemingly, her problem of my wife was gone, forgotten.

I was constantly amazed by Melissa's overwhelming love for me. Yet, in tense moments together, when the subject came up, I could feel her anger at my decent treatment of my wife, and her forgiving me for it at the same time.

The evening of the final preview performance, Lester came out of the auditorium and onto the stage to speak to the cast. Everyone listened intently.

"Tomorrow, we're going to have two dress rehearsals, at ten in the morning, and at three in the afternoon."

He paused while we either made a written or mental note. "I want you to have Monday off, except, of course, for the Broadway opening that night. I think it's important for you to take it easy that day, before that performance. I suggest that you watch television, walk around town, shop—do anything except think about the play. That was always my philosophy at school—I studied up to the day of a test, then took that morning off. It'll give your subconscious mind an opportunity to think about your lines and blocking. That way, it'll all come to you easily once the curtain goes up. Just spend the time relaxing."

He shifted on his feet. "Whether this play will make it depends on the critics and word of mouth from here on in. There's nothing more that you can do about it except give the best performance of your life Monday evening."

He paused, as if waiting for the cast and crew to absorb and consider his words. "Tuesday morning, early," he continued, "the results will come in. If the show gets good reviews, we can celebrate. If we bomb, well, life will go on. All you can do then is forget about it, chalk it up to experience, and go to your next projects with the same positive attitude that you've shown here."

The tenseness in his voice abated. "Brent has asked me to tell you that he's throwing an opening-night party at Sardi's. He's got the second floor for all of us—the cast, crew, investors, friends and relatives.

Lester lifted a palm and held it high above the cast, as if blessing them. "The best to all of you. It's been a fantastic pleasure working with everyone. I want you to know how much I've appreciated your cooperation and effort in putting The Wrecker's Ball together, from Mark, who wrote the play, to wardrobe, and Stanley, who has always seen to it that everything ran smoothly. But especially to Brenda Williams, who left her worlds of television and the movies to take her chances with us here on Broadway."

Brenda, standing in the midst of the group holding her script, beamed. It was as if all were forgiven and forgotten between the leading lady and her director. It was the last day of school, all of us going off to possibly meet again sometime far in the future, or never again.

During Lester's speech, Stanley had brought the work light to the center of the stage.

He turned it on.

Lester continued. "All I can say this late in the game is that I'll see all of you Monday evening and then again that night after the show. Best of luck."

The cast and crew applauded and the lights dimmed to black. In the subdued illumination of the work light, everyone drifted into the wings.

Monday evening, as I was fixing my tie in the mirror in my bathroom at the hotel, there was a knock at the door.

"It's unlocked!" I called.

Shirley came in. "It's me. Are you all set to be the newest successful playwright on Broadway?" I watched her reflection come up behind me. She wore a countenance of victory.

"Your flowers are on the bed." I said. "But don't take all of this too seriously, or you'll never be able to stand up to the bad reviews and my failure tonight."

"Oh, Mark, you're so pessimistic. You have as much chance as anybody else who ever had a play produced."

She went off, and I heard paper rattling in the other room.

"Oh, how beautiful!" came her voice. "They just match my dress!"

I went into the bedroom, still tugging at my tie, and told her, "By the way, Brent has invited all of us to a party at Sardi's after the show."

"Oh, how exciting! To celebrate your smash hit!"

"I'm telling you, Shirley, you'd better not count on it. We didn't get the greatest reviews out of town, and the New York critics are the toughest."

"Well, I think that Brenda Williams is going to carry the show, which was your opinion from the start."

"I don't think so now."

"Why? Isn't she any good?"

"Yes, she's good. Competent, that's it. But please don't quote me. Nobody praised her during the tryouts." I looked at my watch. "Time to go."

"I just have to fix my face," Shirley said, going into the bathroom.

"Please don't take two hours," I begged.

After, for her, an abbreviated make-up session with herself, we left the hotel.

We stepped out into the cool night and walked over to the Longacre. A fairly large crowd had already gathered in front of the theater. There were many fur coats. The owners, no doubt, were the backers' wives. We walked through the group of people and into the lobby, which was also crowded.

I heard a voice behind me. "Mark." It was Brent. He was with Melissa, who said, without even looking at me, "Hello, Shirley, how are you?"

"Fine, thank you," Shirley replied. "How are you?"

Shirley took advantage of the next moment, as Brent and Melissa exchanged a few words. "What's her name? I remember meeting her once or twice."

How ironic, I thought. "That's Melissa, Brent's wife."

"I know she's his wife, but I just didn't remember her name. She's very pretty, isn't she?"

"Yes," I said.

Couples were beginning to go through the doors into the theater.

I handed Shirley a ticket. "Here's yours. It's for the front row mezzanine, center. I'll be at the back, downstairs, pacing."

"Why don't you sit next to me and enjoy the show?"

"Too restless."

She was disappointed, I could see that, but I could also tell that she was resigned to accept the manifestation of my anxieties.

I led Shirley to the door and watched her mingle with the crowd that was leaving the lobby to find their seats.

After she had disappeared from sight and I went back into the lobby, Melissa came over to me. She looked ravishing, her long blond hair set high on her head in swirls, her lovely face, under the lobby lighting sculpted to a goddess-like form of dark and light curves and planes. The jewelry around her neck scintillated. Nothing could have convinced me more than that living vision I was seeing that I was in love with her.

"This is it, Mark," she told me with a faint, enigmatic smile. "Tomorrow you'll know."

I laughed. "I'm afraid I know now."

"We'll see." She put out a hand. "The best, Mark."

I took the delicate fingers that I knew so intimately. "Thanks so much for all you've done, Melissa. You made tonight possible, however it turns out."

She smiled and went off, leaving me alone to await my fate.

When the lobby cleared, I went into the theater and stood in the back. The wait for the curtain to go up seemed interminably long.

At last the house lights dimmed to half. The New York debut audience took longer than the others to settle down to quietness because these were the people most close to the show, and I could perceive that they didn't feel the obligation, as other audiences did, to show full respect. After all, in one way or another, they owned the production. At last there was silence, and the theater went completely dark.

The curtain flowed slowly upward into the fly loft, and the stage lights came up to half on an empty set.

There was heavy applause to praise Christopher Thomas's work, and because it was the start of a production on which many had money riding.

Brenda entered from the wings. Strode moodily to center stage, and faced the audience.

A blast of light targeted and surrounded her.

The audience went wild with screams and applause.

For almost a half a minute the chaos continued, until Brenda had the creditable presence of mind to make a slight move, showing that she wished to get on with the play, astute for someone who had never before been on the stage before an excitedly unruly packed house.

Music up.

The young man who played the role of her husband appeared at stage left and began methodically making his way to her. When he finally reached the star of the show, he brought his hand to hers, and she took it.

When Brenda spoke her first words, her voice projected more depth than I had ever heard from it before, the tone clear, resonant, filling the theater. "This," she said, "is the past that you have spoken of so often."

I could feel the audience settling down for an enjoyable evening. They had sensed that they could look forward to an hour and a half of true theater. I hoped that they were right. We were off and running.

At the first intermission, I wandered through the crowd, trying to pick up words of opinion about the play. During the first several minutes I overheard comments that didn't in one way or another pinpoint any definite trend of thought, but soon conversations turned to other subjects.

Shirley appeared. "I was looking all over for you," she complained, perturbed. "How do you think people are taking it?"

I told her my just-upgraded opinion of Brenda.

"You see? I predicted that your play would do well." As if she were interested in my writing rather than the money.

"I have to admit," I said, "that the cast is putting more into this opening than they did in any of the other performances."

She was looking off, and tugged at my arm. "There's Brent and Melissa. Let's go over and see what they have to say."

We made our way through the large group that had formed in the lobby.

"Mark," Brent said, as we came up to them. "What do you think so far?"

"Pretty good compared to out of town," I told him. "But it's too soon to tell."

I could see in my peripheral vision that Melissa was looking Shirley over intently.

"Looks good to me," Brent said, which made Shirley all smiles. "In my opinion," Brent continued, "we have a damn good chance. If Brenda can give us good word-of-mouth, we can stay open long enough to build ticket sales through advertising."

Melissa had nothing to say. She just looked from me to Shirley and back again. I took her silence as a hint not to start a conversation with her. But I wondered what she was thinking.

The lobby lights blinked, and the audience began to return to their seats.

The second-act curtain went up and the cast continued putting their best foot forward, to my surprise, but I still wasn't as convinced as the others about our having a successful play, or even one that was adequate enough to make our weekly break-even costs.

During the second-act intermission, I fought falling prey to the illusion that we'd get good reviews, which was what was happening to Brent, Lester, and many of the backers.

Lester was ecstatic. "I knew it. I just knew it!" he told us. "They're a fantastic bunch of troupers. I knew they'd come through!"

When the curtain rang down at the end of the final act, the Hollywood cast took deep bows to thundering applause by friendly backers, acquaintances and relatives. Curtain calls were demanded by the audience one after another, which obviously impressed Lester, who didn't know any better. Finally, Stanley told me afterwards, he made number six the last. "It was getting ridiculous," he said.

It was only a few steps to the maitre d's desk from the doorway to Sardi's. "We're upstairs with The Wrecker's Ball," I told him, and he nodded.

Shirley and I climbed the stairs.

Brent's guests were beginning to assemble. There was relief in the air. The ordeal was over. We could all drink together, eat, enjoy ourselves and let fate deal us what it wanted to. By the time the news came, we'd be in enough of an alcoholic state to be able to accept the worst.

I went to the bar to get a daiquiri for Shirley, and a double martini for myself—which I had been thinking about since before the curtain went up that night.

It didn't take long for the room to become jam-packed. Strange faces were everywhere. Brent, of course, knew almost everybody, and he was greeted with congratulations constantly throughout the evening; especially by his backers, who were convinced that since the play had made its way through opening night, and they liked it, that it was a smash hit.

Brent's press agent, like every other Broadway press agent, had entrée to the newspapers, and advance copies of the reviews were expected some time around midnight. Curtain time for opening nights was 7:30 p.m. so that the critics could get back to their newspapers to write their reviews before deadline time for the first edition. The press agents got tear sheets of reviews early and rushed to the opening night parties.

Although the reviews hadn't arrived by eleven o'clock, Lester, who had gotten quite high on the free-flowing booze, began to beg Brent to let him read them to the crowd when they did get there.

Brent, without his jacket, and with his tie pulled down—unusually informal for him—waved his drink at Lester. "All right, Mr. Director. You can have that honor." He laughed in advance of his next comment. "Or dishonor."

The first review to show up was from The *Herald Tribune*.

Brent was the first to read it—to himself, Melissa taking it in from over his shoulder. She passed it to me, wearing a poker face.

My eyes raced through the type.

"Hey, let's see it, Mark," Lester said, cheery and groggy, crowding us. "What did they say?"

I passed it to him and he looked it over, during which time he seemed to sober up.

Shirley, worried, came up to me. "Did they like it?"

"Let me put it this way," I told her. "It isn't exactly a rave review."

Lester handed the clipping on to Tom. A crowd, which included Brenda, who had just returned from the bar, gathered around him.

Stanley sat in the corner with the wife of one of the backers, observing our reactions with a wry expression, keeping the lead on most of us with the number of drinks he had put away.

The next review in was from the Daily News. It didn't exactly make us overjoyed.

Lester read the sheet of newsprint and passed it along. "The New York Times is the one that counts," he told us confidently "Not these other shit newspapers."

The *New York Times* review was the one that turned up next, and no one volunteered to do any announcing about its contents, as most of the backers, oblivious to the fact that the verdict coming in was not too much in the affirmative, continued their carousing.

The New York Post's review followed, and concurred with the others, that the play was average, with some high spots of drama, nevertheless, but that Brenda Williams didn't fulfill her expectations.

"Listen," Lester told everybody at our table, which included Brenda, "there are lots of people out there who want to see Brenda Williams, whatever vehicle she's in." He winked at her. "And this is a damned good play." He looked at me tipsily. "Right, Mark?"

I nodded my head and forced a smile. I knew it was all over. And so did Brent and Melissa.

I'd seen a number of plays with such elements: their producers thinking that 'beautiful people' of the screen would carry the show. These productions managed to hang on for a few weeks, if at all, but after they exhausted the stars' fans, the box office take fell below the nut, and they went under.

I was certain that the same would happen with us. And I was afraid that Brenda didn't have enough clout with theatrical audiences because they weren't television habitués.

(By the way, The New Yorker magazine review was favorable, and praised Brenda, but that one wasn't published until a week later.)

For the record, here are some general comments by the critics about The Wrecker's Ball. It was what I had expected, but hoped wouldn't be the case.

"What is Hollywood doing on Broadway?"

"This wunderkind movie director makes us wunder."

"Although Brenda Williams brought pathos to the character in most of the scenes she played, a few more rehearsals of other scripts in front of the TV cameras wouldn't exactly be to her disadvantage."

"If Mr. Gessel had something promising on paper, it either wasn't transferable to the stage, or it wasn't transferred correctly."

Brent posted the closing notice backstage at the end of the second week. He had intended to accept losses until the play caught on. But so few tickets were sold once the play was reviewed that in a very short time the weekly losses would have wiped out all of the play's capitalization.

Lester and his friends went back to Hollywood, and Brenda returned to the TV screen and an occasional movie.

As for myself, fortunately, I didn't remain unemployed for long. When the play became history, Melissa went out of her way to see that Brent kept me on as a stage manager with one of his productions.

Chapter 27

I continued with my writing.

Shirley was pleased that I was earning a steady, solid income through Actors' Equity, which stage managers must be members of, since the union requires a good salary and benefits.

Melissa continued to meet me, often. At first, after the shows. We had our trysts at some of the smaller downtown hotels, where we least expected to be seen by people we knew.

But then she began getting bolder, to the point where she didn't give a damn any more about whether anyone found out about us.

She started to show up backstage, in the wings of the theater I was working at, just before the final curtain, and I was quite concerned that Brent might learn about our affair. After she came a few times to the theater where I was working, I finally took her aside after the cast had made their final bow. "Melissa," I whispered, "you've just got to stop coming here. All of these people know Brent."

But something profound had happened to Melissa. She had become even more unabashed in her attitude and actions.

"When is it going to be my turn to enjoy life," she began saying. "I don't really give a damn about Brent. It's you I love."

She even began neglecting her children, leaving them home with the maid to take them places, and spending full afternoons with me, walking through Central Park.

She started to lengthen our days together to the late evening, insisting that I phone in sick to the theater and later call Shirley with excuses.

I met her at a bar on 14th Street one afternoon, the morning after meeting her for two consecutive full-length days and not showing up during that time at the theater at which I was working.

"Melissa. We've got to stop this! You're going to be in serious trouble, and I'll lose my job."

"I got you your job in the first place, didn't I? I'll see to it that you don't lose it."

"But you'd have to tell Brent why."

"If I had to, I would." She sipped her drink, then said, "I've been tied up in this marriage now for 15 years. I'm sick and tired of Brent. I love the kids. But I love you, too. And I want to be with you."

"Things are just fine as they are. Why don't you leave well-enough alone?"

"Because it's my turn to live."

"Do you want to ruin your life? Your kids' lives?"

"Don't worry. I won't."

"What if Brent divorces you?"

"He never would. He loves me."

"Are you that sure?"

"I'm positive."

"I'm telling you, Melissa. At this rate, Brent is definitely going to find out about us."

"I don't care.

It finally happened, though. At a cast party for the first anniversary of a musical that Brent had produced.

The curtain rang down on the performance that marked one year since the opening. The cast of 31, crew of eight, three wardrobe mistresses, the musicians, the doorman, general manager, press agent, others connected with the show, many friends, and newspaper reporters and photographers poured onto the stage as delicatessen treats and beverages were rolled on.

Most of the cast members were still in their costumes and make-up. The mood was festive. Smiles were on every face, as the celebrators dug their forks into cold cuts, and filled their paper plates with salads and pickles, and cups with beverages. Employment was fairly well guaranteed. Having a role in a successful musical meant a well-paying, leisurely, secure life for a very reasonable run—perhaps for years.

Brent, formally dressed in a suit and tie, arrived shortly after the party got going.

Melissa was already there. She had come alone earlier and stood by me backstage throughout the final dance and chorus scenes and curtain calls, as everyone in the show bowed amidst a blaring medley of brass and strings from the orchestra pit that recalled the hit songs of the show. Many of the tunes had already been heard on home and car radios across the country— which audience members hummed to themselves on the way out.

Shirley showed up late. "I don't want to be the first one there," she had told me at the apartment that morning, but I knew that she'd never be on time because once she got in front of the mirror with her make-up, excessive time would go by, as usual.

Melissa stuck by me from the start of the evening.

As we both put our second sandwiches together, I said to Melissa, "Don't you think we should separate a bit?"

"Of course not," she answered, putting her palm to my cheek.

"Christ!" I announced, roving my eyes around at faces, until I picked up Brent's eyes looking directly at us. In them, I saw the moment of realization.

After that experience, which was to become indelible in my mind, and would subsequently, and continually, affect the three of us, a fourth was added—Shirley. But in her case, it was a direct result of Melissa's actions, a consequence of Melissa's now full desire to be completely free in her actions.

Rather than be repetitive with the week-to-week, and finally day-to-day, discord between Melissa and Shirley, I've put together a scene that represents it all.

So, here's an example of this "love triangle."

It is two o'clock in the morning. I've just returned home to my apartment in Newark, and I'm in my study, working on a play. I have just, about an hour before, left Melissa, after being with her from curtain time of the production for which I'm a stage manager.

The phone rings. At my desk, where I'm writing, I answer it, but Shirley has picked up just an instant before from her extension in the bedroom. I hear Shirley say, "Hello."

"Is Mark there?"

"Who is this?" asks Shirley.

"Melissa."

"What are you doing calling here at two o'clock in the morning!" Shirley screams. "You woke me up."

"I want to speak with Mark."

"Here I am," I say.

"Melissa!" Shirley shouts. "Get off the phone. I want to sleep!"

"I didn't call you. I called Mark!"

"Shirley," I say, as calmly as possible. "Will you please get off the line?"

"No! I want her off the line."

"I'm not getting off the line."

"Shirley," I tell her. "Just hang up. We want to talk."

"You had all day to talk with her. You don't have to talk at two o'clock in the morning."

Exasperation in her voice, Melissa says, "Get off the goddamn phone, Shirley, and let us talk!"

"You get off the goddamn phone!"

"I'm not going to."

"Leave my husband alone."

"Why? You're not interested in him, and I am."

"You lousy bitch! Keep out of our lives!"

"If you don't let us talk, I'll come over there, shove my fist down your throat and grab you by the cunt or whatever it is you have down there!"

I recall a session years later, with one of my psychiatrists to whom I mentioned this incident, after I had slipped into another depression, who told me, "You like the idea of having women fighting over you, don't you?"

I disagreed with his interpretation. This was different. One was my wife. She didn't count.

But after much thinking about it, I had to admit to myself, he was probably right.

Chapter 28

Even though Brent now more than strongly suspected our liaison, Melissa was unconcerned. "He's just going to have to put up with this affair," was her outlook on the situation.

"But he's not going to take it for long," I would counter.

However, she was right. But only at first.

Let me reconstruct what happened in her life. I can do this because she spared me no details about what she experienced in her marriage (as I did with her in mine)—and what Brent eventually tolerated, to the breaking point.

Brent didn't at first bring up the subject with me at all. For about a month after the party, he just observed Melissa while she worked at the office and at home, and asked discreet questions at the theater where I was working for him as a stage manager.

Then he began showing up unexpectedly at matinees and evening performances, purportedly for a routine check on the production, and found her backstage with me a number of times.

Yet, at that point he still said nothing.

"I told you he'd be afraid to speak up," Melissa informed me after about the fifth time he saw us together.

She was wrong.

One morning he was waiting up for her when she entered their Fifth Avenue apartment at five a.m.

"Where the hell were you?" he asked her. "With Mark?"

"That's right."

"Have you been seeing him often?"

"Yes."

"Why?"

"Because I love him."

"I hope you realize that you're risking this marriage."

"I'll take the risk."

There was nothing more said. She undressed and went to bed.

She called me the next day, and I met her late that afternoon for a walk through the Central Park zoo.

It was a cool, fall day, the air drenched with the spicy scent of yellowing leaves. Sunlight coated the green and reddish landscape with a pale yellow cast. We walked quietly along dirt paths, enjoying each other's company and our silence together. Just being with Melissa had become a delight that I had never known before, or since.

She was wearing dungarees that braced her still-flat stomach, enhancing her slim, womanly curves.

"Isn't everything beautiful?" she finally said.

Her comment confirmed that her feelings at that very moment were the same as mine.

We continued on, still adrift in a harmonious state of tranquility.

Finally, she spoke. "So he knows," she said. "So what?"

"So you can lose everything you have."

"I have my own bank account. Brent was generous to me over the years."

"But what would you do if he divorced you?"

"He won't. He loves me."

"What about you? Do you love him?" I asked, attempting to hide my jealousy.

"No. I never did. If I had it to do all over again, I'd never marry him. He's so caught up with theater. I'm just a plaything to be used and shown to his friends and business acquaintants. He never appealed that much to me. But I was very young when I married him, and I didn't know any better."

Jealousy still consumed me. "Did you ever love anyone else?"

"No, never." She looked at me as we strode at a quick pace over a pathway of brick. "You're the first man I ever really loved."

As we walked together, I almost euphorically watched the way she moved, because she was totally mine. When I was with her, I had no charitable feelings toward Shirley or Brent, no concern about the world around me. Only selfish thoughts of Melissa and myself alone together as we were now.

I was happier than I had ever been in my life. And she, too, was complete. The experience was the fulfillment of a dream that I had never even dreamed, that was beyond what I could ever imagine, especially after having suffered through the depths of depression.

I had gone from one end of the spectrum to the other, from the despair and pain of despondency to ecstatic joy.

Not many people reach either extreme during their lifetimes.

But perhaps it's impossible to appreciate bliss without having ascended from the nadir of anguish.

In the midst of our growing relationship, I had found that I was quickly being influenced into absorbing Melissa's philosophies. That was why, I theorized, I had discovered that I was no longer concerned about anything else except our being together.

But then, as we continued walking, she made a comment that I was to hear many times again, that brought me up short in my new, devil-may-care way of thinking about her.

"Aren't you going to ask me to marry you?"

A notion out of nowhere. "What?" I almost gasped.

"You love me, don't you?"

"Of course," I stammered. I knew that she was paradise to me, but I still wasn't certain that it was love. Even after all of the joy I had experienced with her. For a brief moment I thought about how marriage might destroy our feelings for each other. Could that be the cause of my quandary? She had told me once that I couldn't live without my creature comforts, that I had a deep-seated fear of basic change. Was that it? The serenity of being settled into a routine way of life? Or was it my upbringing? My distrust of love along with my desire for it?

Those few exchanged words, my hesitancy, and her concern, had slowed us to a stop. We sat down on a bench.

She looked at me with her clear, gray eyes. "Don't you want to marry me?"

I didn't know what to say.

I felt myself move my hands and arms awkwardly. "I'm married. I have a family," I explained. I thought for a moment. "You do, too."

She put her hands to my cheeks. "I would give up everything for you, because I love you. Wouldn't you do the same for me?"

"I haven't even thought about it."

"I have. Often."

"But things are good as they are now."

"Are they? We have to sneak around to be together."

"That's true, but look what you'd be giving up. You have money. I don't. Your husband is rich. You'll always have everything you want. With me you'd be struggling."

"Mark, there are no guarantees in life. Ten years from now Brent might be broke. You might be successful. But that doesn't make any difference. The main thing is, we could have each other."

"We have each other now. Everything is fine as it is."

She let go of me, turned away, and said nothing more that day on the subject.

I was hardly spending any time at home anymore, making up excuses that began to sound ridiculous. Eventually, Shirley's subconscious suspicions surfaced.

"What are you doing with all of your time?" she finally asked me one day.

"Oh, I've been at the library in New York, researching material for my next play," I lied. I felt justified in being untruthful to her, considering the drab existence she was giving me compared to the pleasure that Melissa had brought into my life.

"At five o'clock in the morning?"

"Well, sometimes after the show, some of the crew and actors get together for drinks, I added, also untruthfully."

"Do you mean actresses?"

I was surprised that she didn't mention Melissa specifically.

She had a right to be suspicious of my being interested in other women. She held me a sexual hostage. Fuck her, I said to myself. Especially now that I had Melissa.

Ironically, Melissa was concerned over my fidelity to her, too.

Whenever we walked along Fifth Avenue, if I so much as glanced at another woman, she'd let me know. Her comment would be something like, "You've got me; what are you looking at her for?"

"It's subconscious. I wasn't even aware that I was looking."

"If I meant that much to you, you wouldn't even want to look at someone else."

She had become even more possessive than Shirley. But at least Melissa had good reason to be possessive. She was totally committed to me more than to Brent, and even her children.

I continued wondering, as I wonder even now at age 88, and as I stated earlier; whether my love for Melissa was purely sex combined with what was to me overwhelming beauty and magnetism. Especially her unquestioning love for me, which went beyond any that I had ever known, even from my parents, and a nature that merged with mine to make us one. She insisted that she felt love for me and me only, that it was the reason she gave herself to me beyond my requests and desires, that I didn't have to prove anything to her with fame or money. That I had only to be me.

Some days, as we made love endlessly in a motel or hotel room, the window light seemed to pass through ageless transition. And when we returned to the reality of our present mundane existences, six, or eight, or more hours had vanished. I doubt that there was any marriage either of us knew of that was as intense with passion as our relationship. The need for our giving and taking of mutual physical love was insatiable. Was it because it was forbidden fruit that the fire of our passion and lust for each other blazed higher each time we embraced?

As our affair became more ardent, Brent seemed to surrender in the fight for his wife.

My peaceful, and celibate, life with Shirley was soon disrupted when Melissa began to boldly call me at home on a regular basis.

Shirley, being a reader of detective novels, had no problem in quickly putting two and two together, and began screening my calls. But I really didn't give a shit. If she didn't know how to keep a husband, that was her problem.

However, it created problems with Melissa.

"Why don't you call me back?" she began to complain.

"Did you call?"

"Yes, I left a message with Shirley."

"She didn't mention a word about it."

"Why the fuck do you let her run your life?"

"She doesn't really."

Sarcastically. "No?"

Melissa was becoming another person. I hardly recognized her anymore. She was no longer the same somewhat demure woman I had first met. But it made no difference to me. Her intense devotion ruled out any criticism that I might have felt deep down. I suspected, but didn't want to admit to myself, that I was in some kind of state of insanity. All of my thoughts seemed to revolve rationally around her. Yet, from time to time I would wonder whether my outlook was actually irrational. I was aware of the conflict within me: reason versus emotion—with emotion the victor. But seeing her, being with her, making love with her, was all that mattered to me. Money, my job, my writing, my family, all faded into the background.

Shirley interpreted my new disposition as "middle-aged madness with that bitch!"

But where Shirley's comments about me would ordinarily have affected my thinking, they no longer had any influence. I accepted my rational obsession of emotional insanity.

I began spending weekends with Melissa, beginning after the final curtain of the Sunday matinees, when I could get someone to cover for me for the evening performance, and continuing through Monday, when the theaters are dark, and even sometimes into Tuesday morning.

Brent, Melissa told me, had reached a state in which he began going into uncontrollable rages at their apartment, threatening to throw her out and fire me.

But she was indifferent and unconcerned, and countered, she said, with a warning to him that if he continued with his tirades, she would start divorce proceedings. That, of course, turned everything around. He did love her very much, as she had assured me.

But then one evening she called me backstage at the theater during the show. (She no longer tried to reach me at home. Shirley made every effort, at least from there, to keep Melissa away from me.) I was giving cues, and told the doorman I'd call her back, but he returned and said that she insisted I speak with her immediately, that it was imperative.

I had one of the other stage managers take over my duties and went to the pay phone.

"This is no time to call me, you know that," I admonished her.

There was a faint trace of demand in her voice. "It's important. I've got to see you."

"I was planning to go home tonight," I told her, somewhat embarrassed saying it.

"It's important," she repeated.

"What's so important? Can't it wait for tomorrow? I'll meet you in the afternoon, before the matinee."

"Brent beat me up."

I was aghast. My words sputtered. "I can't believe it!"

"You would if you took a look at me."

Still, as cruelly as I knew I was behaving, I requested as gently as I could, "Can't it wait until tomorrow? If we get together tonight, I'll never get home until early in the morning. And Shirley will make my life hell."

I could sense irritation in her voice. Without her telling me, I was certain she was thinking that if the circumstances were reversed, she would leave the theater without a second thought because of her concern for me.

This interpretation was either perception or paranoia. But definitely experience; she always made such comparisons.

But she knew me well.

And, sure enough...

"Still putting Shirley first?"

"Well, look," I explained. "She's making life miserable enough for me as it is. You know that. Seeing you tonight instead of tomorrow won't make that much difference. Why don't you just take a hotel room somewhere?" A horrible suggestion at a time like that, I was aware.

There was a long silence that I assumed was the result of her contained anger. But, as usual, Melissa was unpredictable, still a mystery to me.

"I don't think it's that necessary," she finally said. "He got it all out of his system, and he regretted it afterwards. He just went crazy. When I started out the door, he stopped me and apologized desperately. He was almost on his knees. He said he'd never do it again, because he loves me. He said I was the only one he ever loved, and that he'd let me do anything I want. When he told me he was sorry, he never even mentioned you."

I questioned my reaction. I should really have gone to see her immediately. Was it the fear of disrupting my home life, or that I really didn't love Melissa? I still didn't understand myself, either, my thinking, my motivations.

But I couldn't bring myself around to saying to her that I'd meet her immediately or after the show. "Tomorrow? Central Park West?" I asked. "Eighty-first Street?

There was another momentary lapse in the conversation. Then I heard a tone of resolve in her voice. "Oh, all right," she conceded.

The next day, I headed to the Museum of Natural History, an area where Melissa and I often met, and entered the park at 81st Street. I found her sitting on a bench, wearing jeans and a soft, pink blouse. She had dark glasses on.

We looked at each other, silently. Finally, I realized that I would have to be the first to speak. "How are you doing?"

She didn't reply, but just brought a hand up, removed the sunglasses, and lowered them slowly. The skin encircling one of her eyes was delicately tinged with black and blue that, as she moved her head, showed other colors of the rainbow. She also had a few scratches on her forehead and a bruise on one of her handsome cheekbones.

She waited for a comment.

The reality of what I found myself involved in triggered momentary panic inside my gut.

What came from my lips at first surprised me, but on immediate subsequent analysis, seemed logical.

"I think we'd better call an end to all of this," I told her. "It's not doing either of us any good. It's just not right."

As she spoke, I couldn't help but direct my sight at the ring of discoloration that surrounded her eye. "Now that I've gone through all of this for you because I love you, you want to end our relationship. Is that what you think of me?"

"Maybe it's for the best. I'm sure you don't want Brent to beat you up again."

"For you, I wouldn't care if it happened a million times more," she said softly, waiting for an answer, but I couldn't think of any words of reply. So she asked, "Would you go through this for me?"

"I don't know. I guess I would."

"No, you wouldn't. You say you love me, but you really don't. And you're afraid of Shirley."

"No, I'm not," I said, but neither of us was convinced.

"Let's go to a hotel and make love," she said, her voice and attitude revealing obvious annoyance with my attitude.

"Well, okay," I replied.

After I locked the hotel room door, she moved face-to-face with me and I could clearly see the raggedness of her welt, the abrasions, the shininess, in the room's light, of the delicate purple skin that surrounded an eye looking at me with love and desperation. "Be different this time, Mark," she whispered. "I need it."

I took her in my arms.

She responded to my feelings of love with kisses of passion and abandon.

Her hand took mine, leading me to the bed. She kissed me again and I moved my mouth from hers to her neck, down to the bare skin above her blouse. I kneeled slowly; my lips against each button before I freed it, kissing her breasts, belly, narrow waist, mons, sliding down the zipper down...

"Oh...that's what I want." she whispered, as I buried my face into her wet softness.

Chapter 29

Let's jump ahead now.

It's two years later, and Melissa and I are still going together. In fact, our appetites for each other have not abated, but grown even greater.

By then, our affair was quite open. We were seen everywhere like a married couple. In fact, on occasion, people greeted her as Mrs. Gessel.

Shirley and Brent both grudgingly accepted our relationship.

Our lovemaking sessions had grown more and more intense, and Melissa eventually refused any kind of birth control protection.

In passionate moments, when we were one, she would cling to me, begging, "Give me a baby!"

Why I went along with her insanity, I'll never know, but at any rate, I did make her pregnant.

We discussed the problem at a restaurant on the East Side, at an outdoor table. It was a bright, hot summer day, and we sat amidst the background and sounds of Third Avenue traffic and its thin, blue, odorless haze of exhaust. Crowds moved along the sidewalks: people on their way to luncheon dates, jobs, or to shop, their blank expressions showing no acknowledgement of their obvious New York travails.

Despite the pregnancy disaster, I also had a subject to talk about that was on the positive side.

I had optioned a play. It was the script by the successful off-Broadway playwright friend of mine, and I was busy trying to raise money to produce it on Broadway. However, I found that capitalizing the project was more difficult than I had anticipated.

First, however, I launched into the most important item on the agenda. "I don't know why I let you talk me into being so careless," I said to Melissa.

She stirred her vichyssoise slowly, not looking at me. "You weren't careless, and neither was I." She seemed to be hypnotized by the swirling, cold, white liquid. "We knew what we were doing."

"It was clearly you who knew what we were doing. I was just a fool."

She didn't answer.

"Well, Melissa, what are we going to do now? Hope that Brent assumes it's his?"

"That's impossible," she replied, finally looking up. "I haven't been giving him sex for over a year. I just haven't been able to. After...us...I find him...well... terribly unappealing."

"Great!" I said, exasperated.

She was silent, still making a small whirlpool with her spoon.

"Are you absolutely sure?" I asked. "Is there any possibility that you could be wrong?"

"None. My gynecologist is positive."

I waited for her to speak again, but she said nothing. So I spoke. "Well, what's the next step?" I asked. "An abortion?"

Irritated, she put her spoon down and looked at me with a lackluster expression. Her face was pale, without makeup, sensual, as if she had come back to the world after hours of early-morning lovemaking. "I want to have your baby. I told you that. It will be us, the fruit of our love, a human being who will be alive long after we're both gone."

"Jesus Christ, Melissa! You're crazy!"

"Mark, I want so much for it to be a girl. And I want to call her Tara. You know, the name of the plantation in Gone With the Wind."

"You've got to be practical, Melissa," I said, noticing a tone of stress in my voice. "You can't have this child."

"I want it," she insisted. "Yes, I did stop sleeping with Brent, but when I suspected my pregnancy a couple of weeks ago, I started again. I've been wearing my most provocative lingerie, and been as seductive as possible, and he's been having me two or three times a day." She looked off. "I hated it."

For the first time, I didn't feel jealousy. I was, in fact, relieved. "Still," I said, "he can make a simple calculation. And besides, he knows that we're still seeing each other. Often."

"No. I told him that I'm not seeing you any more, that we broke up. We'll have to stop our affair for a while. Then, after I have the baby, we can get back together again."

"Melissa, he'll always be suspicious. Don't you think that he could figure this out? Especially if we start meeting after the baby's born? You've just got to have an abortion. That's all there is to it."

"Mark. I want your child."

"Absolute insanity! You'll just be creating problems for the both of us. Someday you'll get into an argument with Brent, and blurt out the truth. It's bound to happen with your temperament."

She looked at me with a half-smile, or was it a face of pain. "Let me have this baby. I know you'll want it when you see it. It will look like both of us."

I clasped my hands together. "Melissa, I implore you. Don't go through with this."

I could tell by her attitude that she was intransigent, so I tried another strategy. "The worst of it all is that we won't be able to see each other for months. Do you want that?"

"It would be worth it. I'd want you even more when we got back together."

I attempted another tactic. "We have no right to have this child. It would be unfair to it. We'd have to live a secret life. And you know that it wouldn't be secret for long. You were going to be discreet about our affair, and that wasn't for long, was it?"

Melissa let out a short breath. "All right," she said. She was seething, but controlled. "If you don't want a living symbol of our love."

"I do, but not this way."

Then, as if she had thought of it for the first time, she asked, "Should we both get divorced and marry?"

"Oh, God, Melissa, please don't create more problems."

"It would end our problems."

"I couldn't afford it. You know I'm just scraping by."

"It's that you still love Shirley, isn't it?"

"Please, Melissa, don't be ridiculous. You know how I feel about her. The same way you do about Brent. If not worse. But it would be you who would suffer the most."

She cast her eyes down.

I reached across the table and touched her hand. "Melissa, haven't you ever wondered what our relationship would be like if we ever married?"

"Yes, I have."

"And what conclusion did you come to?"

She hesitated. "That it would be beautiful."

"I don't think you really believe that. I think you realize that marriage would ruin everything for us."

"No, I don't," she replied unconvincingly. So she had her doubts, too.

"Melissa, you know I love you, don't you?" But even saying it, I wasn't sure. Despite the extraordinary relationship we had, I was still doubtful about our living together permanently, legally; I was certain that it would end the bliss of our relationship. (Considering the situation years later, I was certain; even now, in this nursing home, I am.) Was it that I wasn't capable of loving? Or that I loved and wasn't actually positive that I did? That I needed the marriage I had? That I had set or been influenced into patterns in my youth that fettered me to Shirley?

Melissa tossed her spoon down with dismay. "I don't think you love me."

"But I do."

"Oh, I don't know." She put both of her palms over her face. "I just don't know anything."

I took the fingers of one of her hands and brought her arm awkwardly to me, leaving the other half of her face still covered. "Melissa, you're making this worse than it is. It's not so terrible. You wouldn't be the first woman to get pregnant and have an abortion. Just take care of this the way it should be taken care of, and we'll go on."

She dropped her other hand to the table and looked at me sadly.

I smiled. "I do love you, Melissa," I said, as sympathetically as I could.

She looked at me wearing an expression of hopelessness.

"There," I said, "you feel better already, don't you?"

She drooped her head forward, her neck curving more than seemed natural. I had never seen her so dejected.

I took both of her hands in mine. "It's not that important, Melissa. We have each other. Isn't that what's most meaningful to us? Don't you realize that a child could destroy it all? It might actually make us enemies in time."

"But when I'd see her," she said, raising her eyes, "I'd see you."

"You can see me now. Here I am," I told her as tenderly as I could. And uncontrollably, the words, "I love you," gushed forth again. I meant it. I felt it.

She smiled halfheartedly. "You really do?"

"Of course," I consoled her. "And I always will."

Her body seemed to slacken again as she went silently back to eating her lunch.

I said nothing more.

Melissa had the abortion, but after that she was recognizably different, changing even more from the person I had first met. She now seemed more distant. When we made love, it appeared to be more for the pleasure of the act than the giving and taking of affection, as it had been at first.

In time, she no longer seemed serious about sex. A major sign of this occurred not too long after the abortion. It happened one day at a motel in Paramus, New Jersey. We had just gotten settled for a routine afternoon of love. I was stretched out, still dressed, on the bed, my head on a pillow propped up against the headboard.

This time it was her performance of outright buffoonery, as she acted like a prostitute. Whatever put that into her head, I'll never understand.

She was standing across the small room by the bureau mirror, naked, looking at me over her shoulder, her hands on her hips. After glaring sensually, she wiggled her backside. "Hey, baby," she said in a licentious tone of voice. "You want some?"

I found myself totally turned off. I was seeing a totally different Melissa. And her actions made me feel like a customer. In fact, I was unable for the first time in my life to have an erection.

"Oh, come on, Melissa," I said. "Really."

She came over to me and began unbuttoning my shirt and tugging at my belt, eventually pulling all of my clothes, as I acceded to her whimsy. "What's the matter, Honey?" she questioned after she was done. "Can't get it up? Let me help you out."

"Please," I begged, feeling stress that I had never experienced before in any relationship. "Let's just be ourselves."

"I am myself, Toots. I'm your sexy girlfriend. Remember?"

"Maybe you think this is funny, but I don't."

"Why not, Sweets? Don't you think I'm sexy?"

"Yes, of course I do, but..."

"You're an old prude. Don't you dig a gal who has the hots for you?"

"Melissa. This just doesn't appeal to me. I mean, what is this? Some kind of game?"

She was quickly out of character, disappointed. "I'm having fun. Don't you have a sense of humor?"

"I don't know. I see you as a tender lover. Maybe that's it. The way you're behaving is—just so gross."

She sat next to me, back into the role of the hooker. "What's the matter, Pal?" She took a quick look at my loins, then my face, and wearing a half smile, asked, "Don't you love me anymore?"

"That's not funny, Melissa. You know I never had this problem before."

"Like I said, Hon, I can fix you up."

"I don't want to be fixed up. I just want to make love to you the way I always do. Tenderly, romantically."

She was serious again. "Don't you ever just feel horny, sometimes?"

"Not with you."

"Don't give me that, Mark."

"Don't you feel love with me? Isn't that what you always want? To feel love? Didn't we discuss the fact that with us sex is only part of it all?" I asked.

"Sometimes I just feel horny. What's wrong with that? It's normal, isn't it? Can't a woman feel horny?"

"Well, I guess so," I confessed.

"And, of course, I do love you," she told me, now the Melissa I first met, as she moved her lips toward mine.

Still, there were later incidents, as the situation became worse.

Melissa was really getting far-out. I suspected that the trauma of the abortion may have affected her. Yet, that may not have been the reason at all. I just don't know what did it, what put her on the sex track. With my overall limited experiences in sex, I was constantly surprised to see a woman who had the attitude of sex that went with male teenagers I had known, including myself, who thought about the subject constantly in high school and were called 'sex maniacs' by our female counterparts.

One evening I was late arriving to meet her at a New Jersey bar. When I got there, she was well into her drinking. And she was wearing a cowboy hat. I don't know where she got it. Most likely from one of the three men I had seen her flirting with at the bar when I came in.

I pulled myself up the barstool next to her, as the guys drifted away.

Melissa lifted an alcohol-weakened hand to the bartender. "He'll have something," she said to him, a slim man past middle age with an angry scowl on his face.

He came up the other side of the bar, wiping a glass vigorously, not asking what I wanted to drink; he just continued looking at me with a penetrating stare, and spoke directly. "You'd better tell your girl, here, to mind her manners, buddy."

"What's wrong?" I asked, immediately ready to defend Melissa. She had a thing about our standing up for each other. She stood up for me all the time, she insisted, and I should reciprocate.

"She keeps talking about getting eaten," he continued. "I don't like people talking like that around my place. Especially women."

Behind me there was laughter. Obviously from the men she had been speaking with when I first entered. Melissa, facing forward and looking at no one in particular, held one hand around her glass and raised the other one under the front of the hat brim, pushing it upward, tilting it back, and turning to me. I had to admit that she looked cute. But I still felt more and more alienated by her newly forming personality. I figured, hopefully, that it would eventually go away. An unrealistic assumption.

But I couldn't restrain myself from complaining as I sat next to her at the bar, so I said to her, "You're always upset if I look at another woman. How do you think I feel about you flirting with these guys?"

She had no reply.

"How would you like it if I flirted with the women here?" I questioned her, at last satisfied that I was getting through.

She tilted her head, putting the cowboy hat at an even more rakish angle. "If I ever caught you flirting with other women," she told me, "I'd rip your cock out of its socket."

Chapter 30

Assuming that my plans for optioning and producing Philip Carlton's play would go along with minor difficulties, I rented space in an office building on Broadway, just north of 52nd Street, and had stationery printed with the name 'Aegis Stage Productions' on a shield. A magazine illustrator-friend of mine designed the logo, and it was quite impressive.

I hoped that the play would be just as striking as my stationery, and a hit. A story about a loveless marriage that endures, it was titled *Parameters of Love*.

I had problems at the start getting Phil to change the title of his play to that. It was originally called *The Shards of Time*, a real turn-off, in my opinion.

Just as there had been a transformation in Melissa's personality, there had been an alteration in my outlook on Broadway plays. Being a producer now, I looked at the Broadway situation from a more commercial viewpoint. Perhaps it was because I was discovering that money from Broadway investors was not easy to come by. The fact that angels insisted on highly profitable returns, in addition to the excitement of owning part of a play, was brought home to me by their resistance.

But money wasn't the only challenge I had to overcome. My initial serious discussion with Phil about the Broadway production of his script gave me a glimpse of what lay ahead in my dealings with an intractable playwright. I had certainly never been like that with Brent and Lester.

This first ordeal took place at a coffeehouse in Greenwich Village, just prior to my optioning of Phil's property. The experience should have been a sign to me of grim events to come—a suggestion that I drop the project. But I liked the play, and I'd known Phil for some time and had gotten along with him very well on a personal basis.

However, when it comes to an author's creation, upon the signing of a contract, or even in negotiations before that, an invisible wall can immediately materialize between producer and playwright. I now learned that again—from the other side of the fence.

As we sat at the small, round table in the dim room waiting for our espressos, I briefly reflected, almost subconsciously, on my problems with Brent on The Wrecker's Ball. I suppose that I expected Phil to be as relenting as I had been. He had given in to having the title changed, so I was convinced that he'd be understanding about other issues.

"We have to consider the commercial aspect," I told him. "Uptown you've got more of a practical audience. You've got a lot of businessmen coming into town and taking guests to the theater. You can't be over-artistic, if you know what I mean."

God, I was beginning to sound like Lester.

"I get your point," Phil said, "but it's wrong to sacrifice integrity just to satisfy what you think are going to be an audience's demands. They're looking for a writer's viewpoint, a voice that's different from their own, a play that will let them ponder its author's philosophies, make them think. And titles aren't that important anyway. That's why I've given in on that point."

"I personally feel that a title is very important. But you agreed on changing it, so that proves to me that we can work together."

Phil Carlton was about 27, a very mature, tall and swarthy but moody young man, who had published his first novel at 22. The accomplishment had been a stepping-stone to his becoming a client of EMC, short for Entertainment Media Corporation, a top-flight agency representing not only writers of novels, stage plays, TV dramas, and screenplays, but actors and directors, as well as comedians, recording artists and others in show business. They were determined to move him along the road of fame and money, in either order. As a result, the first play he ever wrote was produced Off-Broadway. He was praised for it in the New York newspapers and a good number of magazines, and tickets sold well enough to keep it going week after week for about 10 months. Yet, although he was to be considered to have written a financial success, Off-Broadway theaters didn't bring in as much royalty as those in the uptown commercial district—where a small percentage of plays lasted longer than a few weeks. As a result, he was still struggling to pay his bills in the Village, where he lived, and was disappointed with the discovery that money didn't necessarily come with success, at least in the New York theater.

His second play, also produced Off-Broadway, received even more raves than his first, but still, despite the reviews, the drama didn't bring in full houses. It did have a six-month run, another prestige situation. But during that time, his royalties were meager. Nevertheless, he received some highly respected awards for his plays—after they had closed.

"You've got to think more commercially," I explained, "if you want to make money."

"You thought commercially on The Wrecker's Ball," he criticized. "And it didn't last long."

"That was more than commercial. It was Hollywood garbage. What I'm saying is that you can't feed a Broadway audience long passages of poetic dialogue that don't develop the plot. You can say what you want with your play, Phil, and still keep it from being too quote-artistic-unquote." I tried to get my point across by marking the air with two fingers twice as I said it.

He moved his gangling, slumped-over form to a slightly new position. "Well, I don't intend to give in to everything you want. I want it to be my play that's up there on the stage."

"That's the way it's going to be. I told you. I got a copy of your script to Jesse Bahnister, and he called me the next day to say he wants to direct it. And you know that as a director, he's the best. He said that he'd want very few sections rewritten, if any.

"Sure, the play is damned good!" he replied, angling his head as if searching for a posture of modesty.

Looking back, I can see that I was making a mistake by getting involved with him. But hindsight is not foresight.

(You see, with this 'autobiographical' novel of fiction, or whatever you want to call it, I can let you know, now, the results of my first theatrical enterprise as producer. However, how it happened, and how Melissa became involved, not only with the production, but with Phil, as well as with other related matters, is an important part of this story. You'll find out how she so drastically affected my life and the lives of others. I'll get to that.)

Phil shifted again, this time into even more of an uptight position. "Okay. I'll just have my rep at EMC draw up a contract."

"Good. I'll have my lawyer look it over."

My lawyer was Sanford Ellis, one of the best show business attorneys in the business. I had met him through Brent, whom he represented on a musical that had been running with packed houses for over a year. Ellis and I got along well from the time we were first introduced at a rehearsal. After reading Phil's contract, he advised that I make some drastic changes. There were too many escape clauses, he explained. Phil would have complete control over the production. He'd be able to drop my director or any of the actors at any time during rehearsals. So I would only be able to cast roles with people who were willing to be let go at Phil's whim.

"You're looking for trouble," Ellis told me. "Unless whoever you sign up is willing to give in on those important points, you'll never be able to get them to go along with you. Personally, I'd drop the whole undertaking and produce another play by another playwright."

Good advice, which I didn't heed.

The next time I met with Phil was at Sardi's, with contract in hand, and Melissa by my side. I had decided that in order to live with myself, I'd have to follow my own beliefs.

I had brought Melissa because I wanted to share the excitement of my first production with her. As if she hadn't been through this many times before with Brent.

In the cab, on the way to the famous theater-district restaurant, Melissa had agreed wholeheartedly with Ellis. "Don't give in to anything," she told me. "Just tell him that his agent was unwilling to make the changes in the contract, and that your lawyer advised you to option the play only if Phil has him strike out those clauses. You shouldn't even be meeting with him until that contract is rewritten."

But I was desperate to produce Phil's play, which I thought very highly of. I was confident that with the minor changes in the script, as Jesse Bahnister and I had discussed, we'd have a hit.

I told her that she'd like Phil.

She did, it turned out. Considerably.

After Phil showed up, and while the three of us were waiting for our table, I made the preliminary introductions. By the time we were shown to our seats, and before I could get the contract out of the envelope, they were both heavily involved in conversation. It was as if they had known each other for years. They didn't even seem aware that I was sitting with them.

When I finally broke through their conversation, helped by the interruption of our entrées being put in front of us, Melissa was agreeing with Phil that the escape clauses weren't so bad.

"I doubt if I'd ever have to use them," Phil said, as they both looked at me, smiling. I had a strange, otherworldly feeling that they were the dates and it was I who had been invited as their guest.

Phil continued. "EMC insists on putting them in all their contracts automatically." He raised his shoulders and looked at Melissa. "I doubt if any client of EMC ever took advantage of them."

I took a sip of my drink. "Melissa, your husband is a producer," I said. Then I asked her, rhetorically, "Would he allow those clauses in any of his contracts?"

"I don't think they'd bother him," she replied. I could hardly believe what I was hearing; she had made a complete one-hundred-and-eighty-degree turn. She was not, of course, being truthful with me. I regretted that I had brought the contracts along, because I was now afraid of being influenced, two against one, into completing them. I regretted, in fact, that I had brought Melissa along. I had planned to cross out those clauses at the table. Now, it was impossible, because it would be too difficult."

The almost instantaneous rapport between the two of them bothered me. But I couldn't think too much about that at the moment. I was too concerned over the play.

No, I thought. I would fight Phil. I had to be bold at the start. Despite Melissa's over-friendliness with Phil, and her protecting him, even though he was a stranger to her. I had to look out for myself. This was not just show business, it was business.

"I would feel better," I said cautiously to Phil, "if we would delete those clauses."

Melissa leaned back with a wide smile. "Mark, don't be silly. Phil's right. Come to think of it, I do remember seeing those kinds of clauses in some of Brent's contracts. And I don't know of any instance where they were acted on."

Phil turned to her with a warm grin, which was returned.

Dammit! I felt like a double loser.

"All right, Phil," I said weakly, caving in. "But you have to give me your word that you'll never take advantage of me on those clauses."

A weak and stupid statement!

"Of course, Mark."

Melissa raised her drink as if in a toast. "Sign the contracts, the both of you," she kiddingly demanded, but there was seriousness in her voice at the same time.

I reluctantly laid the contracts out and took a pen from my pocket. I thought for a moment, then I replaced it.

"You're being so ridiculous!" Melissa said. "All right, then, let's have dinner."

Through the meal, Melissa and Phil continued their avid discussion on subjects ranging from theater to literature to food, laughing over what seemed to me to be trivial inanities. Whenever I tried to introduce a topic, it was met with indifference.

Chapter 31

I had raised front money for *Parameters of Love* from an uncle of mine who had a booth at a diamond exchange on 47th Street. He had always wanted to be a comedy writer, but was satisfied having his original puns published by some of the New York newspaper columnists he mailed them to.

He had the vicarious pleasure of being part of my enterprise by putting up the risk capital of $5,000 for a double percentage in shares of ownership in the general partnership. In thanks, I listed him as associate producer.

Melissa put me in touch with a number of Brent's investors, but they were skeptical of the play and me.

One day, after a matinee, when she and I were having dinner together, she gave me what she thought was good advice.

"Just sending the script around isn't going to get you investors. You've got to have a backers' audition."

"I've been to Brent's backers' auditions, and he's always ended up getting very little or no money there. I just can't afford the investment. I have limited funds."

"Frankly, Mark, it doesn't look too good. Nobody wants to invest in a play by a first-time producer of an unknown playwright whose work has never been on Broadway."

"Melissa, this is my chance to make a start for myself in theater. One hit. A break. And I'll be in there like Brent." I looked at her, thought a moment, then reconsidered what I said. "Well, not quite like Brent. He's well established. But I can work my way up from this success."

"As a producer? I thought you wanted to be a playwright."

"I do, but I'm learning fast about life's compromises."

"You don't have to compromise. As far as I'm concerned, you just have to be yourself. You know that. I've told you enough times. You don't have to impress me."

"I have a feeling that I do have to impress you. And I'm desperate to do it."

Her answer to that was a penetrating stare, but no comment.

"So much so, in fact," I went on, "that I've come up with an idea that you won't think is me. Especially after what I went through with The Wrecker's Ball."

An incipient smile appeared on her face. "And what's that?"

"Get a Hollywood star for the male lead."

Her smile quickly matured fully. "I don't believe it," she said, pitching her head back slightly. "Shades of Lester!"

"Actually," I said, self-consciously, "I was thinking of calling him."

"Why not? You two weren't exactly enemies, despite your differences."

"Then you go for the idea?" I questioned, incredulous.

"Of course, I do."

"I love you."

Her facial expression transformed into a tender grin, but she didn't repeat my words. I found it disturbing.

Lester returned my call promptly from LA.

After I had explained the situation to him, he told me jovially, "Sure, I'll be glad to check around for you. The only problem, though, is that escape clause, the business of being fired. If you can remove that from the contract, you'll be getting rid of a huge hurdle."

"I can't. It's standard for EMC."

There was silence.

"Bullshit," Lester finally said. "Your writer is handing you a line. I never heard of such a thing."

"He gave me his word that he'd never use it."

"Well, Mark, all I can say is that I'll try. There may be someone out here who's desperate enough to go along with it, just to get that break on the boards." He was now, no doubt, using theater jargon to impress his Hollywood colleagues.

"I appreciate it," I said.

"A New York theater credit like that can mean a lot to a film star. Financially. I can tell you that. He'll come back here hotter than ever. Okay, let me see what I can do. I'll give it a try. And give my best to Brent."

Two weeks later, I got a message from Lester to call him immediately.

"Listen, Pal," he said in a businesslike manner when I reached him. "I've got you Kenny Bruce. He's coming out in a blockbuster movie in three months. And I don't have to tell you how well he's been doing. He's the new Sean Connery. He said he's been begging his agent to look for a decent Broadway script.

"That's fantastic!"

"But there's only one catch."

"What?"

"He's willing to go along with your author's escape clause on three conditions."

"What are they?"

"First of all, he gets a good advance. Second, if you drop him, his salary is still continued for the run of the play. And last, if your playwright wants him out, the press releases have to read that it was Kenny's idea. And he wants that written into his contract. And, of course, he has to like the script. We can only take Bahnister's word for it so far; after that, the property has to speak for itself."

"That sounds fine to me. Let me talk to Phil Carlton and the people at EMC, and I'll get back to you."

"Righto," he replied enthusiastically. "If this works out, he'll owe me a favor. And I've got a terrific screenplay in the works."

"Still making deals?" I joked.

"That's me."

I had to wonder about Lester's enthusiastic interest in ladies'-man-type Kenny Bruce.

I met with Phil in the office of his agent at the plush New York offices of EMC. It was the first time I had ever seen Phil wearing a suit and tie. Somehow I suspected that the meeting had been arranged formally just to intimidate me. We could just as well have had our discussion at Phil's place or my office, or anywhere else over a cup of coffee.

Phil sat in an ornate chair at the side of Brad Effinger's desk. I was offered an antique wooden chair facing them. Both wore stern expressions.

Brad, who wore a rich-looking, light-brown suit, had the bearing and confidence of a new-car salesman, and spoke in a similar fashion.

"You have to understand, Mark," he said, "that it's our job to look out for our client." He waved a hand in the air almost carelessly. "But we're not a mean bunch of people. We'll work with you. We'll bend over backwards to keep things running smoothly for you with your production. We know how much stress and anxiety there is as you approach your opening night."

I looked from one to the other. "Your escape clauses present me with problems. I can't hire people or cast the show with such an unstable arrangement."

Brad put his hands flat on the desk in front of him. "We never expect to use those clauses. They're just there as a safety factor. We know that once a production gets underway, and the cast and crew become a family, that any destruction of that family can disrupt the bonds and lower morale. And that would be deadly not only for you, but for our client."

"Those clauses are not common," I insisted.

Brad looked down at his hands, then at me again. "They are for our new, young playwrights. They need extra protection. But still, if there's a complaint, a few of us here will take a look at the production. We just don't take our client's word for it."

"To tell you the truth," I said. "My attorney advised me not to go with this play unless those clauses are out." I pressed the point. "I have a well-known screen actor who is interested in this play. And I just can't approach him on those terms, or he'll back out." I figured that I'd hold out, if I could, on those difficult contractual terms. I had nothing to lose.

Brad grinned somewhat cynically. "I don't know who he is, and I'm sure you're not about to tell me. But there's no guarantee that he's going to accept the part after reading the final script. We have to take that into consideration. We also have to consider the fact that you may turn around and cast some unknown who you think is very talented, but may not be able to come through in the clinches, and our playwright will look bad."

"There's no guarantee that I'll get the play on, either."

"True. But if you don't, someone else will."

"That's not necessarily true. There are a lot of plays making the rounds of producers' desks, by writers more accomplished and well known than Phil. And finding a producer who's interested in putting them on is not easy. Before a producer is going to invest time and backers' money, he has to be strongly attracted by a script. Or at least see tremendous potential in it."

Brad looked at Phil, who was staring directly at me. "But," he said, "there aren't many around who have the proven talent that Phil has."

"I think there are."

Brad shrugged. "Well, then I suggest you find another playwright."

He had put me on the spot. It was then that I should have shown strength and walked out. But I balked. I couldn't think of an immediate tough response. It was obvious that I was desperate for the play. I knew it would be a long time before I'd find a another script that I'd want to devote a valuable part of my life to.

I explained the conditions under which my choice as leading man, Kenny Bruce, would approve of my contract. Brad and Phil went along with them.

So, against my better judgment, I accepted their escape terms, signing the contracts right there on the spot. After Brad handed me my copy, the atmosphere warmed. Brad came out from behind his desk and put his arm around me. "Mark, I wish you both the best of luck. I have a feeling that everything is going to go well."

Phil stood and joined us.

Their friendliness gave me hope.

My next hope was that Kenny Bruce would like the script.

I shipped it out to him, and a week later, he phoned me personally.

I have to admit, I was thrilled; it was actually Kenny Bruce's voice on the phone speaking to me. I always found dealing with celebrities exciting, but I'd seen the same reaction in other producers. Maybe that's part of the exhilaration of show business—the side that counterbalances the difficulties.

There was a suppressed elation in his voice that I recognized from his performances on the screen. "I read the play as soon as I got it, and it's just right for me. I may want a few minor changes here and there, but basically it's what I've been looking for."

Changes, I thought. I hope it doesn't cause too much of a hassle with Phil.

"When do we start?" he asked.

Of course, I hadn't as yet raised a cent, except for the front money.

"I've still got to get a theater," I bluffed. "Then there's casting, advertising, and all that." I kept listing other problems expected in any theatrical production.

"You understand, of course," he explained, "that I have commitments. For shooting schedules. I have to have some idea of a date."

"It depends on how things move," I said. "How about six months to a year?"

"You have to be more specific than that."

"Okay," I told him. "Suppose we make it one year."

"Can you give me that in writing?"

"I'm afraid I can't. Not until I'm ready to get underway. When you produce a show, you never know what's around the corner. Let's just keep in touch regarding both our schedules."

"Then you'd better speak to my agent. I'll have him contact you."

Another agent. More trouble, I thought. But I was wrong about that.

A week later, I heard from Milt Rossman. He made an appointment and dropped by my office.

Milt had a square, handsome face. He was middle-aged, with a full head of hair that was prematurely gray around the sides. He turned out to be a very considerate, pleasant guy.

He sat down in one of the two chairs in the small space I had rented and pulled down his tie.

"I just got in from the Coast," he told me. "I'll only be here for a few days. What a rat race!" He sighed and opened his brief case.

"As I mentioned to Kenny Bruce," I said, "I can't make a full commitment at this time." He looked like the kind of person you could level with, and I did, somewhat. "To bring in the balance of the money, I need to be able to say to potential backers that he's going to star in the production. I have to have some kind of assurance, so that I can have my press agent get some releases out to the newspapers. And I'll need some hand-out photos of him."

"Consider it done. You can make the announcement now. Even if nothing works out, we can always use the publicity."

"Great!"

"But please keep us informed about your progress. I'm going to keep his schedule as clear as I can for your planned opening date. But you can well understand that screenplays keep coming in all the time, and if he finds one that he likes, he'll want to go with it. If the play is a go, I can always delay a picture he wants to star in. Any movie producer or director would be willing to wait six months for him. However," he continued. "He's not interested in a run-of-the-play contract. Six months is enough. He just wants a little bit of sophisticated exposure in New York."

"I get you, and that's fine with me. As far as I'm concerned, once the play is established, I'll be able to attract almost anybody I want for his part. And at less salary."

Chapter 32

It was already dark when Melissa and I got out of the cab in Greenwich Village.

Jesse Bahnister and Phil were waiting for us at a small bar on Macdougal Street for our first meeting about the play.

I was grateful to Melissa for Jesse Bahnister agreeing to direct the play. She was using all of Brent's contacts to help me. Bahnister was known for successes primarily with dramas, although he had also had a couple of hit comedies. However, he aspired to direct a musical, and Melissa had talked Brent into tentatively signing him for his upcoming musical on the condition that Bahnister would agree to do Phil's play. Brent, of course, didn't know of those conditions.

When we entered the Greenwich Village establishment, we found Bahnister and Phil already drinking. Melissa joined right in, sitting down and ordering two Bloody Marys. "So that I don't have to wait for the second one," she explained to the waitress.

Melissa had insisted that our first meeting to discuss the script be at a bar. She had been drinking more and more lately, and was becoming somewhat whimsical in her attitude, words, and actions.

Our overall mood at the outset was somewhat grim, because Bahnister, as Melissa and I knew, had some serious reservations about the script and was ready to make a few statements. Although he didn't announce the fact at the start, his attitude had conveyed this to Phil, it was easy to see, as we removed our coats and settled in. But Melissa downed her first drink with a long swallow, and changed the atmosphere to a jovial one—though briefly.

"I have a great idea, boys," she laughed, starting on her second Bloody Mary and ordering a third. "What do you say I rewrite the script, at least the female lead's part—since I can do better than any of you with a female's outlook? In fact, I'm listing myself as co-author. But don't worry, Phil. You can always drop me with your escape clauses."

Phil guffawed and put his arm around her. She turned to me, sitting on the other side of her. "See that, Mark? What you need is to get away from all this serious shit and have fun doing the play. It's the plays that are fun to do that are the hits."

Bahnister cleared his throat. He was a tall, thin gentleman, who looked to be past 55, with thin, white hair. He wore a zippered leather jacket and a white shirt open at the throat. His stoic features were angular and craggy. He spoke formally. "There are a few things I want to say that I'm sure are worth considering." He tapped the script, which was on the table in front of him. As the tips of his fingers repeatedly touched the title of the play, embossed in small gold letters on its black cover, he said, "I'd like you all to think about these few points very seriously." He made the statement without looking at any of us.

With his eyes still on the mimeographed book, he informed us: "I had a long talk with Kenny Bruce today, long distance—for over an hour. And he agrees pretty much with what I'm going to say."

He lifted his eyes to Phil, whose posture seemed suddenly spring-tight.

Bahnister smiled, obviously to relieve the tension he discovered he had created. "First, though, Phil," he said, artificially warming the tone of his voice, "I want to say that this is a very fine, artistically-wrought play. And I'm proud to be associated with it." He tapped the manuscript again, this time more gently than at first. "You are a tremendously talented young man. I've seen your other plays, and as good as they are, this is your best."

It was easy to see that Phil was unmoved by Bahnister's flattery, which came across as mechanical.

Bahnister continued. "The poetry is just fine. But I feel that in certain places it needs some significant changes." Phil moved forward slightly, about to speak, but Bahnister held up a palm, a sign that asked for a moment more.

"Most of these changes can be made once we get started with rehearsals," he went on. "But I'd like to have some general rewrites made here and there now to save time when we get started after Kenny Bruce arrives."

The director waited for a reply from Phil, but there was none. Seconds went by with no words spoken by any of us.

Then Melissa, after taking a huge gulp of her second red drink, broke the silence. She smacked the glass down on the table, and as the ice clunked, said, "Hey, Bahnny, don't you think Phil can save some time at the typewriter if Kenny Bruce is with the both of you for a discussion first? In fact, to get what you both want, you can rewrite it together with Bruce, as second-unit playwrights, as they might say in the movies, and then pass it on to Phil for his approval." She laughed, lifted her glass, and drained it to the dregs. Only Phil joined in with her mirth.

"Oh, come on, Melissa," I said. "Let's be serious. We all have one common goal—to have success with this play."

"Don't be such a party pooper," she replied to me, waving to the waitress for another drink. "You guys are just making a mountain out of a molehill. I read the play, and it's just fine for starters. I've been in the business for twenty years, and I can tell you that this is a great script that will play well. What more do you want?" She turned to Phil. "Tell me something, Mr. Playwright. Do you agree with me that this is a terrific play?"

"Melissa," he said. "I'm very critical, you know that. But after a great deal of consideration, I think I have to go along with you."

"You're most kind," she said to him, freezing a very profound expression on her face. Her head wavered slightly from the incipient effects of the alcohol.

Bahnister looked unhappily at me.

"Why don't you and I go over the changes you want," I said to him, "and then Phil and I can discuss it all further. For starters." I looked at Phil. "How's that?"

"Fine," he replied, rising and going off into the darkness.

Bahnister opened the script to the first page. "Mark," he said. "I think we want a slightly different level of dialogue for the opening."

"Okay," I replied as pleasantly as I could. "What do you suggest?"

Bahnister had certainly been doing his homework. He practically knew the play by heart, and he had some very definite suggestions, most of which I had to agree would improve the production.

He drew me into his ideas as he went over sentence after sentence and paragraph after paragraph of dialogue and stage directions. I was quite impressed, certain that if Phil had been willing to listen, he would have learned a lot from this master director. Not only had Bahnister directed a good number of successful plays on Broadway, he had led the way for several new playwrights, some of whom, in time, earned prestige, respect, and even fame—at least in their generation.

Looking back now, I can say that a couple of them would, in a few generations, have their plays revived by the yet unborn at the time of that evening's discussion.

I wasn't sure of how many minutes had passed, having been so engrossed with Bahnister's original analysis and thoughts. I looked up, hopeful that Phil was there, listening. But he wasn't. But neither was Melissa, whose coat was also gone.

I called the waitress over.

"Do you know where the other two are?" I asked.

"They left a while ago," she said. "Why? Do you want the bill?"

I felt panic. "Yes. Please."

She began writing it up on her tray.

Bahnister looked somewhat dour. He wasn't, of course, concerned over Melissa, not having any idea of my relationship with her. "I hope this young man is cooperative," he said bleakly. "I get the feeling that he's not going to be too amenable to changes. At our first meeting of importance, he disappears."

"You won't have any problems with him, Jesse, I'm sure," I said, almost by rote. My thoughts were on finding Melissa, to know whether they really went off together and, if so, where.

I paid the bill, and quickly bid Bahnister good-bye. I was unconcerned with his annoyance over the bum's rush I gave him.

I hurried to the pay phone; then, gripping a handful of coins in my pocket, hesitated. If Melissa had gone back home, she might not be there yet. But Phil's apartment was only ten minutes away. I dug out Phil's number, dropped coins into the slot and dialed.

The ringing went on and on. No one was home.

Should I go over to his place?

No. I'd have a drink at the bar, wait, then try calling again. Maybe I should try Melissa's home number, anyway. Although I tried to keep away from Brent on a personal basis as much as possible. I decided, no.

I went to the bar, bought a beer and nursed it. I tried not to think about Melissa. But, still, thoughts of her raged through my mind. Had I taken her too much for granted? Did she no longer love me? Had I not shown her enough affection? Was there now a special attraction she felt for Phil that put me out of the picture? I felt a terrible loss. My ego was hurt. I realized now, more than ever, how much I loved her. How much, at least, I needed her. It took another man in her life to bring that point home to me. But was Phil, after all, another man in her life? Or was it my imagination? Melissa dominated my thoughts utterly now. She meant more to me, I realized, than Phil's play. More than anything else in my life. Had I been a fool to get involved with Phil's Parameters of Love? No, that was ridiculous. Illogical. If it could happen now with Phil, it could have happened with someone else. I felt so terribly jealous. Lost. She was mine. She always told me she was. How could she leave with someone else without telling me where they were going? Didn't she know that would hurt me?

Maybe they were coming back.

That was it.

She was discussing Bahnister with him, and they'd return. Maybe I shouldn't have brushed Bahnister off so soon.

No. That was minor, unimportant. We could all meet again another time.

I'd wait, then call; at worst, go to Phil's place. But the thought of finding her there with him was agonizingly painful. I was certain I couldn't bear the reality of it, that I'd never be able to live through the experience. That was how much I was discovering at that moment, because of this traumatic episode, that I was so deeply in love with her, or else so terribly infatuated.

I let time go by. Maybe it was a half-hour, maybe only minutes. I wasn't sure. Then I called Phil again.

Still no answer.

I braced myself, dropped the returned coins again into the pay phone, and dialed Melissa's number. If Brent answered, I'd think of something to say. I just didn't care. I had to be sure that she wasn't with Phil, that she wasn't intimate with him. Giving him her love, her body.

There was no answer.

I had no other choice but to go to Phil's place.

I went back to the bar and dropped a bill next to my half-emptied drink, made my way through the glass-clinking darkness to the outside, and then through the Village streets to his residence.

His lights were on. They were there together, I was sure.

Hesitating until I drew up the courage, I entered the lobby and rang his bell, waited for him to press the buzzer to let me in. I dreaded confronting the both of them together.

I wanted him to be there without her. That would mean that she was on her way home or back to the bar.

There was no response.

I tried again, waited minutes. Still no answer.

I was tremendously relieved.

He most likely forgot to switch off the lights when he left to meet us.

There was probably no place he could take her to make love. Only to his apartment. Everything was all right.

But maybe I was judging Melissa unfairly. She wouldn't suddenly become involved with him, I was sure. But she had changed so much lately. She had become so different, no longer the woman so breathlessly in love with me.

Had I changed her? Turned her away? If I had, I swore to myself, I'd return our lives to the way they were.

Could I take her back if she had made love to Phil?

No, I could never touch her again. I'd hate her.

But pondering further, I knew that I'd tolerate—no, more than tolerate—her, if she was fleetingly his mad lover. After all, I had put up with her having her husband at any time. Still, that was different. I knew that she didn't love him—at least as much as she loved me. According to what she told me, anyway.

I was confused.

But with this experience of tortured love, I suddenly felt that I understood about second marriages in which in the darkness of the night and confirmation of the flesh, thoughts of someone else's previous love of one's lover was disturbing but endurable.

I went back to the bar, certain that Melissa and Phil would never show up, but hopeful that they would.

I sat there drinking for at least two hours.

My horrible speculation proved to be correct. Neither appeared.

The time was approaching midnight. I tried again, called both numbers. There was no answer at either.

Again, I walked over to Phil's place. The lights were still on. I rang the bell. No answer.

There was nothing more I could do. I went to the parking lot at Port Authority, and drove back to New Jersey.

The next day, I went to my New York office early, hoping that Melissa would show up, and I'd find out that nothing had really happened the night before. I felt physically strange, as if I were glassily in some other galaxy. Everything seemed totally hopeless. The magical world that Melissa had created for me was gone. I found that I had now begun to lose interest in the theater and Phil's play. I had lost Melissa. Nothing would ever be the same again. Was I slipping into a depression? No, that wasn't possible. I wasn't mentally and physically incapacitated. At least, not yet.

To pass the time, I went over some of the papers on my desk, not really reading them. I looked out of the window. I paced the small room.

I wanted to take lunch, but I was afraid to leave, fearing that I'd miss Melissa if she came by. So I ordered a sandwich and coffee by phone.

By noon, I was toying with the idea of calling her. But I just didn't feel like having Brent answer the phone at home, or know that I was calling his office.

Finally, in the late afternoon, the door opened, and there she stood, neatly dressed, postured as if nothing had happened.

"Where did you disappear to last night?" I asked her angrily.

"I don't know."

I saw white.

"I'm sure you don't believe me," she said, "but it's the truth."

"No, I don't believe you."

"All I remember is that I went to the ladies' room at the bar, and when I came out, Phil was standing there with my coat. He suggested that we go to another bar. He said he just didn't feel like going over the script with Bahnister that night."

I listened intently, not only for her explanation, but to try to determine by her movements and tone of voice whether she was making up the story.

"Then, what?" I asked, incensed. "You went with him?"

"Yes."

"And then?"

"Well, we had quite a few more drinks." Her eyes penetrated mine, as if she were making every effort to be convincing. "Too many, I guess."

"Then what?"

"That's where it all begins to fade. I vaguely remember his helping me out of the bar. I could hardly walk. I told him to get me a cab, and I'd go home."

"Did you go home?"

"I'm not sure."

"You're not sure?"

"Look, Mark. I could tell you anything, but I'm trying to tell you the truth. I just don't remember."

"You remember, all right. You went back to his apartment with him."

She faltered. "I don't think I did."

"You don't think you did?"

"Okay, yes, I did. But I was fairly drunk, practically unconscious, to be perfectly honest. I was out of it."

"Did the two of you make love?"

"I don't remember."

"You don't remember?" I said, infuriated.

"No, I swear to God, I don't remember. But how could I have made love in that state?"

"Easily. You could have let him. Or he could have taken advantage of you."

"Don't be ridiculous. I'd never let that happen."

"I'll bet you wouldn't!"

"Mark, I was dead drunk. I couldn't move. Nothing could have happened."

"A lot could have happened. I just don't know what to say. I'm angry. I'm pissed off!"

Now it was her turn to show outrage. "Don't you believe me? Do you really think I would lie to you? Is that what you think of me?"

There was no sense making the situation worse. I had to accept what she said. What else could I do? "All right, all right, Melissa. I believe you."

She seemed to physically tighten up, like a cat arching its back in self-protection.

"Then I'll tell you something else that I remember. And let me know if you believe this!"

"What?"

"When I woke up the next day, Phil was in the kitchen making coffee. I heard him as I was fixing my make-up in the bathroom, getting ready to leave. When he came in with it, he told me that he had slept on the couch and given me his bed."

I felt relieved. She was obviously telling the truth. At least it sounded that way. And I wanted to believe it. No lover wants to believe otherwise in a situation like that.

But then she said, "I know you won't like what I'm going to say now about something that did happen. But it did. And I'm telling you this because I want to be honest with you."

"Telling me what?" I asked impatiently. "What is it?"

"Before I went into the bathroom, I saw my panties lying in the flower pot next to the door."

"You what!"

"I don't know how they got there. But I know I didn't do anything. I know that. I'm sure of that." She paused and looked at me intently. "Do you believe me?"

I was shaking. "Yes, I do!"

She hesitated, looked at me with a blank, immobile expression. "Well, you shouldn't. Because that was a lie! Everything else was true, but the bit about the panties is a lie! You just don't trust me, do you? I trust you, but you don't trust me!"

"I don't believe you! Now! What you're saying about the panties not being true. I think it is true!"

"Then live with it!" she exclaimed, walking out.

I lived with it.

I couldn't live without her.

Chapter 33

Over the next six months, Melissa contributed considerably to the show. In addition to helping me acquire Bahnister as director, she was also responsible, though indirectly, for bringing in most of the $100,000 I needed to produce the play on Broadway.

Half of the capitalization resulted from a suggestion that she made.

Up until that time, most Broadway shows were backed primarily by private investors. Her advice was to approach cosmetic companies that might want to use the name of the play—*Parameters of Love*—for a perfume. A brilliant idea.

I contacted all of the major companies in the industry whose headquarters were located in New York, most of which showed great interest in talking with me about it. I had a good number of lunches with officers of those corporations.

One of the less important companies, Tarkington Cosmetics, was the firm that finally came through.

At first, despite the interest shown by backers and the cosmetic companies, I had encountered some resistance. But when Phoebe Shannon was cast in the part opposite Kenny Bruce, that was the determining factor. Her name, associated with his, brought in the final dollars.

Phoebe Shannon was another top-flight movie star, a tremendous talent who had started out on the New York stage. The daughter of a theatrical family whose parents had made names for themselves as paired actors of note; she made the switch to Hollywood.

After she was out there for a while, the Gay White Way slowly faded from her aspirations. At first, although she had been eager to return to Broadway, her outlook was altered quickly by her success on the Coast. Earnings, national fame, and the California way of life were instrumental in keeping her at her lovely home in Bel Aire.

She was never without offers to return to New York. Scripts by established playwrights were sent regularly to her agent, but she never bothered reading them. They were returned with her representative's comment, "Although Miss Shannon found your play to be first-rate, contractual commitments for movies prevent her from taking advantage of your proposal for her to play in this extraordinary vehicle."

But Kenny Bruce and Phoebe Shannon had starred opposite each other in two films which, though they weren't blockbusters, had been highly regarded by the critics, and made substantial profits. In fact, Bruce and Shannon had been hailed as the new, young Tracy-Hepburn twosome. Movie producers were optioning novels and developing screenplays that would appeal to both, with the hope that their production companies could cash in on the current mass trend of interest in these two popular stars.

It was Kenny Bruce who talked Phoebe into joining the cast after five years at her impressive home, with pool, in the sunny hills of LA.

"It'll be fun," was the way he put it to her, he told me the day he arrived in New York for the rehearsals of Parameters of Love. "I said that I need her," he explained, "and ever since we met and worked together, we've gotten along well both professionally and as friends. So, I was able to persuade her to take the part. I convinced her that with her experience, she would be helping me as a personal tutor. And that as a result, in a few short weeks, she could actually give me years of dramatic training. And she wanted to help me."

Melissa, who had put me in touch with Brent's investors, talked up the play to them. She emphasized the value of having Kenny Bruce and Phoebe Shannon in the leads.

My relationship with Melissa became stable again over the year. As we worked together, we were once again fast friends and lovers, as if nothing had happened, although the panty incident was always in the back of my mind, when that undergarment was in any special way involved in our lovemaking. At those times, I felt certain that she was judging my reactions. And despite doing my best not to show any reference to it, through comment, or even by any superficial bearing, I always felt that her perception was attuned to my subconscious thinking. Nevertheless, she, too, never brought up the subject.

But I always found myself tense with Phil during our get-togethers, most of which regarded the script. We were now both extremely serious when we met and no longer friendly and philosophical with each other. Our once smooth rapport had become strained and, in a way, I had at times almost dèjá vu-like moments when I felt as if I were Brent, and Phil was me —with Melissa.

Eventually, I left script changes up to Bahnister. But I did keep close check over the production. I was not about to let this play get out of hand, as mine had. I planned to consider both sides of the issue without bias.

I dropped by the rehearsal hall often, to let my presence be known, beginning with the first reading of Parameters of Love by the newly gathered cast. But I made comments about the production only to the director.

As we got into the rehearsals, it was hardly necessary to use my advertising budget to inform the public of this show starring Kenny Bruce and Phoebe Shannon to create interest among theatergoers and film fans. Spurred by my production's press agent, who regularly sent out press releases, many of them highly inventive, as well as comments by columnists, articles about Kenny and Phoebe, and word of mouth, interest in the show grew like wildfire. We began to get calls from individuals and groups inquiring about the availability of tickets for the New York opening and run, which was about two months off. So we had tickets printed and put on sale, and placed ads and notices in the newspapers. Pre-opening sales would hopefully get us a foothold despite mediocre or even bad reviews when the show arrived in town, and bring in enough cash to keep the show going.

As I became more and more caught up with the details of the production: booking the out-of-town theaters, set-construction, and the myriad other particulars that are involved in producing a show on Broadway, I found myself increasingly busy. As a result, Melissa and I met less and less regularly on a social basis, although she was consistently at rehearsals.

Being sensitive to the incident about the panties, I was especially attentive to how she and Phil reacted to each other when they occasionally chatted together. Every attitude, every body movement, came under my close scrutiny. Sometimes I even forgot that I was watching the play being put together by Bahnister when I saw them conversing for long lengths of time. Could she be so interested in the script changes that there would be such protracted conversation, or was something else going on?

Still, neither of them gave any sign of intimacy that I was able to observe.

By the time we were into the third week of rehearsals, I began to notice a pattern. After rehearsals ended, Melissa would leave, and approximately ten minutes later, Phil would follow.

It at first became evident to me subconsciously, but when I checked the situation with my watch, I discovered that the timing was almost like clockwork.

So after a few days of observing this pattern, I tried to think of a way to investigate the situation without raising suspicion. I attempted to convince myself that there was no hanky-panky going on. Or, I at least, wanted to be assured that there was none. I realized that my outlook regarding hanky-panky should really be reserved for husbands, not lovers, but my love, need—or whatever emotional phenomenon or dynamic it was—for Melissa, made me jealously possessive.

Finally, I decided what I would do. I couldn't follow Melissa, because that would discourage Phil from taking off after her, if that was their nightly plan. I couldn't call either of them about an hour later, because if I got Brent on the phone, it would be too uncomfortable a situation. And if I called Phil, and she was there, he would never admit it.

So the only tack I could take would be to follow Phil. Which I did one night.

I kept a good distance behind him, keeping close to the buildings, so that I could dart into the shadows of the arcades and entrances to stores should he by chance look behind him.

But he was so intent in reaching his destination that he rushed ahead, unconcerned about any possibility of being followed.

After we were several blocks from the rehearsal hall, Melissa appeared out of nowhere.

As they casually embraced and exchanged a quick kiss, I felt the temperature of my blood increase substantially, or did it decrease? The scene before my eyes was unreal. I stood in the midst of what seemed to be a lucid dream, knowing that what I was seeing wasn't really happening, that I would wake up and have returned to reality.

I watched as Phil hailed a cab. One swung to the curb, and they got in. It pulled out into the evening traffic.

I raised my hand for a cab. Another pulled over, and when I said, "Follow that cab," I felt as if I were in a grade-B movie.

Phil and Melissa were headed toward the Village and, just as I feared, after the ride downtown, their cab finally stopped in front of Phil's apartment.

Melissa was the first one to step out. Phil followed, counting out bills. He handed some to the cabdriver, and with a wave of his hand, indicated that the man should keep the change.

"Pull over down there," I told my driver.

I watched them as they went into his apartment house.

"Okay," I said, tensely wrought. "This is fine."

His tires screeched at the curb, and I got out and paid the fare.

I stood there alone, looking frantically up and down the street for the nearest pay phone. When I spotted one, I went to it, almost running. But when I reached it, I stopped and waited, realizing that I was, at that moment, too overemotional to call. I waited, breathlessly, trying to calm myself so that my voice would sound reasonably composed.

Now, definitely knowing that Melissa was in Phil's apartment, I was desperate to hear what Phil would say. Strangely, my illogical optimism was high, because I was still foolishly hopeful of the possibility that they weren't having an affair, that there was some absurd chance that when I reached Phil he might say, "Mark, by coincidence Melissa is here. Why don't you drop up? We're about to talk about the play." I knew, of course, that I was being irrational to wish for that, when the rational conclusion had to be otherwise.

Still, I had to know the truth by words that definitely incriminated them. Why, I don't know. I steeled myself and dialed.

Phil's phone rang and rang. No answer. I didn't count the rings, but when I sensed that I had let it ring more than long enough, and was about to hang up, I heard a click.

Phil's voice sounded faint, far away.

"Hello."

"Phil?"

"Yes, who is this?"

"It's Mark."

"Oh, how are you doing? What's up?"

"I'm in the neighborhood. I thought I'd drop by."

I paused. He said nothing.

"To talk about the play," I continued. "Just a short chat. A few important items."

"It's awfully late for that," he said in an innocent tone that briefly erased my suspicion. "I'm exhausted. Let's make it another time."

My anger made me forceful. "I'm down here right now. In the Village. Let's just get together for a short time. Just a few minutes."

"It's too late in the day, Mark. I've been working on the play all day at rehearsals. I just can't think anymore. We'd accomplish nothing. I'll meet you early tomorrow, before rehearsals. Okay? We can talk then."

Word games. What I had expected. I had to be clever, overcome his verbal parrying.

I persisted. "There's just one important scene I want to discuss with you."

"Definitely not. I'll see you tomorrow."

"I insist!"

"There's nothing in our contract that says you can harass me around the clock. Good-night!"

There was a solid click.

I found myself incensed, frustrated, angry, holding a dead handset to my ear. I yanked it down on the hook and rushed almost mindlessly in the direction of his apartment building, seething, blind, almost deranged.

I tore the front door open and was confronted by the dull brass battery of mailboxes with pushbuttons. Knowing that if I rang his apartment so soon, he'd never buzz the door so that I could open it, I rang all of the bells except his.

There was almost immediately a return buzz. I pushed against the inner door, and it snapped open and swung wide. More buzzing followed.

I rushed to his apartment and banged on the door.

"Who is it?"

"Me. Mark."

"I told you, I'll see you tomorrow."

I threw my shoulder against the door, but it responded with an unyielding thump. I tried again and again. It wouldn't budge.

There were no further words from inside.

I could picture Melissa standing on the other side of the door, a worried expression on her face. I could have been wrong about the expression.

Finally, frustrated, out of breath, my arm in pain, I left.

After that, Melissa stopped attending rehearsals. She didn't come to the office, either. She just disappeared from my life.

Neither of us contacted each other.

I assumed it was all over, and to diminish the pain of my loss I threw myself mentally and physically into the production, keeping busy with every significant and insignificant detail that related to the play and its production. At moments between these business and artistic diversions, thoughts of Melissa tortured me.

It was apparent that she was seeing Phil, and each time he and I were together, which was often, the anguish of knowing that they were lovers was renewed, and tore me apart.

As for the play, I found myself so close to it that I was unable to judge from an unbiased standpoint how it was progressing.

We wound up our last rehearsal after four intensive weeks. And, surprisingly, everyone was satisfied with how they had gone. As the cast members got their belongings together to meet again in Philadelphia, at the Shubert Theatre, I asked Jesse how he thought we had done. "It looks good to me," he said, "like we're going to get a good response from the critics on this. I don't think I've ever had as much cooperation with a cast as I've had with this one. Even our understudies for the lead rolls are excellent." He looked around furtively. "To tell you the truth, Mark. They're as good as Phoebe and Kenny—if not better." Then he dropped his secretive attitude. "I think we're right in the ballpark as far as an audience goes. The play is a bit artistic, but interesting. We might have a winner."

I detected doubt in his demeanor and the tone of his voice. I didn't want to believe it, but I suspected that his desperation to direct Brent's musical was the impetus for his doing Phil's play. He might have felt that an artistic failure wouldn't harm him as much as an out-and-out bomb. In addition, having directed two Hollywood stars wouldn't hinder his reputation, either.

As Bahnister went off, Phil approached me.

Even despite the tension between us, I was pleased that Phil took the time to talk with me. He put out his hand. "Mark. You did a great casting job. Your suggestions to Bahnister and your publicity on the show have been excellent. I couldn't be more pleased. And I can tell you that Brad is happy with everything, too. And so are Kenny and Phoebe. You can be sure there won't be any escape clauses used." He smiled.

For a brief instant, the bitterness I felt about his taking Melissa away from me vanished. But only briefly. I took his hand and shook it. What the hell, I thought. Life goes on. I had my moments of joy with her. Three memorable years. Now it was gone. Such is life.

Chapter 34

I was sitting in the Shubert theater in Philadelphia, watching the set being put up for the world premiere of *Parameters of Love*, when Phil came down the aisle to ask me if we could get together for a drink. He wanted to discuss something with me, he said, that was quite urgent. I agreed to meet with him at a nearby bar.

He was sitting at the bar, waiting, drink in hand, when I arrived a half-hour later. His mood was gloomy.

"Did you change your mind?" I asked him. "Are you unhappy now with the production?"

"No, that's not it."

"What is it, then?"

"It's Melissa. And the play."

I didn't feel like discussing Melissa. That was over. I didn't want to think about it anymore. But since the problem also included the play, and that was all that I had left in my life, with her gone, I listened interestedly.

He tilted his glass on the dark wood, and tapped it a couple of times, not looking at me. "Mark, first I want to say that I'm sorry about everything that's happened with Melissa. I really had no control over the situation. I guess, as your friend, I should have shown a bit of restraint, more concern about you."

"There was nothing you could do about it," I told him. "It was just...natural circumstances."

"Melissa is a very aggressive woman," he went on.

"I know," I said, hurt by all of the implications of the comment.

"It's over with us," Phil said.

I was startled. "It is? So soon?" But I was very pleased. And immediately hopeful now about seeing her again—to my surprise.

He took a sip of his drink and looked at me. "I just went along with it. I don't have to tell you how appealing she is, how flattering it was to have her show interest in me."

I was wounded even more. My transitory elation vaporized. I could think of nothing to say.

"It was over just about before it started."

Was there hope that they never made love? Of course not, Mark you idiot!

There was no further discussion for moments. Then he said, "Now she's after someone else."

I burst fully wide-awake, my body surging with adrenaline. "Who?"

"Kenny Bruce."

I couldn't speak at first, but then I repeated, "Kenny Bruce? But when...?"

Phil interrupted. "I didn't say anything was going on. I just said that she's interested in him."

"What do you mean?"

"She told me that she's madly in love with him."

"She did?"

"Yes. We had a long talk, and she said that it's possible for a woman to love more than one man at the same time."

What was happening to Melissa? I thought I knew her. Was she going out of her mind? What about us, at first? What about her love for me? She said I was her first love, that I'd be her only one. At the time it seemed so true, so natural. She had been so serene in our relationship, as if it were classic, eternal. But now, how quickly she had changed. She was no longer the same Melissa who had been shy, naive. I was confused. Should I hope that she'd come back to me or was she too far gone? Should I forget about loving her? Or forget about her altogether?

As I once again became aware of Phil's voice, my consciousness returned.

"Right after we began seeing each other," Phil said, looking away, "she suddenly realized that she had a crush on him. That was the way she put it." He turned back. "She said it was important that she let him know...that they consummate..."

I quickly interrupted him, not wanting to hear another word. "I'm surprised that he became interested in her, I said. He's a family man."

"Exactly. That was her problem. But now she wants him out of the play."

"Out of the play!" Not only was Melissa going off her rocker, she was becoming dangerous!

As Phil described the situation that had developed with Melissa over Kenny, I gradually no longer heard his words. Instead, they faded into the dark corners of the bar and scenes appeared before my eyes created by what he was telling me. As he spoke, my imagination, through my experiences with Melissa and Kenny, established the settings and the interactions that took place between them in a vision before my eyes. It was the same effect as when the words of a novel fade away and the reader falls headlong between the lines and into the author's fantasy.

Melissa had observed Kenny Bruce during rehearsals more and more closely until his appeal had begun to overcome her. He rapidly grew on her was the way she put it. But she felt all conquering, that just a sultry look from her would bring him to his knees, as had happened with Phil and me.

But either Kenny's upbringing or his fondness for his wife kept him firmly committed to his family. He was a private person, granted few interviews (he had been generous to us with a couple for the play's publicity), and spent as much time with his wife and two children as possible.

Now, tied up with rehearsals and a possible a six-month run on Broadway for six days a week, he would be unable to commute weekly to Bel

Aire. So he planned to allocate what would be the airfare of his budget to lengthy phone calls.

Even knowing that, Melissa had become so self-confident about her appeal—not having had much experience in the game of love—that she went avidly after Kenny Bruce, certain that her charm and beauty would result in his infatuation with her.

Melissa had begun her overtly passionate campaign for Kenny Bruce in Philadelphia. She took a room for herself. There was no doubt, though, that when she told Brent she was leaving for a week or two, he assumed that it was for the out-of-town tryout of *Parameters of Love*, and that she would be staying with me.

Melissa got together with neither Phil nor me. I spotted her through the first week, though, now and then, in the hotel lobby, at a restaurant, or just hanging around backstage.

I could have restricted her from being with the cast, as Phil could have done. And even Kenny Bruce. But I felt that taking such action would be cruel. I understood her emotional nature, and the least I could do, even as a now-unrequited lover, was let her have her way. I was jealous, of course, but undoubtedly I still felt enough love for her to be unselfish in that respect—if love was the feeling I had for her. I still wasn't sure.

At any rate, I noticed that she was talking occasionally with Kenny backstage during rehearsals over the weekend in what seemed to be casual conversations.

We opened on Monday evening, and the next day we studied the reviews. They were all generally average. The Philadelphia Bulletin pointed out some slow spots, The Philadelphia Inquirer stated, frankly, that the stars came through beautifully "despite, at times, the overly poetic monologues which with they had been burdened," and The Philadelphia Daily News reported that, "as a whole, the play works. The audience didn't show any signs of boredom during the fortunately few dreary scenes." All of the critics, however, were consistent in their praise for the stars of the show.

"I'll be perfectly honest with you, Mark," Bahnister told me at lunch after we had discussed the reviews. "We've got a problem. The play is good. No doubt about that. But with my experience, I'd say that the 'names' we have will only carry us for a short while, if that. This play is far from sparkling. We've got to bring it up to that point, or you'll never make your weekly break-even ticket sales. I could be wrong, but that's what my intuition tells me. I do feel, however, that at this point it doesn't look necessary to close out-of-town."

"What do you suggest?" I asked him.

"Tighten some of the scenes. Take out the long speeches, or cut them down. A lot of it is superfluous; it's just there to create mood and we have that. The play has to move." He lightly axed the palm of one hand with the edge of the other and spoke in an almost hushed voice. "It has to go bang, bang, bang; it has to have a regular beat throughout. With no let-up.

We've got to capture the audience's attention and keep it."

"Does that mean considerable changes?" I asked.

"Not really extensive. But close to extensive. And it does mean a bit of rewriting and that the cast will have to remember a fair amount of changed dialogue and new cues. We can slip up now and then here in Philly, prompt them and throw them cues from the wings. We're trying out. So we can get away with it."

Since we were booked for a two-week run in Philly, I thought, it gives us all a chance to relax and, without excessive stress, work out the script problems. The way I saw it, we had much to do. But nothing really terribly drastic, thankfully.

"Do you think we can make it in New York?" I questioned.

Bahnister spoke cautiously. "That remains to be seen. We can only do our best to doctor it up. Nobody can predict how the New York critics will feel about it after we make the changes. All we can do is make those adjustments and hope for the best."

Through the first week, it was quite difficult for the cast to go through the matinees and evening shows without flubs, but only a pro would have noticed them. The smoothest of all was Phoebe, because of her early life in the theater. In her scenes with Kenny, a few times when he was about to falter, she gave him confidence by improvising, with hints, until he could pick up his line. They worked together like troupers.

About the middle of the week, I found a sealed letter with my name on it, marked 'Confidential', tacked to the bulletin board backstage. It was from Kenny. He wanted me to call him about a private get-together. I hoped there were no problems.

I saw him in his hotel suite.

He was wearing a black turtleneck sweater. "Mark, how're you doing?" he said pleasantly. "Make yourself comfortable. This will only take a few minutes."

We sat down opposite each other in padded ball-and-claw-footed chairs. "If there's something wrong," I said worriedly, "you can count on me to straighten it out."

"Nothing really serious," he said, "at this point."

"What is it, then?" I asked.

"Well, it's like this." He rubbed his chin. "There's this gal, Melissa Lourdes. I think she's a friend of Phil's. At least, I saw them talking to each other often during rehearsals."

He paused, looking at the floor. I waited anxiously for what he had to say.

"She's very nice. I want to mention that." He scratched his head. "But she's been hanging around me. And she's become sort of an annoyance. I take this opportunity you gave me very seriously. I want to do my best out there on the stage. I'm the kind of guy who has to be by myself, alone, even when I'm in a crowd, if you know what I mean. I'm always thinking about my part in the play. It's my first time on Broadway, so I have to concentrate, even while I'm not up there."

He hadn't explained his problem enough for me to make a comment, so I waited.

"As I said, she's a pleasant woman. But I get the feeling that she's...well...she's trying to start up a relationship." He flashed a palm. "Now, I don't know if I'm right about that. But the point is, I'm married, and happily married. And whether she has those intentions or not, I don't want people thinking that something's going on with me and her." He paused uncomfortably and shifted in his seat. "That's the last thing I need. To get a mention about that in a gossip column. Or even have Phoebe think there's hanky-panky. Phoebe is a close friend of my wife's, she knows me, and she thinks highly of me—especially compared to other guys out in Hollywood who are carrying on right and left."

I was still trying to think of what to say. So I remained silent, hoping that he would comment more.

The time that I left open stimulated new thoughts in his mind.

"The thing is," he went on, "I don't know what to tell her. Frankly, I want to get her off my back. But I'm afraid of offending Phil. That's all I have to do to break up the chummy relationship of the cast."

"I understand," I said. "Don't bother yourself about it. I'll take care of everything."

He put out his hand, relieved. "Thanks a lot, Mark. I knew you'd be the one to talk to."

"Please feel free to come to me about any problems at all, Kenny," I said.

My next step was to talk directly to Melissa. I dreaded it. But it had to be done.

Going into the second week, after Bahnister announced that there would be no further changes in dialogue or blocking, the acting became almost flawless. After that, the cast members began to concentrate entirely on their own individual characterizations.

Melissa continued her stay in Philadelphia. I had checked with the hotel desk.

Early in the week, I decided that I'd wait until I ran into her accidentally, and chat casually with her, finally getting to the subject of Kenny Bruce.

But as life usually works, when I wanted to see her, she wasn't around.

After the Wednesday matinee, Kenny stopped me as I was on the way out of the theater. "Say, Mark. I hate to bother you about this again. But have you had a chance to speak to that Melissa gal?"

"No," I said. "I really meant to, but I've been quite busy. Sorry I let it go. Why? Has she been bothering you?"

"Well, yeah. She's been calling me and even dropping by my suite, knocking on the door. I'd really appreciate it if you'd do something about it."

"I'll take care of it right away."

"Thanks a lot, Mark."

When I got back to the hotel, I went directly to the registration desk.

"Can you tell me the phone number of Melissa Lourdes, please."

The well-dressed gentleman went off to look it up, then returned. "That's room 471."

"Thanks." I picked up the house phone on the counter and called. No answer.

"I'd like to leave a note please."

All I wrote was, "Please call me. Mark." I would go into details when I saw her.

By late the next afternoon I still hadn't heard from her. There was no return call or message. Obviously, she was avoiding me.

I decided to try harder. I tore a page from a tablet on the registration desk that had a drawing of the hotel with its name and address at the top, and wrote, "Melissa. Please contact me. Important. Mark." I asked the deskman for a piece of Scotch tape and went up to the fourth floor, found 471, and taped the note to the door. When I turned to leave, I realized that I hadn't called her first this time. She might be there. Why not knock at the door.

I did.

Her voice was dull, relaxed. "One moment, please." She spoke as if she purposely didn't want to sound surprised. She might have thought it was Kenny. I waited silently.

The door opened. She stood there in a long, plain, dark blue dress that reached her ankles.

"Oh, Mark. Come on in."

She closed the door behind me.

"I was just about to take a shower."

"Then don't let me interrupt you. I can come back later."

"No, that's all right. What do you want?"

"Well, first of all, I wanted to say hello to you," I told her, attempting to warm up the atmosphere. "I've been so busy, I haven't had time to even get together for a chat."

"Really?"

"Yes." I sat down on the bed.

She reached behind her back to unzip the dress.

"But there's another matter," I continued, "that I want to discuss with you."

"And what's that?"

"Kenny Bruce."

She pulled the top of her dress to the edges of her shoulders and let it fall to the floor, standing only in her slip. "What about Kenny Bruce?" She bent over, took the hem of the slip, pulled it up over her face, and dropped the glittering lingerie in a heap by her side.

As she looked at me with a passionless expression, wearing only her delicate undergarments, I hesitated, trying to think about what to say, at the same time aroused by the spareness of her brassiere and tightness of her lace-edged panties that firmly bound her torso and bulged at the crotch.

"You're interested in him," was the only way I could put it.

"Haven't you ever been interested in other women?"

"That's not what I mean. You're chasing after him." I regretted putting it that way, but that was how it came out.

"So what?" she said.

"He wants to be left alone. He doesn't want any problems. He's married. And he's afraid of gossip."

I stood and went to her, face to face. "He's not interested," I told her.

"We'll see about that."

"Don't you care for me anymore?" I said, not knowing where the question came from.

"Of course, I do," she answered, putting her arms lightly around my shoulders.

She kissed me, rekindling the embers of our love. Fleetingly.

The Parameters of Love Company was approaching closing night in Philadelphia, and we were all looking forward to one more week out of town, in Baltimore. The cast, crew, general manager, myself, some of the backers who anxiously turned up—everyone—were beginning to feel some confidence in the production.

Now we had to see what a fresh set of critics would think of it.

That Saturday, after the matinee, I went back to the hotel and routinely asked for my messages. There was one from Brent, asking me to call him.

What could he want to speak with me about?

Obviously, Melissa. But with regard to what?

Did she say something to him about our getting together again? Were we together again? Did he know that we had split up? I wasn't anxious to find out what was on his mind. But there was no avoiding him. I had to return his call.

I went up to my room and sat by the phone for a while, bracing myself for what would probably be an unexpected conversation.

Then I dialed his office in New York.

He was there.

"Mark," he said. "Is Mrs. Lourdes still down there?"

"Uhhh...yes..." I sputtered, losing all of the bearing that I had mustered because of the way he had put the question.

"Who's that slut with now? You? Or Kenny Bruce?"

"I really don't know," I lied. "I've hardly seen her for these past two weeks."

"A likely story."

I couldn't believe that I was speaking with Brent. It didn't sound like him—the words, or the tone of voice.

"You'd better tell that whore of a wife of mine to get back up here to New York."

I thought that he might be drunk. Whatever, he sounded as if he had reached the end of his tether.

"I'm just fed up. She has a family, and she should be here with us."

"If I see her, I'll tell her to call."

"You'll see her, all right. Don't give me that bullshit. I've been calling her and leaving messages for the past two days, but she hasn't answered them. I called Kenny Bruce, but he says he knows nothing about her."

"I'm sure he doesn't."

"What are you so sure about? She told me she was seeing him."

"That's impossible," I said, making my voice sound as confident as I could. "That I can guarantee you."

"Guarantee!" he said, exasperated. "What the hell is she doing there, having orgies?"

"I really don't know, Brent."

"You sure as hell do. She told me that she's owned by nobody, and that she's free to do whatever she wants."

"I'll look for her, Brent. I'll make a special effort. But I'm busy, and I'm not sure whether I'll find her."

"Well, you'd better find her, and have her call me."

"Okay, Brent," was all I could say.

He hung up.

I dialed her room.

The phone rang several times, then the operator picked up. "Who are you calling?"

"Melissa Lourdes."

"We've been asked to hold any calls. Would you like to leave a message?"

"Yes. Tell her that Mark Gessel called, it's important, and to call me back right away."

"Yes, sir."

I hung up and sat there for a while, my thoughts in disarray.

Melissa and I finally got together in her room on Sunday. She was packing. I didn't have to notice a half-full bottle of Jack Daniels on her bureau to know that she had been drinking.

"Are you going back to New York?" I asked.

Her attitude was cold. It was as if nothing had happened between us. That we were still, basically, strangers. "No, I'm going to Baltimore to see the try-out there."

"I think you should take Brent's call into consideration."

"Why?"

"Because he's your husband."

"Since when did that ever bother you?"

"Lately."

"Just a couple of days ago?"

"You might say that." I waited a moment for a reply, but she was busy stuffing clothes carelessly into her suitcase. So I continued. "Brent doesn't sound like the same person we know."

"You mean the same person you know, not that I know. I know him better than you do. Mark, I'm sick and tired of him. He's a bore, a stuffed shirt. Everybody thinks he's a man of the world because he produces plays. But actually, he's just a narrow-minded individual who puts on plays by writers who know their way around, who have lived and thought about the world."

"Melissa, you just can't go on like this."

"You wouldn't say that if the situation was different with us."

She was right. Romance was not in the air.

"What are you going to do?" I asked her.

"I'm going to go to Baltimore."

"To be with Phil?" I questioned, with pain.

"To be with whoever I want to be with."

"Does that mean Kenny?"

She stopped her movements with the clothes and sighed. "I don't know what it means."

Neither of us said anything. Then I asked, "What about us?"

"Maybe you can answer that question."

"Me?"

"Yes," she said. "You're the one who knows how you feel about me. I don't."

"But you do." I was, I'm sure, unconvincing, because I was unconvinced, myself, still unsure if it was really love that I felt, even as much as I wanted her to be mine.

"Mark," she told me. "I'm a free human being. I can do as I wish. Nobody runs my life, except me."

"At this point," I said, "the best thing for you to do is go home. Straighten out your relationship with Brent. That's most important. Then you can go back to being yourself. The man is getting out of control. You can never tell what he'll do to you. He beat you up once."

"I'll take that chance," she said with finality.

Chapter 35

When I arrived in Baltimore to check into my reserved room, there was a message waiting for me. It was from Brent.

Melissa had registered at another hotel than the members of The Parameters of Love Company. She had told me in Philadelphia that she wanted to avoid hearing from him.

I didn't know what was happening with Kenny, or whether to ask him if Melissa was still bugging him. But he hadn't said anything, so I left well enough alone. Only if he brought up the subject with me would I pursue it further.

I went up to my room and killed time unpacking slowly. Anything to avoid calling Brent. Although I knew that I'd eventually have to.

Finally, after I hung most of my clothes in the closet and stacked the rest neatly in the drawers, I had no further excuse to put off calling him. So I did.

As soon as he was on the phone, he asked, "Where's Melissa? They say she's not on the hotel list."

"I really don't know, Brent." Then, to throw him off the track, at least insofar as my being with her, I said, "I haven't seen her for days. Maybe she went back to New York." Since she wasn't with me, I didn't feel too guilty telling him that.

"She's not here," Brent told me. "I left word with the maid to have her call, or for the maid to let me know if she shows up. But Baltimore is the only place she could be."

"Well, I can't help you."

"Is she with you?"

"I told you, Brent. I haven't seen her."

"Is she with Phil? With Kenny?"

"I really don't know."

"I'll call them, too, damn it!" he shouted, and hung up.

I immediately called the hotel that Melissa was staying at. She wasn't there, so I left a message. I had a few hours before meeting Bahnister at the theater, so I decided to stay around and wait, hopefully, for her to call back. Feeling somewhat fatigued, I decided to take a nap.

I was sharply aroused from my sleep by the phone ringing. I reached for it.

"Yes?" I said groggily.

"It's Melissa."

I was disoriented. The room came into focus, and I remembered that I had been sleeping. The pressure of the play had tired me more than I suspected it would. "Oh, yes."

"You called?"

In seconds, I recovered completely from the deepness of my little nap. "Yes. Brent was in touch with me. He wants to speak with you."

"I don't want to speak with him."

"He seemed up in arms."

"That's too bad. All he wants is an argument. I told him he's not going to control my life."

"But, Melissa..."

"I don't want to discuss it any further."

"He asked me if you were with me." I waited "Or with Phil. Or Kenny."

"That's none of his business."

I had to know myself. "Are you with Phil or Kenny?"

"That's none of your business, either."

"Melissa, you're looking for trouble."

"That's my problem. Not yours."

Opening night went well. The audience seemed to appreciate the play. They were quiet during the serious scenes and laughed with delight at the humorous lines. After the show, Bahnister agreed with me that the possibilities looked good. Not great, but good.

Our opinions were confirmed by the reviews.

Following the final curtain on Wednesday, he stopped me in the lobby.

"I want to talk with you," he said.

"Sure," I replied. He didn't seem very happy. I was afraid that he had re-evaluated the play and was feeling differently about it. What else could it be? "Let's go back to the hotel and chat there," I suggested.

"We can talk on the way over," he said.

We left the theater and walked through the dark streets, and he immediately brought up the subject that was on his mind. "Melissa is a troublemaker."

I felt panic. "Why? What is it?"

"Frankly, I don't know exactly what's going on. Phil came to see me just before the performance tonight and told me that she was upset because Kenny was ignoring her. Why that should bother her, I don't know. At any rate, he said that she insisted he drop Kenny and Phoebe from the show and use the understudies."

"That's insane!" I said. "Just ignore her," I told him. "I'll tell Phil to ignore her."

"My agreement," Bahnister pointed out, "if you remember, was that I would direct Lourdes' new musical if I did this show for you."

"Yes, that's true," I said. "But Melissa would never do anything drastic like drop the stars just as we're about to go into New York. She's bluffing."

"I have to consider the possibility that she's not," Bahnister said. He must have been desperate, because he followed with, "I've mentioned to you much earlier that Kenny and Phoebe's understudies are damn good. In fact, as I also told you, they're better. But, of course, they're unknowns and wouldn't have the drawing power of stars."

"Jesse," I said unbelievingly, "you don't mean to tell me that you would actually consider replacing the leads in this play with the understudies?"

"Yes, I most certainly would. I have to think about my career. A successful musical would open new doors for me. There's more money there, to begin with, than in any straight play. And it might give me good exposure for films, which have eluded me all these years."

"Take my word for it, Jesse. She'd never back out on her promise to you."

"She's a strange woman, Mark. She could very well carry out her threat. And I can't afford to take the risk."

"I know for a fact that she wouldn't be able to get her husband to back out on his commitment to you. Believe me."

"I'm afraid I just can't take you at your word on that," he replied.

"Jesse, please do," I implored. "I swear that you'll direct that musical. Please."

He hesitated for a moment. "Well, all right," he said with sympathy toward me in his voice. "But we're going to have to convince Kenny that it's to his benefit to at least appear to be interested in her."

Bahnister arranged for the both of us to get together with Kenny the next day for breakfast in a coffee shop near the theater.

Bahnister explained the entire situation to Kenny as we all dug into our choices of eggs, bacon, sausages, toast, rolls, jams, and hot, freshly brewed coffee. "Just play her along," was his advice to the show's male star.

"I guess I can go through with it," Kenny said. "It's not just your future; it's Phoebe's and mine."

Bahnister looked at me. "And Mark's, too."

"It's everybody's, the whole cast's," Kenny summed up. "I'll just explain the situation to Phoebe. She can call my wife and tell her what it's all about, so that Marilyn can give the story to her friends in advance, and they'll know what to expect. That way, it'll be just another anecdote about show business, and we can all laugh about it later on."

"Good idea," Bahnister said. "If we make it on Broadway, you only have to put up with her for the run of your six-month contract."

"That's all I'm going to do," Kenny replied to him. "Play along. I'm just not interested in her. Or anybody else. Only my wife. This is just plain ridiculous."

"We know that, Kenny," Bahnister said. "Just do all of us this favor."

Subsequently, Kenny gave regular descriptions of his experiences with Melissa to Bahnister down to the very finest points, and Bahnister passed them along to me. I was, of course, quite interested in hearing all about them. But none of it made me very happy.

Kenny said that he acted very warm to Melissa; in fact, he kissed her once, telling her that he finds himself very inhibited about having an affair.

They began going to many of the well-known downtown restaurants together. Finally, as expected, their names showed up together in a Philadelphia newspaper gossip column. It was picked up shortly after by a few New York columnists.

The news spread rapidly to Hollywood. Before closing night in Philly, Kenny's wife called to give him the news that word had reached a newspaper out there. He said that he immediately bought a copy of the Los Angeles newspaper in Philadelphia at a newsstand that carried out-of-town newspapers.

Kenny let Bahnister know that he was running out of excuses for not sleeping with Melissa.

Bahnister gave me an account of one incident in all its particulars.

Kenny had told him, "What I did last night was invite Harry Kurtz, the prop man, to dinner with us." (Kurtz was a young man of about 25.) "I told Melissa that he had asked me for advice, since his goal was to be an actor. He didn't know whether he should stay in New York and pound the pavements casting for shows, or go out to Hollywood and try the studios." Kenny told her that since he had experience in films and Melissa was experienced in theater production, they both could evaluate Kurtz's goals and looks, and give him combined advice.

"Actually," Kenny told Bahnister, "the kid had flipped out over Melissa after seeing her around, and I figured it would be a good opportunity for me to ditch her. When I proposed the idea to him, he really went for it."

"That's fantastic, Kenny!" the young aspiring actor had said. "I'm dying to meet her. I really appreciate this."

"They all met at a bar around the corner from the Shubert," Bahnister said. "She really lapped up those drinks," Kenny told me. "Like there was no tomorrow. And the plan worked perfectly. Kurtz took her back to his room; he said she could hardly walk."

"And what happened?" I asked with dread.

"Kurtz told Kenny the next day," Bahnister informed me, "that he had made out just like that. He said she was a pushover." He smiled cynically. "I congratulated Kenny on his great idea," Bahnister said, his joy fading. "But it turned out to be a one-night stand. She didn't want to see Kurtz again. She told him so the next day when he phoned her. Then, wouldn't you know it, she called Kenny and said that they should have dinner together that night."

Hearing this devastated me, not just to learn about the quickie, which was a terrible blow to my pride that considerably altered my opinion of Melissa and my feelings for her, but because it meant a continuing problem with keeping Kenny and Phoebe in the play.

Everything was such a mess, but the anger I felt sobered me to the point where I was certain that I could deal coldly now with Melissa.

We were getting close to opening night, and Kenny was becoming agitated. Not because of the play, but because Melissa was upsetting him again.

"Listen, Mark," Kenny told me before the next performance. "I heard from my wife. She found out that a lot of her friends are laughing at her behind her back. Even though she told them in advance about the situation with Melissa, most of them don't believe her. They suspect that she set up the situation to avoid later embarrassment. And now she's worried that all of this business about my philandering that's in the columns out there is going to hurt my reputation and the possibility of my getting more movie contracts. I've been getting cast opposite Phoebe as a clean-cut husband type, and all of this might just ruin my image—and career."

"Okay," I said. "I'll take care of it. I promise you."

My next step was to deal directly, and emphatically, with Melissa.

I called her. Fortunately, she was there.

"It's Mark. I have to get together with you. It's urgent."

"About what?"

"I'll tell you when I see you."

"Tell me now."

"It's best if we're together to discuss this."

"Oh, well, all right. Come on over."

I went to her hotel as fast as I could, waited impatiently for the elevator to reach her floor, rushed to her room, and knocked at he door.

She opened it and looked at me without a smile. "Come in."

As I went through the doorway, I said, "Kenny told me that you're still hanging around him."

"That's right."

"He's not interested in you." It made me feel good to say that. "And he'd like you to leave him alone."

"I find him very rude," she said.

"Rude?"

"Yes, rude. He just completely ignores me. I'm not saying he has to be friendly. I'm just saying that he could treat me like a human being."

"Why don't you just forget about him."

"I'm not forgetting about him. I want him out of the show. And Phoebe, too."

"Just a minute, Melissa. I think you're carrying things too far. This is my show. And I don't intend to have you wreck it just when it's about to open in New York."

"The reason that your show got as far as it has is because of me. I'm the one who got you Jesse Bahnister. And, as a result of that, Kenny Bruce and Phoebe Shannon. Not to mention that, in addition, I was responsible for most of the investment that came in. So I have every right to have them dropped from the cast."

"I don't want Bahnister threatened. He's put up with a lot to get this show on. I'm not going to let you destroy all of this. Besides, do you really think that Brent, after what you've done to him, would even listen to if you tell him to drop Bahnister as the director of his musical?"

"Yes, I do. If I tell Brent I'm coming back to him."

"Do you mean that you would lie to him?"

"Haven't I been lying all along? What would another lie mean?"

"Melissa, I can't believe that you'd be that kind of a person."

"I'm a free agent. You know that. I don't have to prove it to you."

"I give up," I said. "Just tell me what to do."

"Ask Kenny to have dinner with me tonight."

"I can't do that. It's out of the question. He wants nothing to do with you. You're blemishing his name, damaging his career."

"That's too bad."

"Melissa, there's nothing I can do about it. I'm not forcing him to get together with you, and that's that!"

Trying to persuade her to be logical about the situation was impossible. I left.

But that evening, just before performance time, I found out that she had meant business.

Bahnister took me aside backstage. "Mark, I've given notice to Kenny and Phoebe."

"You what!"

"They've already made reservations to fly back to LA. The understudies are going on tonight." He put his hand on my shoulder. "Don't worry about it. The understudies are good. No, not just good," he assured me. "They're excellent. They know the lines and they'll have everything down pat for opening night in New York."

"This is insane!" I said.

"Mark," Bahnister told me calmly, "I took a risk with this show to do that musical. Melissa called me last night and gave me the word. Either the leads are out, or I don't direct her husband's show. I believe her. I'm not taking any chances."

"But Kenny and Phoebe are our ace in the hole for New York. We'll never last. We have several weeks of theater party tickets sell-outs. I'm counting on the advance sales to carry us through. Those people will want their money back when they learn about Kenny and Phoebe being out."

"This is the kind of a show that has to stand on its own, Mark. Advance sales might mean just a few weeks of holding on if the play is right. That's all. But in the end you're going to have to depend on the show itself. It will rise or fall by itself, regardless of who's in the lead roles."

"That's not true, Jessie, and you know it. Those two names mean everything."

"I'm sorry, but that's my decision."

"Listen, Bahnister. I've just got to be tough on this. I'm the producer, and what I say goes, not what you say. And I say that Kenny and Phoebe are going to open in New York and stay with the show."

"You may be the producer," Bahnister said. "But Phil holds the cards. He's the one who controls the escape clauses. And he's concerned with Kenny's problem. He already called his agent, and those contracts are off."

"He can't do that!" I said. "He'll ruin his own chances. His problem is that he thinks artsy," I said. "In my opinion his play will bomb without those names over the title."

"I think that he also feels some kind of sympathy for Melissa."

"I wouldn't doubt that," I told him sarcastically. "Is he around?"

"He was backstage just about ten minutes ago."

I had no more to say to Bahnister, and rushed backstage. I found Phil talking with Melissa. The stage manager was just giving the opening cues and the hum of the audience was diminishing to a hush. As I made my way solemnly to them, she looked up and saw me. Her expression was cold.

I ignored her. "Phil," I said. "Can I see you for just a moment?"

"Okay," he replied. "At the back of the theater." As we went off, leaving Melissa standing there alone, I noticed that the understudies were waiting to go on.

I followed Phil into the darkness of the side aisle, which brightened partially as the curtain went up. I turned and looked off toward the stage as we made our way past the rows, and saw Phoebe's understudy walk slowly into the center of the set. There was a mild, broken applause. No doubt, according to equity's rules, an announcement had been made that the main roles would not be played that night by the famous screen stars that we had advertised. And I was certain that ticket holders were given an opportunity to get refunds because the house was half-empty.

We stood at the short wooden wall behind the final row of seats in the orchestra, and said nothing to each other as we watched the understudies in their roles for the first time before an audience.

Our stage manager had rehearsed them well between practice run-throughs and regular performances. I had to admit to myself that they carried their parts off well, at least so far in the opening of the first act.

"They're damn good, aren't they?" Phil whispered to me as he watched straight ahead.

"Not bad," I said feebly. "But Kenny and Phoebe were better," I added.

"I don't think so. I think you're too hung up on names."

"Phil, it's names that can keep your play going. This play you've written is a fine one, and I think Bahnister's production of it is going to be received well. But it's not a blockbuster drama. And that's what you need if you want it to keep it running. And you can't do that unless you have names."

"I don't go along with you, Mark. Just watch and listen to this for a while. You'll see what I mean."

We were silent as the characters on stage delivered their lines and went smoothly through their movements. It was an impressive performance, but I still wasn't sold on Phil's theory.

"Listen, Phil," I said, after a while. "Get Kenny and Phoebe back. There's still time. They may make other commitments tomorrow, and you'll be out of luck."

"No way, Mark. My mind's made up."

"We'll be lucky to run a week in New York."

"Let's just see about that."

Before we ended our run in Philadelphia, I called my press agent and asked him to send out the releases that had been approved by Kenny and Phoebe announcing their replacements in the leads of Parameters of Love. The notices appeared in the New York newspapers before our first preview there. As agreed, Kenny and Phoebe were let off the hook. The reason for their departure from the play, it was stated, was because another Bruce-Shannon screenplay had come along and they had no choice, because of its schedule, but to regretfully leave my production. They were quoted as praising Phil's play with the hope that its movie would come their way. Of course, no knowledgeable theatergoer would believe such an outright lie; they could only assume that the play was in trouble.

Chapter 36

New York.

Fortunately, none of the theater parties had backed out, and only a few tickets had been returned. But, essentially, sales had cooled down, which might have happened anyway. We had probably drawn most of the people who were either interested in seeing Kenny Bruce and Phoebe Shannon, or Phil's new play.

As soon as I arrived in Manhattan, I walked over to the theater to look at the marquee.

There it was. The stars' names replaced by the understudies' names. It was too short notice to reprint the posters, which would have been expensive, anyway, so the new leads' names had been pasted over the previous ones. Ordinarily, unknowns would have had their names below the title; however, I had no choice but to leave the credits where they were.

Our week of previews gave the two newcomers the opportunity to brush up and perfect their lines and moves, and we all listened intently to comments at the intermissions between the acts.

But there was no telling what the general opinion was. Comments ranged the gamut from great to so-so.

It would be up to the critics, especially the one from The *New York Times*—which carried the most weight.

I didn't know during those final tense days what the situation was with Melissa and Brent, but I found out later that she had briefly moved in with Phil.

I was quite busy, and whenever I ran into her at the theater during the previews, she was quite chilly toward me. So I just avoided her. I could never have guessed at the time what was going on with her and Phil.

And I didn't much care. I was resolved to concentrate on my career as a producer now, not as a writer (which was, of course, to change later in my cyclical life), and forget about Melissa. But whenever I saw her with Phil, or alone, my past experiences with her flashed through my mind in an instant, the way a person's life is described as being recalled just before the moment of death, and I felt a physical pang each time.

At any rate, Bahnister's contract to do the musical hadn't been canceled—not that it would make any difference, it turned out.

I never did find out what had happened between Melissa and Phil by opening night of Parameters of Love. But I was surprised to see her show up with an actor who played a lead in one of Brent's comedies that had been running for over two years. He was about ten years her junior. He seemed quite proud standing in the lobby before the show in the company of Melissa, whose slim, black gown and long, gold earrings enhanced her devastating beauty.

Phil, talking to a few people in another part of the waiting crowd, acted as if she weren't even there. I could easily see myself standing in his shoes. That's exactly how I would have reacted. Not that jealousy didn't overpower me now, too, as it was.

Our opening-night party was set for Sardi's, as had been the one for my play. In just several hours we would all know our fates.

When the opening night curtain rang down, the critics rushed off to their respective desks to give their important decisions, and the people associated with *Parameters of Love* eventually showed up around the corner, at the party.

I went there directly, but Shirley returned to the hotel to fix her make-up. She didn't get to the party until over an hour later.

Melissa and her new boyfriend also appeared in the crowd at Sardi's.

Neither Phil nor I spoke with her the entire evening.

But, surprisingly, Brent appeared.

He was unshaven and generally unkempt. It was unlike him to look other than neat at any theatrical occasion. He also seemed agitated and surly.

He, naturally, went directly to Melissa, who was calmly sitting at a table with her new, young acquaintance.

I studied the three intently, as Brent vented anger at her. I couldn't hear what he was saying in the distance, because of the noisiness of the excited crowd, which was anticipating the outcome of the reviews while at the same time enjoying the festivities.

Melissa looked not only unruffled, but almost totally ignored Brent. Consequently, his temper seemed to be increasing. Finally, he left, fury showing in his attitude and gait.

A few hours later, the results began to come in. The reviews were mild. There was praise for the two replacements, but the critics hadn't exactly been overawed by the play. In general, the script was described as pleasingly poetic and fairly competent. The understudies received high marks. Bahnister's efforts were lauded; he was found to have worked a miracle with thin material.

To be honest with myself, I had to conclude that I would probably be able to keep the play on the boards for only a month or two, the length of time paid for by the theater parties; then I'd have to close it. Which is the way it turned out. There was a loss of about 50% of the capital.

Movie rights were never sold (Kenny and Phoebe never showed interest in them), but royalty from amateur productions over the next two decades brought in enough money to balance out the deficit.

Such was my experience as a legit producer.

But Brent made news on the day following the reviews. The front page of The *New York Times* carried a one-column headshot of him below the fold, with a story that began with a heading that shocked the theatrical community.

The story went on to say that at age 25 he had produced his first play, which was an immediate artistic and financial success. Then it went on to chronicle his early life and accomplishments in the theater.

When the notoriety of Brent's death wound down and the incident was no longer news, Melissa took over her husband's productions. I learned of this only through a few newspaper articles that appeared afterwards.

I had tried to contact her, but she refused to speak with me, so I didn't attend the funeral. I thought, under the circumstances, that my being there would be in bad taste.

Phil, too, I later found out, stopped seeing her altogether.

At first, there were rumors around town about her being seen at restaurants, night spots, and premieres with a number of men involved in the theater: actors, backers, stage managers.

But, in time, she faded from the scene.

She hired as an executive producer a business manager/accountant who had provided the budgets on a number of Brent's shows. He wasn't an experienced producer, and all he could do was keep the shows running, not being capable of selecting scripts, or casting. He had only the ability to carry out a producer's orders precisely or do books efficiently.

But since money was never Melissa's schtick and she wasn't the producer type, she eventually let her late husband's dynasty of successful productions slowly expire. Nevertheless, money from their runs, road shows, movie rights, and amateur rights would continue as income for her for many years to come with no effort on her part.

Within a year, she left New York and took her children with her.

Neither her executive producer nor her office would give me, or anyone else, information concerning her whereabouts. She went into Greta Garbo-like hiding.

I missed her at first, but in time my need for her waned.

I was to have more depressions, one immediately following the closing of *Parameters of Love* and my affair with Melissa. It initially lasted for about two years, then recurred occasionally.

Shirley had to take a job so that we could survive.

So I've made a record here about my experience of knowing Melissa, in order for you to understand how important she was to my life. And so that I could view it with my own eyes, in order that I might assess my feelings about her in depth before I die, most likely here, in this old age home. There was no such person in my experience with women before her, or after. And I don't expect a woman like her ever again to appear and love me as she did. Especially now, as this hulk sitting here in this wheelchair. I had my chance. And it's all over.

If one did, by chance, show up at this time, I'd probably put her to work helping me with the printout of these final pages, here in my little room.

I'd have her tap this key, wait for this last page of this novel, put it at the bottom of this manuscript next to me, and give it to my son to see if he could get all of these memories published.

With the hope that I have, at last, made somewhat of a contribution to literature.

www.ingramcontent.com/pod-product-compliance
Lightning Source LLC
Chambersburg PA
CBHW071244130626
46556CB00003B/1159